drown me gently

FLIPPED FAIRYTALES

TEREZA KANE

For those who aren't afraid to reach into the abyss...
and hope it reaches back.

Trigger Warnings

Sexually explicit scenes and language
Intimacy involving non-human anatomy
Abduction and Imprisonment
Torture
Medical Mutilation
Body horror
Threat of SA
(Includes non-consensual touching)
Emotional Abuse
Self-harm
Suicidal Ideation
Violence and Gore
Death
Psychological Trauma

Chapter One

Auren

Shivers ran down Auren's back as he pressed himself against the cool marble column. His heart thumped steadily. Not from fear, but anticipation. The thrill of the escape. He'd memorized the palace schedule. Knew exactly how long the guards, with their golden tridents, held post at the outer gate.

This was far from his first time ditching royal attendants.

The sea was velvet-dark, its silence broken only by the faintest whisper of current sliding over sand. The palace of Atlantis loomed over him. Grand, immense, carved into the cliffside with a craftsmanship fit for a god of the sea. Its white marble columns reached high into the gloom, wrapped in vines of glowing kelp and gilded with pearls, a testament to Poseidon's divinity. Braziers lined the gates, blue flames twisting inside glass globes and casting warped reflections on the marble archways.

Auren exhaled slowly, the soft tissue of his gills fluttering. His fingers curled tighter around the strap of his satchel. Inside were the usual tools—a dull blade and a bit of food—nothing fancy, but enough. The blade was for cutting through obstacles at the wall; the food, for waiting out a guard rotation if needed. He'd turned escape into a science, and tonight was no different. The sound of heavy motion sliced through the water behind him.

"Magister, we cannot locate him, we've searched—"

"Don't bother. I'll get him." A heavy voice replied to the frantic palace guard.

Auren's stomach sank.

Shit.

A moment later, the water shifted beside him in a whoosh, and he didn't need to turn around to know who it was.

"Auren."

There was that voice. Auren could recognize it from leagues away. It was deep and rumbling, like the blackest part of the ocean floor was settling into place. Auren winced, letting his head thump against the column in defeat.

"How'd you find me?"

"You aren't as clever as you think, spriteling."

Auren grimaced and turned.

Ulric hovered a few meters away, arms crossed, hair drifting around him like ink in water. His face was carved from rigid discipline and patience worn thin. Twin eyes, black as trenchwater, fixed on Auren with all the disappointment of a weary mentor and all the judgment of a high priest.

Even the tips of his obsidian tentacles twitched with irritation where they pooled at his waist like a living sash. Nine in total, sleek and gleaming like polished jet, ringed with pale suckers that caught the blue firelight. He made for a murderous sight, but Auren didn't flinch.

He met the Kraken's gaze head-on. "You gonna keep staring, or do you plan to drag me back by my tail?" Auren muttered.

Ulric's brow twitched. "Don't tempt me."

"I'm not scared of you."

"You should be."

Auren scoffed. "Yeah, right. Big scary Kraken. I've survived your temper a hundred times."

Ulric's skin was coppered bronze, sunless but burnished. His shoulders were broad and imposing, his chest inked in curling black tattoos. Dark lines curled over his collarbones, ran down his arms, and disappeared into the inky shadows of his lower half. Runes etched near his ribs marked oaths too old for most to remember in a language long since forgotten. His face bore a trimmed beard, neatly kept, the same color as his hair—deep black, threaded with streaks of iron-gray.

He wore no armor—just a dark leather wrap across his chest, a long, curved fang from some deepwater beast hanging from one ear, and a carved whalebone holding his hair half up. The only mark of his rank was an embossed trident on the leather, a symbol that set him apart as the Court Sorcerer.

He was Kraken.

Not Merfolk.

The water shifted around Auren, vibrating in response to the Kraken's anger. Ulric was one of the few marked to carry Poseidon's magic, the brands on his skin pulsing with power. Combined with his obsidian eyes, it was no wonder most Merfolk found the Kraken unsettling. Even terrifying. A creature of the ocean pits.

And still, Auren refused to back down.

"You aren't as scary as you look." Auren snapped at his mentor.

Ulric snarled, revealing pointed shark's teeth.

"Ever the sea-sprite," he hissed. "You know the meeting with the Tidelord begins in under an hour."

Auren bristled at the demeaning nickname.

Ocean sprites—is that what Ulric saw when he looked at him? Not a threat, just some flitting little thing causing trouble for the sake of it. A nuisance, not a danger.

"Don't you think it's time to let go of the nicknames? I'm a man, not a Merling. And I'm getting tired of you forgetting that."

"Yet you continue to shirk your responsibilities like a petulant child."

Auren crossed his arms, gills flaring in irritation. "I'm not shirking. I'm selectively avoiding."

Ulric raised a brow. "Ah. So you're *strategically* disobedient. That must be a great comfort to the Queen."

"Don't act like she'd even notice I was gone. She has twelve other heirs to smother with ceremonial garlands."

"You're still the prince," Ulric said, arms folded. "And it's the prince's duty to attend these councils."

"My twelve older siblings can handle it," Auren groaned, flicking a piece of kelp off his shoulder. "They *live* for that nonsense. They're all too happy to grovel and gossip."

"It is your responsibility as Poseidon's heir—"

"—to sit there and smile while they drone on about border negotiations and sand tariffs?" Auren spat. "Hard pass."

"You are royalty," Ulric said flatly. "Start acting like it."

Auren bristled. "You're the Court Sorcerer. Not my guard."

"No," Ulric muttered, "though lately, I feel more like a babysitter."

Auren glared at him. "Haven't you grown tired of this? You've been dragging me back into these walls since I was twenty."

Ulric sighed. "And I'll continue to do so until your magic manifests at thirty. Three more fun-filled years."

"Do I look like I need protection?" Auren snapped, letting his arms fall to his sides as if to display himself.

He wasn't fragile.

His body was lean from years in the sparring rings, honed by daily drills where he often bested older, stronger opponents. His chest was firm, shoulders broad, arms corded with muscle from training with tridents and blades. Even his tail—thick and sculpted—cut through water faster than most surface currents.

Ulric didn't even glance down.

"It's not about what you look like. There are powerful forces in the sea. And every one of them would smell the magic in your blood long before they ever saw your crown."

"So you keep reminding me," Auren muttered, scowling. "Yet thirty seems awfully late for Poseidon to grant me access to that magic."

"Thirty years is not long."

"Maybe not to you—fossil."

He meant it as a jab, but his voice lacked venom. The truth was, Ulric didn't look a day over forty. But Auren had a creeping suspicion that the Kraken's years stretched back like trenches. He hadn't aged a day since the moment they'd met.

"Watch your tongue," Ulric warned, though there was a hint of amusement behind the threat. "Prince, you might be, but I'm not above dragging you to court myself if you don't hurry."

For a moment, Auren considered resisting. Just to see if he'd do it. To feel the Kraken's tentacles wrapped tight around him, dragging him bodily through the currents.

He sighed instead and turned toward the palace. "One of these days, I might try to force my way past you, old man."

Ulric's mouth tugged into something between a smirk and a threat. "I'd like to see you try."

The Hall of Currents was a marvel of shells and limestone. Towering columns reached toward a domed ceiling painted with grand depictions of Poseidon's power. Shoals of shimmering fish swam lazily through archways, and the great throne of Queen Tritheya sat elevated on a shell-shaped dais.

It was beautiful.

And it made Auren want to grind his teeth into pearl dust.

He sat near the far end of the long, crescent table, one of thirteen royal heirs draped in ceremonial sashes and surrounded by floating scrolls. His sash itched. The golden shoulder pin—Poseidon's trident—dug into his collarbone every time he shifted. His siblings sat upright, poised, and polished like the statues lining the hall.

Auren clenched and unclenched his fists under the table.

The nobles spoke in circles, their words as slimy as eels, winding through the ever-present concerns about territory, border strains, and the recent rise in surface pollution. They bickered politely, all sharp teeth behind gilded smiles.

They're like scavenging wolf eels looking for scraps of power. They don't give a damn about Atlantis.

In all fairness, Auren never applied himself enough to seem devoted to Atlantis. But at least he didn't come before the Queen and lie about it. Listening to those nobles made him want to press a trident's tip to their throats and watch the color drain from their faces.

His bored gaze drifted along the table until it locked with Ulric's. The Kraken floated near the dais, arms folded, still as carved stone. Watching him. Judging him. Probably counting the number of eye-rolls Auren had made so far. Auren made a show of yawning widely just to watch the Kraken's eyes narrow.

Auren didn't care what the court thought of him.

He was the youngest. The thirteenth. The unimportant one. A prince by blood, but too brash and temperamental to be seen as anything more than a figurehead. His siblings were scholars, diplomats, and generals.

Auren?

He spent his time in the training yards, splitting spears on sandbag dummies. He preferred steel to politics. Salt to syrupy formalities.

No one expected anything of him.

And he liked it that way.

Well, nobody besides his mentor. Ulric refused to go along with everyone else's dismissal, still hounding him like Auren's involvement was the last thread keeping Atlantis from falling apart—old nag.

The meeting dragged on for another hour, filled with more titles than substance. The Lord of Drift spoke for fifteen minutes straight. Rambling on and on about trade currents between reef colonies. Auren stared at his clenched knuckles to keep them from spontaneously punching something.

Queen Tritheya sat unmoving, her face a mask of polished stone. If the nobles' bull-shit irritated her, it didn't show. Not once did her silver gaze glance in Auren's direction.

Just when Auren was beginning to think he'd perish from scale rot, the court dispersed. Auren cast a quick glance around the room. Ulric was locked in conversation with the Lord of Drift—whose mouth moved at such a relentless pace it was a wonder his gills kept up to supply him breath. Auren smirked.

Serves you right.

And with that, he slipped from the courtroom unnoticed.

Auren didn't flee the palace—he slipped from it like a serpent through the reeds. This wasn't rebellion. It was routine. A well-practiced escape, executed with the ease of someone who'd done it many times before and fully intended to do it again.

The outer walls of Atlantis loomed above him—vast slopes of coral and volcanic stone carved with ancient runes. Glowing wards shimmered faintly along the perimeter, pulsing with a dull blue hue meant to keep intruders out and royalty in.

He swam fast, slipping past patrol routes and darting through blind spots between columns. The city guards were too predictable. Too loud. Auren could hear the steady beat of their Orca mounts long before they ever turned the corner.

The Deepguard was the elite force assigned to patrol and protect the borders of Atlantis. Warriors clung to the dorsal fins of black-and-white giants—Orcas who served not as enslaved beasts, but as willing partners. Proud and intelligent, no Orca would suffer reins or harnesses. They swam with the Deepguard by choice, bound by honor and instinct. The Deepguard operated on a bite-and-subdue basis. They didn't ask questions. Not until you were bleeding.

Auren respected them.

Which was why he wasn't about to risk tasting the full power of those teeth.

He angled down, swimming toward the lowest section of the wall, where old rock met tangled seaweed and the current pulled strongest. A forgotten seam in the foundation. A crack no wider than a conch shell.

Most Merfolk steered clear of the wall, afraid of the current's strength. But Auren met it head-on, his powerful body slicing through the drag, muscles straining and winning with ease.

Auren shoved his shoulder into the opening and wedged through with a grunt.

It wasn't as easy as it had been in his youth. Sand scraped his ribs. A jagged bit of shell scratched his bicep. He cursed softly under his breath and flailed his tail harder.

Damn it. I'm stirring up too much sand.

But before anyone could notice the disturbance, he popped out on the other side and into open water.

The current here was colder, the shadows thicker. Poseidon's magic warmed the waters within the city, keeping the residents of Atlantis comfortable. But beyond the towering walls, the magic ended in a harsh, cold line. Seaweed slithered past like curious fingers, brushing against Auren's skin. He flicked his tail once and shot toward the western reefs.

He swam a short distance before reaching his destination. Hidden between a cluster of ancient searock was his sanctuary.

His secret cave.

Auren darted through the narrow entrance and exhaled in relief as the familiar shape of his hoard came into view. His creations. His discoveries. His obsession.

Tangles of leather straps and bridles hung from bone hooks. There was even a completely intact saddle Auren had once dared to steal from a half-sunken galleon. Bits of fabric lay in organized piles along with an endless supply of fraying rope. But the pride of his collection stood at the center. A sculpture he built himself from discarded bits of human leather, twisted wire, and scraps of metal polished to a shine. He spent weeks fine-tuning it until it was just right. It resembled a creature—tall and proud, with four long limbs and a thick mane made of unraveling rope.

Auren only saw the beast once.

One stolen glimpse, boarding a human ship at dusk. The creature stood at the edge of the dock, snorting clouds into the cool air. Its legs were impossibly slender, its body strong and lean. Its hooves struck the wooden planks like thunder, and when it tossed its head, mane flying, Auren's breath caught in his throat.

He hadn't known what it was—still didn't. But it moved with such grace, such power, that the image rooted itself deep in his mind. And when he returned to his cave, hands itching, he'd begun to recreate it.

If he couldn't *touch* something, he couldn't understand it—and he desperately wanted to understand.

He loved to tinker. To touch. To take things apart and piece them back together until they made sense. There was something alive, almost sentient, about the human artifacts, especially when their stories revealed themselves through his hands. It felt as if they spoke to him, whispering secrets of the surface world with every scratch and seam.

He floated closer, trailing a rapt hand along the creature's arched neck before turning to the back shelf where parchment and ink waited.

Notes. Drawings. Diagrams. He documented everything—ship routes, net patterns, seasons. Habits. Reactions. Names.

He wanted to understand the world above as completely as he did the one below.

But lately, nothing in his cave held his attention like a single, echoing name—not the leather, not the artifacts, not even the shimmer of sun-warped silver. He wrote it again and again, testing spellings, tracing letters until they felt right. It echoed in his thoughts, in his sleep, and sent goosebumps over his skin.

A single name he'd written over and over again in the margins of nearly every piece of parchment.

Elias.

The human with the sky-colored eyes.

Auren had been scavenging human materials from the edges of boats the night everything changed. He thought the cover of darkness would conceal him well enough. Humans slept during the moonlit hours—Auren was sure of it. That's what made it safe. That's what made it *his.*

Yet that night, he'd broken Atlantis's most ancient law.

He was seen.

Auren had just hoisted himself halfway out of the water, the slick wood of the hull damp beneath his elbows, when he felt it—a tightening in his gut.

He turned around, and their eyes met.

The pressure in Auren's chest spiked like a cramp. The world tilted, his balance wavering as a rush of cold panic stole through him.

A man stood just beyond the railing of the ship, tall and broad-shouldered, dressed in a half-unbuttoned shirt that fluttered in the breeze. His skin was fair as moonlight, as if he'd been sculpted from seafoam and whitecaps. Tousled black curls framed a face that was almost unfair—sharp jaw, dimpled chin, and a mouth that looked soft enough to tempt the tides.

But it was his *eyes* that held Auren still. Pale. Blue. The color of a summer sky, undisturbed by clouds, shining with something that made Auren's pulse crash in his ears.

Wonder.

The human wasn't screaming. He wasn't afraid. He was staring, mouth parted, as if seeing Auren was the only thing giving him breath.

And Auren—gods help him—stared back.

Panic and thrill collided inside him. Every instinct screamed *run, dive, disappear*. But he couldn't move. Not when someone was looking at him like that.

Like he was something *beautiful*.

Auren's heart beat hard enough to hurt. He felt *alive*. Exposed. Burning.

That's when the man whispered, so quietly Auren almost didn't hear it:

"I knew you were real."

The sound of it broke the spell. Auren turned, tail flipping seawater onto the deck as he dove beneath the surface. He was already vanishing into the depths when another cry reached him.

"My name is Elias!"

It followed him like an anchor, and Auren let it drag him down, deeper, into the dark.

Elias.

The name echoed in his mind like a bell rung underwater. And even as the cold swallowed him whole, Auren knew: he wanted those eyes to find him again.

He *needed* them to.

Auren couldn't stand it any longer. Living off the memory of Elias alone was no longer enough. He had to see him.

Gathering supplies, Auren left the cave. Outside, the water remained inky. Dawn was still plenty far off. He had time. Auren swam to the cave entrance and gave a short, sharp whistle.

A shape moved in the gloom. A massive orca, streaked with scars, surged forward, letting out a series of playful clicks.

"There you are, Iska," Auren whispered with a smile.

The orca floated to his side, her good eye shining with recognition. Her dorsal fin curved in a graceful arc—at least from a distance. Up close, it was clear most of it was crafted from leather, strapped in place with buckles that wrapped around her belly. The original fin, along with her left flipper, had been shredded long ago. When Auren first found her, the wounds were raw and bleeding, barely clinging to life.

She'd been just a pup, thrashing weakly near the reef, her body surrounded by a haze of red. Her fin was torn off, her left flipper mangled beyond use. Abandoned by her pod, too injured to keep up, she'd begun to sink. Auren dove to her side and lifted her toward the surface. Her blowhole sputtered as she desperately gasped for air.

The healing took moons. With painstaking care, Auren crafted her replacements. He returned day after day, guiding her to the surface when she couldn't reach it on her own. And when he couldn't stay by her side, he built her a floating sling out of salvaged driftwood and woven nets—just wide enough to cradle her body and suspend her blowhole above the waterline. There she'd float, eyes half-lidded with exhaustion, breathing shallowly but alive.

After weeks of healing, Iska swam. Fiercely. Freely. Now she could've gone anywhere. She had the whole sea. But instead, Iska stayed with him.

The orca bumped his chest affectionately and let out a high trill that vibrated through his ribs.

"I missed you too," Auren murmured, brushing his fingers along her scarred side. "Ready to break a few rules?"

She responded by diving under him, letting him rest onto her back and grip the worn strap he'd stitched along her spine.

Orcas weren't slaves. They were never haltered, not even by the Deepguard. But Iska's injuries made straps and leather a necessity. That's why Auren took extra care to ensure every movement she made was her own. Never his command. Iska wasn't a pet. She was an equal—fierce, proud, and untamed, with the right to choose her own tide.

And somehow, she had chosen him.

"Let's go."

With one powerful kick of her tail, she shot forward like a torpedo, dragging Auren through the deep.

To the forbidden shallow waters dominated by Atlantis's number one enemy.

Humans.

The moon hung high and silver when Auren reached the human shipyard. He drew in a long breath, gills fluttering shut along his neck.

He *loved* this part.

The waves rocked gently, cool against his shoulders. The air carried the scent of tar, brine, rope, and fish oil—human smells. He'd trained himself to hold his breath for nearly four minutes. Longer, if he stayed still. Just enough time to poke around.

Iska swam a worried circle around him with a quiet puff of breath, chittering in warning.

"I know," Auren murmured, running a hand down the slope of her scarred flank. "Wait here," he said gently.

Iska whistled and vanished into the darker waters, but he knew she'd remain close enough to hear his call.

Auren swam silently, only the upper part of his head breaching the surface. The fishing boats swayed in their slips, dark silhouettes against the night-silvered water. Wooden hulls creaked. Nets hung like cobwebs. The tide lapped at barnacle-crusted stilts.

And there it was.

The Windless.

A modest cargo ship with faded paint and a crooked mast, but Auren had memorized every plank. The shape of the anchor. The missing chip on the rail. The spot by the stern where a coil of rope dangled, just within reach—and where, weeks ago, he had been seen.

By *him.*

Auren swam to the stern and pulled himself carefully onto the lower deck. The weight of gravity hit like a stone. Water poured from his tail and arms, soaking the wooden planks, making the deck slick beneath him. His arms felt heavy and clumsy, but he crawled well enough to peer around.

Several barrels. Some crates. A flash of copper wire near the railing. Nothing new. He frowned. He'd grab one small trinket. Something useful. Something to take apart and study and keep him occupied while—

A sound.

A single, quiet—

"Oh."

Auren whipped around, heart lurching.

At the top of the stairwell to the upper deck stood a human. His human.

Elias.

Dark curls tousled from sleep, eyes heavy but wide now with recognition. Bare feet. Loose trousers. Rope-burned hands.

But the eyes were the worst of it.

Sky-colored. Piercing. Looking at Auren like he'd stepped out of a dream.

"I knew you'd come back," Elias whispered, a slow smile touching his lips.

Auren froze. Saltwater dripped down his shoulders, glistening in the dark. He must've looked frightening. Foreign. Half-wild.

But Elias looked at him like he was a miracle. Auren's heart thundered in his chest.

Then—

"Wait!"

Auren dove.

The ocean swallowed him in a rush of bubbles and instinct. His tail kicked hard, sending him spiraling into deeper water. But even as he swam, he looked back.

And saw Elias at the edge of the deck. The human pulled something from around his neck and tossed it into the water. It fluttered once before the sea claimed it.

Auren caught it.

He clung to the soaked fabric and swam quickly, his heart a mess of panic, heat, and awe.

"Oh gods. Oh gods, what did I just— Did that really just—"

His mind swirled in a haze of adrenaline, and he didn't stop until Iska rose beneath him, letting him cling to her side.

Neither spoke—not in clicks, or words.

And together, they disappeared into the dark.

Back to the reef.

Back to the cave.

Back to thoughts that would not settle.

Auren was so preoccupied, so shaken, so enamored with the silk treasure in his hands that he swam headfirst into something solid upon returning to his cave. He recoiled, pushing back with a startled breath.

Ulric hovered, arms crossed, taking up more space than the small chamber could spare. The Sorcerer conjured blue flames trapped in bubbles that cast a ghostly light over everything. His tentacles fanned out, exploring the stone shelves, as though each appendage could think for itself.

Of course. Of course, he found me.

"You're trespassing," Auren said stiffly, even though it was his voice that cracked.

Ulric's brow lifted. "I could say the same."

Auren's jaw clenched, the silk scarf still clutched tight in his fist. "You followed me."

"I followed the gaping hole you kicked in the wall." His gaze moved over Auren, noting the scrapes on his shoulder. "You weren't exactly subtle."

"I wasn't trying to be," Auren muttered, waving his tail and swimming deeper into the cave. This was the only place that ever felt like *his*. Anger simmered to a rolling boil in Auren's stomach. "You're not supposed to be here."

"And you're not supposed to be above the tide line," Ulric snapped, voice slicing sharper than a bladefish's fin. "You know the law. We don't breach the surface. You've put yourself in danger. Again."

"Spare me the lecture, old man."

Ulric's form darkened, and several of his tentacles flexed, muscles coiling and expanding. His presence filled the space like a rapidly rising tide. "You think this is a game? If the Queen finds out you've been going above—"

"She won't. Not unless you run to her."

Ulric's nostrils flared, and a few strands of his long, dark hair came loose from the whale bone clasp on the back of his head. "You think I want to? You think I enjoy playing watchdog while you go chasing sailors like a lovesick selkie?"

The words hit like a slap.

Auren turned, eyes flashing. "You don't know what it's like up there."

"I don't care what it's like up there."

"You should!" Auren shouted. "Because I do! Because I feel different up there, Ulric—I feel... lighter. Like I'm not just some spare prince that no one wants."

Ulric stared at him, unmoving.

"And you," Auren continued, voice trembling, "you've been chasing me back into this palace like I'm a misbehaving guppy."

"I was ordered to protect you."

"From what?" Auren gestured wildly. "From barnacles? From a breeze? From myself?"

"From the surface," Ulric said. "From making the same mistakes your ancestors did. From being seen by the kind of men who would take you apart, just to watch you scream."

"They wouldn't—"

"They would," Ulric growled, drifting closer. "And they have. You think they'd be charmed by a prince with a pretty face? They'd gut you on a table and sell your bones to the highest bidder."

Auren's voice dropped low. "Not all humans are like that."

Ulric shook his head, disappointed. Not in anger. Not even in disgust. But something worse.

Resignation.

Auren swam past him toward the mouth of the cave, the silk scarf gripped tight in his hands, hiding it from the Sorcerer. He didn't bother demanding to be alone. What would be the point? Ulric would follow anyway. He always did. Not because he cared.

Auren wasn't naïve enough to believe that anymore. But because it was his duty. His burden.

Auren's fingers tightened around the ribbon.

"Just once," he muttered under his breath, "I wish you'd come after me because you wanted to. But every time you do this, I can tell you don't actually give a damn."

Auren kicked forward, tail cutting the water in a sharp burst of speed as he fled the cave.

He didn't wait for Ulric.

Let the old Kraken catch up, if he could.

Chapter Two

Ulric

If Ulric had known Queen Tritheya's final son would become the most infuriating creature in all the sea, he might have stayed in the depths.

He'd served at the queen's side for a century. Attended every one of her dozen births and watched each of her children grow into scholars, warriors, or courtiers. Each had come into their magic and upheld their duties with grace. He'd seen tantrums, tears, triumphs—and he'd guided them all with patience befitting his post. When the magic inked into his skin warned that this pregnancy would be the last heir of Poseidon's bloodline, Ulric assumed the worst was behind him.

So he left, confident that Atlantis could stand on its own for a few seasons while he was away. The magic in his skin was calling him home.

To the black depths.

To the trench.

To be with his kind.

The Kraken. Chosen wielders of Poseidon's magic—keepers of balance, judges of divine will. They served the old ways. The deep ways. The silence and pressure of the ocean's floor.

Ulric only intended to be away for a few seasons. He didn't notice the years slip away. Time didn't feel the same when it couldn't touch you. But without him knowing, he'd lost decades. And when the magic called him to the surface once more, Atlantis had changed.

And the final heir of Poseidon's bloodline not only had been born, but had grown into a Mer of twenty.

Auren had grown into something wild and ungovernable—crimson fire and storm-blue eyes, with hair that refused to be tamed and a temper hot enough to melt ore. He slipped past guards, crossed forbidden borders, and vanished for hours—only to return with an eye-roll and some smug explanation about how he *"had it under control."*

Ulric blamed himself, at least in part. Auren was the only one of Poseidon's heirs he hadn't mentored from birth—and of course, it was this final child who grew into something feral. Reckless. A creature raised in the palace but born of the storm.

He drove Ulric mad.

And that was exactly the problem.

Because Ulric couldn't stop noticing how that rebellion had shaped him. How his years in the sparring rings had honed his body into a formidable shape—wide-set shoulders, defined arms, a tail rippling with muscle. He didn't carry himself like a court-bred prince. He moved like a warrior.

And gods help him, Ulric noticed.

"If only he kept his gaze in the water, where it belongs," Ulric murmured bitterly.

After discovering Auren's secret cave, Ulirc knew it wouldn't be long before the prince tried for another escape. And sure enough, the moment the palace grew busy and the guards were occupied, the prince slipped away. Again.

Though Ulric had to admit, however begrudgingly, that Auren was good at it. If not for Ulric already predicting the prince's escape, he wouldn't have noticed the Mer disappear in the span of a blink.

But as it was, Ulric was watching. And with a groan, he excused himself and followed. He exited the city, making his way to the now-familiar entrance carved into the stone. Auren was gone— likely off acquiring more human artifacts— but Ulric knew he'd come back. One didn't abandon a hoard this meticulously kept for long.

That, perhaps, was the greatest surprise.

Ulric would never have guessed Auren capable of such fastidiousness. The cave wasn't just filled with trinkets—it was organized. Every object was carefully placed, labeled, and studied. Not a haphazard pile, but a curated collection.

While he waited, he took it all in—a veritable shrine to human detritus. The walls glimmered in the dark, filled with buckles, bridles, twisted scraps of metal and leather. And in the center, a delicate sculpture pieced together from scraps of wire and tanned hide—a horse.

Ulric had seen them many times during his trips to the surface, and he recognized the grace in their form. Auren shaped it well. Unconsciously, Ulric reached up, stroking the ear made from what looked like the tip of a human woman's shoe.

"Never would have taken him as an artist," Ulric said to himself. "And a good one."

The sound of a swishing orca's tail announced Auren's arrival, and Ulric quickly retreated from the sculpture, taking up a stern position at the front of the cave.

Ulric blended so well with the dark stone that the prince flinched in surprise when the shadows of his cave moved. He swung his tail in alarm. "What're you—!"

"Five minutes," Ulric articulated dangerously. "I turned my back for five minutes, and you were already gone."

Auren's jaw set, and his tail twitched with irritation. "I wasn't out long."

"If you keep going to the surface, it's only a matter of time before you're spotted."

"It's nighttime. I was careful."

Ulric barely resisted the urge to roll his eyes.

Stay calm. I'm the mentor. I can't be the one to lose my head.

But damn it all, this sea-sprite was testing him.

"Humans can stay awake in the night, too, Auren. Surely you aren't that foolish."

"I'm never on deck long, can only hold my breath a couple of minutes."

"You leave the water—!?" Ulric closed his eyes and forced himself to take a steadying breath. "Please tell me you don't literally climb aboard human ships. All it would take is a single human with functioning eyes."

"It's not a big deal," Auren said, but he wouldn't look at Ulric as he said it. "Like I'd be so careless."

The Kraken narrowed his eyes suspiciously, then his gaze locked on a silver fabric woven in Auren's hair. He scented it immediately. Human silk. Not fabric made by Merkind. The scent of the oily land creatures still lingered in its threads.

Ulric let out a long-suffering sigh. "You've already been seen," he said, rubbing his temple.

That earned him a glare.

"You don't know what you're talking about."

Ulric leaned forward, his dark tentacles unfurling in warning. "Do not lie to me, spriteling. I can scent human all over that," he said, jabbing towards the scarf.

Auren clutched at his braid, as if the Kraken might try to yank the silk free.

Ulric threw his hands in exasperation. "And yet you cling to that like it's some lover's token." He'd meant it as a joke. But the defiant flush to Auren's cheeks made something volatile coil in Ulric's belly. He froze in disbelief. "You can't be serious."

Auren bristled. "So what if I am?"

"Do you have any idea how dangerous that is?"

"Oh, please, Ulric. Don't start the lecture. I'm not in the mood for politics—"

"This isn't politics." Ulric snapped, tentacles flaring in a rage, spreading around him and eating up any remaining space in the cave. "This is survival. Yours."

Auren moved to push past him, but Ulric's tentacles surged forward, catching him mid-stroke.

"Let me go," Auren hissed, thrashing in his grip.

"I'll drag you back if I have to," Ulric said, even as his heart beat erratically. Even as his hands trembled with the effort not to touch more than was allowed.

The struggle was brief.

Ulric overpowered him with ease. But the closeness... damn it all, Ulric was losing the fight with himself by the second. Auren's body was trapped in his, muscles coiled tight, breath catching. His tail thrashed in anger, hands trying to pry the limbs wrapped around his middle.

This is allowed. I'm taking him back to Atlantis. It's my duty. Nothing more.

Ulric didn't know who he was trying to convince. The magic in his skin, or himself.

I am fulfilling an order. Nothing more.

But even as he continued to deny it, Ulric knew his touch lingered too long, holding the prince long after he'd stilled and admitted defeat. One tentacle remained wrapped beneath Auren's ribs, feeling every breath, every flex of frustration. The imprint of his shape etched itself into Ulric's memory like coral scarring stone.

A single tendril ran down the length of his abdomen, feeling the muscles bunched there.

He's not soft. He's hard and heavy and...

Searing pain flashed in Ulric's skin, the tattoos burning him like a brand.

The Kraken released him with a sharp breath, turning away before Auren could see the heat in his eyes.

"The Queen wants an audience," he said stiffly, trying to shake off the pain.

Auren didn't answer right away. When Ulric turned to him, his stomach dropped. Auren wouldn't meet his eyes—his arms wrapped around himself, as if trying to scrub away Ulric's touch.

"Did you hear me?"

"Yeah, I heard you," Auren snapped. "Why is she bothering to talk to me now?"

Ulric gestured broadly to the cave. "This would be my guess."

Auren's eyes swept across the hoarded treasures. "She doesn't know."

"She might suspect," Ulric said. "The Queen is as old as I am. You will not fool her easily."

"I'm not going," Auren said.

"Yes," Ulric said with a growl, "you are."

Another tense silence. Auren pressed his lips thin in defiance. "You always do this."

"What? Protect you?"

"No. Drag me back. Assume I don't know what I'm doing. That I can't make my own choices."

"It's because you never listen. If you'd stop acting like a child—"

"—then stop treating me like one."

Ulric's voice dropped low. "I'm sworn to protect Poseidon's bloodline. That includes you."

Auren moved closer. "Then protect me from the court. From the lies. From the ones who don't actually care about Atlantis, only their own positions of power."

Ulric flinched, and Auren pushed closer. So close that Ulric felt the wall press against his back as somehow, the prince herded him into a corner. He was close enough that Ulric could see the deep rise and fall of his chest. Feel the tickle of red hair against his skin.

"But you won't, will you?" Auren whispered. "You'll just keep locking me in there with those sharks."

"You're a prince of Atlantis, it is your duty to—"

"But what if I wasn't?" Auren interjected, and Ulric froze at the swell of urgency in his voice. Like this is what he'd wanted to say all along. "What if I weren't a prince? What if Poseidon's blood didn't flow in my veins? Would you still come after me?"

Ulric's jaw clenched, and he said nothing.

Because he couldn't. The magic in his skin wouldn't allow him. Even now, as the honest truth rested on the tip of his tongue, the marks along his skin began to burn in warning.

Because Ulric's magic was conditional. Not born into him like Auren's. His connection to the ocean's power was bestowed after years of training and trial... and an oath. An oath to give himself to the god of the sea and never let his heart belong to another.

He vowed never to take a mate.

A lover.

No tether to anything that would distract him.

He'd promised Poseidon his entire life in exchange for eternal power. The ability to protect the sea and all it birthed. He had never strayed from that path. Nothing had ever tempted him to do so.

Until now.

But the magic threatened. It burned on his skin. So he lied. He lied to those cerulean eyes looking at him with too much earnestness.

"No." Ulric finally said. "I would not."

The court of Atlantis rose from the seabed like a monument carved from time itself. Poseidon, it was said, had always favored the architecture of the Greeks, and so his builders had mimicked the Pantheon's glory below the waves.

But where the Greeks etched their heroes into their temples, Atlantis honored only the god of the sea. Across the inner walls, murals bloomed in sweeping arches: the elegance of the Merfolk, the solemn watch of the Krakens, the wrath of the ocean as it demolished human fleets.

A visual scripture of sea-born power.

Ulric hovered to the right of the Queen's throne, the designated place of the Court Sorcerer. Every tattoo along his upper body hummed with magic. Being this close to another carrier of the god's power always charged the water around him. The queen's magic was second only to his. The chosen Mermaid of the sea.

And kneeling at the far away base of her throne, head bowed before her diamond gaze, was Auren.

Ulric didn't envy his position.

Auren knelt before the throne, tail curled respectfully beneath him. One hand lay flat against the tiled floor, the other crossed over his chest with a bowed head. The only stance one took before Queen Tritheya.

She sat above him like the sea itself—dark-skinned, with coiled black hair and piercing silver eyes. She looked nothing like Auren, nor most of her children. That was the nature of divine parentage. Poseidon's magic had fathered them all, and so they bore little resemblance to her.

Her tail was a magnificent sapphire blue, longer than that of any Mermaid Ulric had known. Ear fins curved from the sides of her head like delicate fans, framing the crown of gemstones and shells that gleamed like they had grown there.

"Mother, I have come at your request," Auren said, his voice clipped. His head remained bowed.

"Yes. I'm sure you came very willingly," she replied, dry as salt.

Ulric kept still, arms folded behind his back.

"There has been a significant increase in human ships above our city," Queen Tritheya said, silver eyes sweeping the room like a tide rolling in. "More than a dozen vessels over the past three moon cycles. One in particular concerns me. Civilian-marked, named *The Windless*. Captained by a biologist, we believe a coastal kingdom has sent it to study the sea. Particularly, right above Atlantis."

Her gaze snapped to Auren, sharp as a spearpoint.

"Do you have any idea why that might be, my son?"

The room's pressure shifted, magic responding to the Queen's scrutiny. Ulric's tattoos prickled across his chest. His tentacles coiled tighter.

Auren's jaw tightened. "I wouldn't know."

A lie. And not a good one.

The Queen's expression didn't change. "You forget," she said softly, "I can sense lies the way sharks smell blood in the water."

"Then you already know the answer."

Ulric's throat tightened.

Don't provoke her, he silently urged. *Not like this.*

"I know you've been playing a dangerous game," the Queen continued. "Swimming close to the surface. Visiting human ships. Endangering every life in this city with your curiosity."

"I was careful," Auren muttered.

"Clearly not careful enough," she said. "Because now the humans are watching. They linger. They probe. You were seen."

Auren flinched but didn't deny it.

"I'm forbidding you from rising again," she said. "You will not approach the surface. If I sense even a ripple near the barrier, Ulric will craft a sinking potion that physically prevents you from crossing it."

Auren's head snapped up, and Ulric's breath stuttered as those eyes swept past the queen and locked on him. Like Auren was silently pleading with him to speak. To contradict her. To come to his rescue, as Ulric had done many times before.

I'm sorry, spriteling.

Ulric held his gaze and forced the words out.

"Yes, Your Majesty," he said, each syllable cutting his tongue. "I can create such a tonic."

Auren's body stiffened, and Ulric felt the betrayal radiating from him like heat from a volcanic vent.

The Queen rose, voice final. "Then we have nothing left to discuss. You are both dismissed."

Auren didn't bow. He turned and stormed from the chamber, emerald tail swishing violently, causing the massive doors to slam in his wake.

Ulric didn't follow. Not immediately.

He floated beside the throne, trying to still the ache that had bloomed behind his ribs.

"Ulric," the Queen said as she rose from her perch. "You understand this is for his protection."

He nodded. "Yes, I do."

Her silver eyes scrutinized him for a moment, and for a heartbeat, he feared she sensed the whirlpool of emotion ravaging his insides.

"Good," she said finally and left the room.

This is for his own good. He's going to get himself hurt. It's for his protection.

Guilt tore through him like a shark at wounded prey. Because what the queen asked of him... what he had agreed to do... It wasn't protection. It was a cage.

And Auren had heard him say yes to the lock.

Ulric hadn't meant to return to the cave.

He'd meant to let the sting of the courtroom fade, to give them both space—time to breathe, to cool the frayed ends of their patience. But something restless churned in his chest. He told himself he was only checking on Auren. To ensure the prince was safe, and therefore, fulfill his duty.

He reached the mouth of the hidden cave only to find it empty. No hint of an emerald tail, no sharp voice demanding he go away, no echo of movement or breath.

Panic struck.

Did he really just go to the surface in broad daylight?

Ulric's tattoos pulsed with unease. His gaze swept the reef's edge. Sunlight fractured through the shallows ahead, far too close to the surface for any Mer to be lingering.

He surged forward.

And then he saw him.

Auren knelt in the sand at the edge of the reef, just beneath the shimmer line where water kissed the open air. His body was still, fins fluttering behind him. His head was bowed low, shoulders hunched.

Ulric slowed, his reprimand already dying on his tongue.

There, nestled in the sand beside Auren, lay a seabird—small, delicate, and heartbreakingly still. One wing was splayed at an unnatural angle, the other tucked beneath its body. Its eyes, swollen from salt, stared blankly through the water. Most of its feathers remained intact, suggesting it had only just fallen... or been pulled beneath the waves.

"I was coming to check on Iska," Auren said quietly, not turning to look at him. "And I saw it hit the water. Its wing was broken. I tried to keep it up... so it could breathe. But..."

His voice caught. "...it just gave up in the end."

Ulric's anger faded, hollowing into something gentler. He studied the gills along Auren's neck, the tension in his jaw, the way he looked at the bird like it had taken something precious and never meant to give it back.

Tenderness cracked Ulric's chest open.

"I can help you bury it," he said softly. "Properly."

Auren looked up at him, and emotion lightened his eyes. Surprise, mostly. Gratitude, maybe. He gave a slow nod.

Together, they buried the seabird in a patch of sunwarmed sand, nestled between the rocks. Ulric said no words. Auren didn't ask for any. When they finished, Auren lingered for a moment longer before turning and swimming slowly back toward the cave.

The silence between them was quiet, but not heavy. Until Auren finally broke it.

"I know it's stupid," he muttered. "Getting upset over a common seabird."

"Death is upsetting," Ulric said. "Even expected ones. Everything dies eventually."

"Except you," Auren said quickly.

Ulric tried not to let his discomfort show as they swam.

"You'll live forever, won't you? Even my mother will eventually fade, once Poseidon's bloodline is secured. But you...You'll just keep going."

Auren didn't say it bitterly. He said it like a fact.

Ulric didn't answer right away.

The Queen's immortal tether had been granted. As the vessel for Poseidon's bloodline, she was ageless only so long as that bloodline needed her. Once it flourished on its own, her tether would dissolve. But Ulric... Ulric had bound himself for eternity. His life was inked in service. And like the creatures that lived at the ocean's deepest floor, he would remain. Unmoving. Unchanged. Alone.

When they reached the reef's bend, Auren darted back through the crevice leading to his secret cave.

Ulric hesitated.

He wasn't sure why he followed.

But he did.

Inside, the glow of bioluminescent moss and reflected metals painted strange shapes across the walls. Auren's cave was a shrine to human curiosity. It was reckless but also brimming with wonder. It drew Ulric like dumb prey to an anglerfish.

Auren turned on him immediately. "What? You have to babysit me here, too? Am I not allowed in my own cave now?"

"I never said that."

"Shouldn't you be somewhere important?" Auren snapped. "Don't you have a beloved mate to get back to or something?"

Ulric gave him a long look. "The Kraken chosen by Poseidon do not take mates. We serve and in exchange, wield his magic. That is our promise."

Auren rolled his eyes. "Gods, how romantic."

"It has been this way since the beginning. A pact between my people and the gods," Ulric said, turning away. "We don't all get to chase foolish dreams."

Ulric's gaze swept the space. His attention snagged on the sculpture again—the familiar shape of four long legs, arched neck, and a flowing tail, all formed from twisted leather and discarded rigging.

"I like the horse sculpture," Ulric said before he could stop himself. "How long did it take you?"

Auren blinked, caught off guard. "The what?"

Ulric realized the mistake too late. Of course, Auren didn't know what it was.

"That," Ulric said, nodding toward it. "The creature."

Auren tilted his head, still watching him. "You know what it is. You said it's called a harss?"

Ulric hesitated. "It's pronounced horse. And I've seen one. Once. On land."

Auren's eyes widened. "Have you been to the surface—?"

Ulric cut him off, sharper than he meant to. "Just get home before it gets dark."

Auren stared at him, something unreadable flickering in his expression. But he didn't push.

And Ulric didn't explain.

He turned before he could say something he'd regret, slipping into the water's gloom.

Leaving behind the shimmer of human scraps.

And the Mer who never looked at the deep.

Only the sky.

Chapter Three

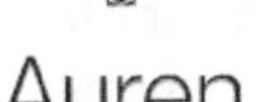

Auren

Auren lasted a week.

A week of torture, caged in palace walls. Surrounded by polished lies and thinly veiled deceptions. The only thing that kept him sane was Elias's silver silk, twisted into a braid down the side of his hair.

He wore it every day.

From the moment it touched his hands, Auren hadn't been able to let it go. The scarf was soft as breath, the scent of humans, of Elias, still clinging in its fibers. Auren twined it into his hair with careful fingers. A token. A symbol. Something he could press between his fingertips when the world grew too heavy.

And he did. Often.

When the throne room felt too suffocating, when the elders' voices buzzed in his skull like biting sea gnats, he found himself reaching up, fingertips brushing that silken thread like it could free him.

He let himself daydream.

About the human.

About the way Elias had looked at him with wonder. Not fear or violence, as his mother and Ulric would have him believe. But something akin to worship. Like Auren was something special. Not a prince, not a pawn, not an heir to anything but the moment they'd shared on that ship's deck.

It had only been seconds. But Poseidon, it had been enough to spark something inside him that Auren hadn't known was missing.

Elias's eyes saw through the glamour of court titles and duty-bound obligations and saw him.

And it made Auren feel... dangerous things. Hopeful things.

He'd never felt that with any Mer.

His siblings had all taken mates by his age, had built lives, and formed families. Auren had been propositioned more times than he could count. By noble Mermaids, bold warriors, even one of his sister's old flames, who claimed they could make the palace *less boring* together.

But none of them ever stirred anything inside Auren. None of them made him feel like the world paused just to make space for his heart.

He'd started to lose hope that such a connection would ever find him. Started to think maybe those feelings would never come. Maybe his bloodline made him too different, too untouchable. Or maybe he was broken in some irreparable way.

Then Elias had looked at him like *that*.

And suddenly, Auren wasn't sure of anything anymore.

Not his duty.

Not his future.

Not the promises he'd been born into.

Only the silver scarf in his hair, and the memory of sky-colored eyes that made him feel completely seen.

But seven days of court depravity were enough. He couldn't do it anymore.

He slipped past the guard under the cover of night, heart pounding with every swish of his tail. The city wall loomed, and Auren could practically feel the cooler waters outside its border. Cool and quiet. The kind of quiet Auren craved.

Another day of court nonsense still clawed at the back of his skull. Hollow words and passive threats. Future obligations and necessary protections.

As if all of it wasn't a noose tightening around Auren's throat.

The idea of being tethered to the depths, of being cut off from the surface forever... his chest went tight just thinking about it. He needed open water. He needed freedom. He needed to leave.

And he was nearly to the wall when a familiar pressure rolled through the current.

"I was wondering how long you'd last," came the low rumble of Ulric's voice behind him.

Auren cursed under his breath and spun in the water. "I'm not going to the surface."

"Then why sneak out under the cover of darkness?" Ulric asked as he drifted over. "Why slip your guards? *Again?*"

Auren growled. "Because I needed to get out. I can't—" He faltered, his chest tightening again. Gills refusing to work.

"Can't what? Bear the responsibility?"

"No, I—"

"Can't handle the task of scribing a few meetings? Honestly, Auren, it's like you're not even trying—"

"I can't breathe in there!" Auren shouted, his voice echoing through the water.

Something in Ulric's expression shifted, just slightly. The stern crease between his brows eased.

"I don't have the strength for a lecture," Auren muttered, and hated the way his eyes stung. "Drag me back if you want. I'm not in the mood to fight."

Ulric was silent for a long moment. Then, unexpectedly, he said, "Go where you need to go."

"You're not going to take me back?"

Auren watched as Ulric wrestled with his better judgment and forced the words out through clenched, shark-sharp teeth.

"If you need space, you need space. Just tell me where you're going and when you'll be back."

Auren blinked, thrown. His shoulders eased a fraction. "There's a bioluminescent storm over the western reef tonight," he said quietly. "I've missed it three years in a row. That's where I was going."

Ulric hesitated so long that Auren assumed the Kraken was about to object. About to tell him that it was too close to the surface. But instead, he said the last thing Auren ever expected to hear.

"Can I join you?"

The words rippled through the water like a current heading the wrong way. Auren blinked stupidly at him, unsure he'd heard right.

Auren's first instinct was to dismiss it as another way for Ulric to play guard and protect Poseidon's heir, as always. But... Ulric had asked. Not ordered. Asked. He'd given Auren the option to say no. And that—that wasn't something the Court Sorcerer ever did. This didn't feel like an obligation. It felt more personal. Something warm stirred in Auren's chest. He swallowed and gave a single, careful nod, brushing the feeling away before it could rise too far.

"Alright," Auren said. "But don't slow me down."

They swam, slipping past guard routes and into the older

ring of stone fortifications. Auren moved toward his usual escape route, already dreading the scrape of stone against his ribs.

"I don't think you'll fit through this one," Auren muttered, preparing to wedge himself through the crack.

"I wasn't planning on it," Ulric replied.

He placed a single suctioned appendage on the stone beside Auren's usual exit and pressed inward. The rock gave with a creak, revealing a narrow but smooth archway. A hidden passage.

Auren blinked. "What—wait, this was here the whole time?"

"It's an old courier exit. Magically sealed, but I keep the enchantment on it fresh."

Auren's mouth dropped open. "You've been watching me smash myself through coral for *years*... and this was here the whole time?"

Ulric's smirk was unrepentant. "A small justice I allow myself."

"You're an ass," Auren muttered—but he was grinning as he said it.

They slipped into the passage lit by trapped flame-bubbles pulsing blue. When they emerged on the other side, Auren moved forward, just as a shadow passed overhead.

An Orca.

One of the Deepguard's long-ranged patrol beasts. They guarded the city even without Merfolk companions. The creature spotted them instantly. It turned, mouth open, ready to unleash a shrieking alert.

Before it could, Ulric surged forward, faster than Auren expected.

A single hand extended, palm open. The tattoos on his fingers lit like brands, bright blue magic flaring to his elbow. The orca shuddered, gaze going glassy. Then it turned away and continued on its patrol at a languid pace, seemingly without a care in the world.

Auren stared, mouth slightly open.

"If you weren't the very reason I have to sneak out," Auren said, "I'd definitely bring you along more often."

Ulric raised a brow. "And here I thought you snuck out just to avoid my company."

Auren grinned. "That too."

He brushed past him in a flurry of bubbles, a grin curling at the corner of his mouth. Ulric followed, then said, "Oh, and uh—don't tell your mother."

Auren couldn't help it. He laughed.

The reef shimmered, the bloom casting everything in ghostlight. Cool blues and glimmering greens trailed like smoke through the water. A colony of sea lions joined the natural wonder. Their slender bodies weaving in and out of the kelp fronds, trailing whisps of blue bioluminescence.

Auren swam and spun with them, knocking aside stalks of kelp, creating bursts of light. The glowing algae clung to his skin and tail like stardust. He knew his hair was likewise coated in dots of luminescence. Behind him, Ulric moved slower, always with control and purpose, never abandon. Auren grinned as he glanced over his shoulder.

"Don't strain yourself, old man."

Ulric's eyes snapped to him. "What did you just say?"

"I said, try to keep up without throwing out your back," Auren called, laughing as he used his tail to flick a whisp of blue light into Ulric's face.

The Kraken moved. A tentacle snapped forward and curled tight around the joint of his tail fin, yanking hard. Auren yelped as he was dragged backward through the water, limbs flailing for balance. Another tentacle caught him mid-waist, spinning him like a hooked fish. He twisted, trying to right himself—but Ulric darted forward, his human half now fully engaged.

Their chests collided, and Auren found himself pressed up against hard muscle and cool, ink-marked skin. Their hands caught mid-strike, forearms straining as each pushed against the other in a sudden test of strength. Ulric's grip was iron. His arms barely budged, while Auren's muscles flexed and corded in resistance, trying to gain leverage.

The heat of it surprised him—not just the friction, but the closeness. The press of their bodies. The sheer, solid presence of Ulric in front of him. Tattoos flashing along Ulric's arms, pulsing with power beneath Auren's fingers.

"Who's old now, you little shit?" Ulric barked, laughter curling in his voice.

They wrestled—if it could even be called that. Auren kicked and shoved, his arms braced against Ulric's shoulders, his palms digging into solid muscle. But Ulric didn't budge. Not really.

He shifted with him, letting Auren think he was making progress, letting him struggle just enough to believe it was a fair fight. But Ulric's core held fast, unmoved. His tentacles coiled and adjusted with lazy precision, keeping Auren right where he wanted him.

And Auren realized, with a startled jolt of awareness, that Ulric was *letting* him fight. Letting him grapple and work out some of his pent-up stress.

Because it was abundantly clear that if he wanted to, Ulric could end this in a heartbeat.

He could break me.

The thought should've unsettled him. But it didn't. Instead, it sent a jolt of electricity down his spine, raising his awareness all the way down to his tailfin.

Auren was panting when Ulric finally let go. The release was sudden—like a line cut from a net—and Auren drifted back, chest heaving, hair partially fallen from his braid and sweeping across his face. His gills flared wide, straining to catch the current.

Ulric winced, and there was a flash of magic along the runes on his arms, but the Kraken shook it off, amusement still dancing in his eyes. "That's what you get for running your mouth," he said with a huff.

Auren didn't answer right away. He was still catching his breath. Still trying to ignore the phantom press of Ulric's hands on his arms, his waist, his back. Still trying to quiet the voice in his head that whispered *he could've broken me.* And didn't.

For a moment... Ulric hadn't felt like his mentor. Or his jailor. He'd felt like a man.

Auren's gaze slid away. Anywhere but that smirking mouth. He needed to gather his thoughts. Get himself under control.

He spotted a pair of seal pups tumbling through a curtain of kelp, squeaking and nipping at each other. It gave him enough distance to pull his frazzled mind back together. To summon up that familiar bite and bickering in their usual cadence.

"Yeah, well, I bet this rock is younger than you—"

He turned to throw the insult, but stopped short.

Ulric was *right* there.

So close that their noses nearly touched. So close Auren felt the pressure of the Kraken's words before they were even spoken.

"What was that?" Ulric whispered, voice low. Ragged.

The current stirred between them, brushing against Auren's lips like a kiss not quite given. His breath hitched. His mind spun in a panic. Why was Ulric talking like that? Why was he so close? Why wasn't Auren moving away?

"I—I don't remember," he whispered back, because it was the only truth he had left.

This close, and in the glowing light of the algae bloom, Auren saw the Kraken like he'd never seen him before.

Ulric's skin was burnished bronze, smooth and defined. The

tattoos etched across his arms and chest glowed in the bloom light, pulsing with the magic that lived in his bones. His beard framed a sharp, grim mouth that for once wasn't twisted in disapproval. Dark hair drifted around his face, framing obsidian eyes that missed nothing.

And Auren's heart stuttered.

Oh no.

Ulric was beautiful.

No—not beautiful.

Ulric was *devastating*.

It hit him like a breach to the ribs. He dropped his gaze before it could betray him, pretending to brush glowing algae from his arm, but the heat had already risen to his face. He felt it in his ears, his gills. Everywhere.

Ulric let out a low chuckle, that same rough, unguarded laugh that made something flutter low in Auren's gut.

"That's what I thought," the Kraken backed away. "All talk until you get your ass handed to you."

Auren swallowed hard, voice hoarse. "I liked that."

"What? Getting tossed around like chum?"

"Hearing you laugh." The words slipped out too quickly, too honestly. Ulric stilled. The water went quiet. Auren winced. "Sorry. That was weird."

Ulric's voice was softer when he replied. "It happens... sometimes."

"You should do it more."

Their eyes met. And something cracked. Something shifted. The water between them held its breath. Auren's thoughts tangled. He didn't want Ulric to scold him. Didn't want his protection. He wanted Ulric to stay—like this. Unguarded and real.

But he couldn't say that. Not when his stomach still twisted with discomfort. Not when he didn't even understand why that look set his skin alight.

He turned away, twisting the silver silk in his braid like a nervous habit.

Ulric's eyes landed on it, and Auren quickly dropped his hand. But it was too late. Whatever softness had been growing on his face turned to stone.

"Let's go," Ulric said, voice tight. "It'll be dawn soon."

Auren didn't argue. Not this time.

They swam back in silence, but it was far from quiet inside the bedlam of Auren's mind.

Ulric. Ulric, the nag. Ulric, the stone-faced Court Sorcerer, who probably remembered the formation of the first rock and had the attitude to prove it. Ulric, who scowled at everything and laughed at nothing, bossed Auren around like it was a holy duty.

Ulric, who'd held him—when he could have easily broken him. Whose laugh was deep, like the rumble of the sea.

Ulric, the strong, beautiful Kraken from the deep.

Auren didn't say a word, not as the shimmer of the bloom faded behind them, not as the familiar shapes of Atlantis rose in the distance. But a smile tugged at his lips, shy and entirely involuntary.

He hadn't expected any of this. Not the way Ulric had looked at him. Not the way he'd felt in Ulric's arms. Not the way something shifted and settled, like a door opening inside his chest that he hadn't known was there.

He should've been afraid of it.

But he wasn't.

He was curious. Hopeful. Like maybe—for the first time—he wasn't broken for wanting something different. Wanting something he wasn't supposed to have.

Like maybe it could become something new.

Something wild.

Something real.

Something unapologetically *his*.

Chapter Four

Ulric

ULRIC HAD TO ADMIT—AUREN SURPRISED HIM.

A full moon cycle had passed since the Queen's decree forbade him from surfacing, and yet the prince hadn't tried again. Not once. Not even with his usual reckless defiance. That alone was enough to make Ulric suspicious. But the truth was...Auren had found other ways to breathe.

He still slipped out of the city— because, of course, he did— but now it was to visit that charming cave of his. Or the disabled orca he'd rescued, who adored him with a devotion Ulric tried not to envy. The boy was wild, yes. But he wasn't disobedient. Not where it mattered most. And Ulric, who had feared this last heir would become his greatest challenge, found himself—reluctantly, stupidly—proud.

Auren hadn't surfaced. Ulric would take the win.

Without meaning to, Ulric grew fond of the cave.

At first, he'd visited only to ensure the prince wasn't secretly sneaking away. But over the passing weeks, it became a habit. A ritual. He would drift inside while Auren worked, sometimes asking about a new artifact he'd found, sometimes just to listen. Auren always answered eagerly, his eyes lighting up in a way Ulric had never seen in the throne room.

Now, sitting amongst the court nobles, Auren looked like stone carved from obligation. Stiff and unsmiling. Miserable. He barely spoke unless spoken to, and when he did, it was short and sour.

But here... here in this space of curiosity and obsession, the Merman transformed into something vibrating with a passion for life.

Auren worked like a scholar. Organized, meticulous. Every item catalogued and arranged. A web of meaning existed behind each bit of broken glass or torn fabric, and gods help him, Ulric found it captivating. He asked about the objects to hear Auren speak about them. Just to watch his hands move with purpose, his lips parting in explanation, his eyes fierce with thought.

Ulric already knew what most of it was, of course. He'd been to the surface far more times than he'd ever admit.

The Merfolk of Atlantis depended on herbs and minerals only the surface could provide. The ocean didn't grow dandelion root or white sage, didn't offer eucalyptus or bitter bark. So Ulric ventured inland— using methods of magic to hide what he was, and blend in with the humans.

He came and went quietly.

In and out. Never lingering longer than necessary.

He avoided the villages when he could, slipping into the forests or overgrown gardens under the cover of mist and early morning light. If he had to enter a town, he did so with care, keeping to the edges, moving like a wraith through human life.

No one ever recognized him for what he was.

And that was how it had to be.

But as Ulric listened to Auren's passionate raves, guilt sank into his stomach like a burning coal, melting through him, leaving sickness behind.

Auren would hold up a bit of snapped metal or a rusted hinge with excitement in his eyes, guessing its function. A cooking tool, he'd say, when it was part of a clock. A blade, when it had once been a piece of a wagon. Or he'd tilt his head, puzzled, asking why a human might wear shoes with spines protruding from the heel.

Ulric would know the answers. Every time.

He knew the name of each object, the shape of its use. Knew the scent of fire-forged steel and the sound of church bells echoing over hills. Knew that the "ugly spines" were spurs for riding boots. He could've told Auren what it meant. Could've fed that quick-burning curiosity, watched the fire in those eyes flare even brighter.

And gods, how he wanted to.

He wanted to teach him everything. Not just about human tools, but about the world above. About birds and wind and bonfires. About books with paper pages and laughter that echoed in wooden taverns. About music that wasn't just sound but story.

But he couldn't.

Because if he did... Auren would know.

He'd know Ulric had touched the world he so desperately longed for.

Auren couldn't know that.

Couldn't even glimpse the idea that the surface was reachable. It would destroy him. Because it would mean the barrier between worlds was not an insurmountable prison. Just a sentence. And that it was his name written on the warrant.

So Ulric said nothing. He just asked questions, let Auren ramble, and watched him burn with life.

And all the while, Ulric remained careful—painfully, obsessively careful. He hadn't touched Auren since that night on the reef. Not in any way that could be misconstrued. Not in any way that might rouse the wrath of the magic carved into his skin. He allowed only the smallest points of contact. The acceptable ones.

A hand on the small of Auren's back to get his attention in a crowded hall. A steadying pass of fingers over his arm as he helped him into royal sashes. The barest brush of his palm to Auren's chest when pinning the golden trident insignia over his heart. Tasks any palace servant might perform. But Ulric always volunteered. Always ensured it was his hands. His touch. If only for a moment.

The magic never burned him again. But it flickered. Just enough to make him retreat.

And still, despite every effort, despite every guarded breath and reined-in impulse, his magic began to fail.

Not in great swells, but in small, insidious ways. The floating blue flames that lit Atlantis's halls began to go out more often. Tonics he'd brewed for centuries started misfiring. Potions for healing, clarity, fertility... all flawed now.

A potion for dreamless sleep made the user speak in riddles for days. A tonic for clean skin had the user referring to everyone as "Uncle Sebastian" for hours. Finally, a draft intended to aid in a healthy birth led to the mother's sneezing bioluminescent boogers.

Once it was determined this wouldn't harm the baby, all was well—but Ulric was displeased.

These errors. This lapse in his magic was his fault.

He knew the rules.

He had carved them into his very flesh.

No mate. No desire. No love.

But Auren had never followed rules.

And Ulric—Ulric was starting to forget why he'd ever believed in them.

Their relationship had shifted. Grown too soft. Too easy. He found himself laughing more. Teasing, even. Relaxing.

It terrified him.

Now, Ulric lounged in the narrow cave, his tentacles lazily sprawled across the stone, twirling a tarnished pudding spoon between his fingers. It had come from a shipwreck Auren discovered a few days ago—one he'd begged Ulric to help lift from its half-buried state. They'd swum through the wreckage for hours and returned with so many trinkets that Ulric could hardly swim for how many of his tentacles were occupied holding the treasures.

Ulric couldn't explain how he'd gone from chastising Auren for this behavior to helping him.

As long as he is staying in the water.

Across the chamber, Auren worked in focused silence. A new sculpture took shape beneath his hands—a seabird, immortalized in wire and gems. When Ulric recognized the creature's form, his chest tightened, remembering the quiet grief in Auren's voice as he'd cradled its broken body on the sand.

The wings were slight and graceful, mid-stretch as if caught in flight. The skeleton was fashioned from twisted brass and smooth, bleached shell, delicate yet sturdy. But it was the feathers that caught the eye. Each one carved from nacre and layered with colored sea glass, their edges tinted in soft gradients of pink, blue, and teal. They shimmered as if still wet with sky.

It was a tribute.

It was Auren's way of giving the seabird the flight it had been denied.

And even half-finished, it was breathtaking.

So was the one making it.

Ulric watched Auren, brow furrowed in concentration, hair falling loose from its braid. His long green tail coiled beneath, fin unconsciously swaying side to side. The way his hands moved, the way his eyes lit with quiet purpose, it had Ulric enraptured, mind, body, and soul.

Ulric had seen nobles dressed in the finest gems and silks the sea had to offer. He had seen warriors wreathed in blood and salt and triumph.

But nothing—nothing—was more beautiful than Auren lost in his own creation.

And still, that damn silver scarf was braided into his hair. Always that scarf. High-quality human silk, tied in a delicate fishtail braid. Ulric tried to ignore it.

"There's another Council session tomorrow," he said at last. "Both of us have to attend."

Auren groaned. "Why? Are they plotting another hour-long lecture about algae allocation?"

"I wouldn't put it past them. But it's a royal appearance, not a debate."

Auren sighed, rubbing the side of his face. "It's going to be hours, isn't it?"

"Probably," Ulric said, then smirked. "But I'll make you a deal. If you sit through it without glaring, groaning, or rolling your eyes, I'll take you to see something afterward."

Auren arched a brow. "What kind of 'something'?"

"You'll have to wait and see," Ulric replied.

Auren narrowed his eyes, suspicious now. "That's what you said before you dragged me to the Murkmire flats."

"It was ecologically important," Ulric muttered.

"It reeked," Auren shot back, lips curling in disgust. "I couldn't get the smell out of my hair for days."

Ulric fought the urge to smile. Even the way Auren complained stirred something in him lately. He kept his voice even. "This will be different."

Auren abandoned his sculpture and drifted closer, his body language trying for casual but failing. Ulric didn't react when he settled so close that their shoulders almost touched. "You're awfully cagey for someone trying to bribe me."

"I'm not bribing you," Ulric lied. "You just need to trust me."

Auren's expression changed. It lost its usual biting edge and settled into curiosity. Almost trust.

Trust. That was dangerous.

Ulric rose and made his way to the cave's entrance before he could say something foolish. "No glaring tomorrow," he said over his shoulder. "Play nice and I'll make it worth your while."

He was so hurried to get out of there, to get out of that stifling proximity, that he almost missed the quiet response.

"I look forward to it."

They left at dusk.

The water shimmered with fading light, orange streaks filtering through the surface like the sea itself had caught fire. The warmth of it kissed their skin as they swam, turning scales and tattoos to molten reflections. Auren stayed close, quieter than usual, though the tension in his shoulders betrayed his anticipation.

Ulric led them beyond the kelp forests and through a shallow underpass, where columns of coral bent with the current like swaying reeds. The route narrowed, then opened again into a wide clearing over the reef's edge.

And there it was.

The Abyssal Bloom.

Not the cold, starlit kind they'd seen before—this was its opposite.

A crack in the sea floor split, and through it, warm mineral waters from deep vents surged upward in long, spiraling plumes.

Caught in the currents were ribbons of sun-reactive plankton, only active for the brief window of time when the light hit just right.

Now, in the magic hour of sunset, they glowed—not with blues or greens, but oranges and ambers. The water blushed with warmth, as though they were swimming through sunlight made liquid.

Ulric glanced over.

Auren's eyes were wide with awe, every sharp edge of him softened by the light. His red hair burned brighter than ever, suspended in the warm currents, his skin kissed in gold.

Ulric swallowed hard. "I thought you might like it," he said quietly.

Auren only nodded, drifting further into the bloom where rays of sunlight turned his hair to flame and fins to glass.

He looked like a god.

Conjured from salt and sunlight.

Ulric watched from a distance, trapped in a tempest of thought.

Why did Auren look so *right* here?

Why did this beautiful creature—this infuriating, brilliant, untamable man—look like he *belonged* in the sunlight?

Why couldn't he bring that radiance downward?

Why was his gaze always cast toward the sun?

Why couldn't he be content in the deep?

With me, Ulric thought, bitter as brine.

He met Auren in the bloom before he realized what he was doing. His tentacles curled slowly behind him, careful, as though to lock them in place and resist the urge to reach out.

Auren was only inches away, looking at him through gold glittered lashes.

There was no playful smirk. No teasing glint in his eye. Just... tenderness.

And *want.*

It struck Ulric like a harpoon to the chest.

That look—the barest tilt of Auren's head, the way his lashes dipped, the slight parting of his lips—*that* was not the look Ulric had grown used to. Not a look of defiance. Or anger. It was the look of someone reaching. Someone yearning. Someone on the precipice of discovering that what they wanted most... was right in front of them.

Ulric's heart kicked in his chest. Too hard. Too loud. The blood sang in his ears. Auren's voice was quiet, but it wrapped around him like a vice.

"I used to think I'd feel trapped forever," Auren murmured, eyes still on him. "That nothing could ever change. But now... I don't know. Things feel different."

Ulric swallowed. This was dangerous. "Auren..."

"I look at you now," Auren said, "and I don't feel trapped."

Ulric couldn't breathe.

He wanted to touch him. He wanted to *grab* him. By the wrist, by the waist, by the mouth—and kiss that hope from his lips before it crushed them both. But he didn't move.

His voice came out like gravel.

"Then why do you always chase the sky, Auren?" Ulric asked, barely above a whisper. "Have you ever wondered who waits for you in the depths?"

Auren's breath hitched, and when he looked at Ulric, those cerulean eyes were glowing, pulsing with magic still to come, straining to reveal itself early. Ulric's magic hummed in response.

"I never had a reason to look down before," Auren said, voice low. "But... maybe now?"

Then, Auren's gaze dropped to his mouth and lingered there. Ulric's stomach clenched. A moment later, he felt the brush of hands against his shoulders. Tentative. Testing. Then firm.

"I think," Auren said, "I should've been looking into the depths all along."

Ulric's throat bobbed with the force of a swallow. His heart was beating like a war drum, his body caught between instinct and rule, desire and duty. Every ancient vow he'd sworn was unraveling like old rope.

He should say something—stop this before it grew out of control.

Instead, he whispered, "And if the depths have been waiting for you all this time?"

Auren didn't answer. Because everything in his eyes spoke for him. Ulric moved. Or maybe he didn't. Maybe it was Auren. Maybe they both leaned in at once. He didn't mean to reach out. He didn't mean to touch.

But his hand slid gently into the prince's hair, fingers brushing the silver silk woven through the braid. His palm came to rest against Auren's cheek, warm and soft beneath his callused touch. One of his tentacles shifted forward until it curled around the delicate arch of Auren's tail.

Anchoring him.

Just for a moment.

Long enough for Ulric to pretend they belonged like this.

Long enough to want it more than the next beat of his heart.

"I think," Auren said, voice trembling, "I might be ready... to be held that close."

His fingers curled on Ulric's shoulders. Grounding. Seeking an anchor in the electric current of emotions tugging them towards each other.

Then, slowly, Auren leaned in.

Ulric did too.

There was only breath. Only closeness.

I'm going to kiss him.

Ulric opened his lips, tilting his head and—

The magic struck.

It was a silent, brutal lash. Like his ribs had cracked open, and the ocean was pouring in. Agony tore through him. One of the runes inked into his skin burned white-hot, then vanished.

Ulric choked, hands yanked back as if scalded, his tentacles recoiling like a wounded thing.

"Ulric—?" Auren's voice was alarmed, confused.

But Ulric was already backing away, pain radiating like fire through his limbs. His breath came ragged, his heart crashing against his sternum like a tortured prisoner begging for escape.

No. Not again.

The gods warned him.

No mate. No desire. No love.

Auren reached out, catching him gently by the wrist. "Ulric, what's wrong?"

But the moment their skin touched, Ulric jerked like he'd been burned.

"I can't," he rasped, the words strangled from his throat.

Then he turned and fled into the dark.

"Ulric!" Auren called after him, but Ulric didn't look back. Didn't slow.

I'm sorry. I'm so sorry. I'm... not strong enough.

That night, he did not return to Atlantis. He told himself it was duty. That the sea needed him elsewhere, that time would dull the ache. But the truth was far simpler. He couldn't stay. Not when he was already drowning. Not when every part of him still burned with the memory of Auren's mouth—of a kiss they'd never shared.

So he made himself a promise: He would bury this feeling in the blackest depths of the sea. Leave it where it could rot. Where it would never rise again. Where it could never ruin him.

Or the Mer who looked to the sky.

Chapter Five

Auren

Auren waited over a month.

A month of silence. Of absence. Of heartbreak. Ulric hadn't returned to Atlantis. He hadn't sent word. Hadn't given a reason. No explanation. No goodbye. One day, they were swimming through golden light, wrapped in a moment that could've been everything. And the next, he was gone.

Auren waited in his cave. Waited in the palace halls. Waited in the dark, sleepless and broken. His mind replayed that moment in the bloom over and over. Ulric's whisper, his touch, the look in his eyes as he fled.

At first, Auren thought he'd done something wrong. He'd gone too far. Misread something. Was it the way he'd leaned in? The things he'd said? The way... Auren's lips were seconds from touching Ulric's.

He buried his face in his arms most nights, gritting his teeth as unbidden tears forced their way free. He was unsure what stung worse—the heartbreak, or the not knowing. Had Ulric been disgusted? Had that flicker of something between them all been in Auren's head?

He'd even gone to his mother, hoping for some truth. Queen Tritheya had barely looked up from her scrolls. "It's not uncommon," she'd said, tone clinical. "The Kraken are attuned to older currents, deeper forces. Sometimes the magic calls them back. It's nothing to fear. He'll return when Poseidon wills it."

That wasn't an answer. That was a dismissal. Ulric hadn't been called. He'd run.

Run from me.

But as the days dragged on and the loneliness thickened, grief gave way to anger. If Ulric was so repulsed by him, so appalled by the idea of wanting him, then he could keep his silence. Auren didn't need him.

And he sure as hell didn't need to obey his orders. Not anymore.

If he can throw me aside so easily, I'll go where I'm wanted.

And in a single, furious act of defiance...Auren broke his promise and surfaced.

The water was calm when he broke through it, stars smeared like spilled salt across the sky above. And there she was. *The Windless.* Her sails were drawn tight, her lanterns darkened for the night, rocking gently in her berth.

Auren didn't rise just yet.

He stayed beneath the surface, watching. Waiting. He knew better than to climb aboard while light still glowed from the Captain's quarters. So he remained beneath the hull, conserving breath, pulse thundering in his ears while his mind wrestled between hurt and hate.

Damn Ulric. Damn Atlantis. Damn all those who dismissed him and cast him aside like unwanted clutter.

Minutes passed, and the light from the captain's quarters finally went out. Now was his chance. Auren took one final pull through his gills and shot from the water. He caught the loose hanging nets, dragging himself up the *Windless's* starboard side, sliding silently onto her deck. He'd barely had a second to orient himself when—the echo of boots on wood. Auren threw himself behind a stack of barrels laden with sweet-smelling fruits. He grabbed his fins, shoving them back, trying to conceal their starlit glimmer. The footsteps drew closer, then paused at the railing. Auren dared peek from his hiding place and...

And there he was.

Elias.

Dark curls tousled by the wind. Pale skin kissed with moonlight. A heavy coat thrown over broad shoulders, one hand braced on the railing as he gazed out into the dark sea. He placed what appeared to be a long, hooked piece of wood into his mouth, and a second later, the rich scent of smoke mixed with the salty air.

He hadn't seen Auren yet. But the way Elias stared into the waves, searching, made Auren's chest tighten.

He never stopped waiting for me.

Auren felt it deep in his bones. The foolishness of his absence. The bitterness of his own fear. He'd run from something that had never once turned away from him. Without thinking, Auren flopped his tail once, the heavy thud vibrating along the wooden deck. Elias's head jerked toward the sound.

Then their eyes met.

And everything stopped. Elias removed the burning wood from his mouth, setting it aside and taking a step toward Auren as though in a trance.

"I never lost hope that you'd come back," Elias said, breathless as he leaned on the ship's edge. "I looked for you. Every day. I never gave up."

The human approached slowly, Auren fighting every cell in his body to remain still. With trembling limbs, Auren extended his arm and placed a delicate shell necklace—white spiral turritella strung on a line of braided kelp—into Elias's hands. A gift. A peace offering. An apology for disappearing. Elias held it as though it were bestowed upon him by a god. Like it was proof of a dream come true.

"I will cherish this. Thank you. You are... a miracle."

And those damned eyes. The sky blue gaze that *saw* him. That touched him without ever making contact. And this time, Auren knew he would never give up on this. On him.

Elias.

From that night forward, Auren returned. Nearly every evening. Even if only for a few minutes. Elias was always waiting. He never pushed. Never tried to touch. Never demanded anything.

Auren sighed in frustration, wishing he could speak above the waves. Wishing he could tell Elias all the things building in his chest. That he was grateful, that he was afraid, that he was beginning to feel something dangerous and sweet in the human's presence. But no words came.

Still, Elias never seemed to mind the silence.

He spoke gently and somehow always found ways for Auren to join the conversation. A flick of the eyes. A nod. The subtle tilt of his head or twitch of his lips as if to say, *Do you agree? Did you like that?* Auren found himself nodding, laughing without sound, more and more.

Their conversations were brief. Four minutes, maybe five,

before Auren had to submerge again to breathe. But those minutes were *everything*. They became the sun around which his days orbited. The one thing steady in the storm.

And Elias—gods, Elias was beautiful.

Always dressed in some half-wrinkled linen shirt, sleeves rolled to the elbow, collar loose and open to the air. The wind loved him, brushing back the dark curls from his face, teasing open his shirt just enough to reveal the smooth line of his chest. Pale skin. Sharp collarbones. The thin line of freckles at his throat. Auren found his eyes drawn to it every time.

Even his trousers, thick canvas tucked into oil-stained boots, enchanted Auren. Everything about Elias was strange and soft and solid. Tangible in a way Merfolk weren't. And Auren drank him in.

And if Elias himself was beautiful, his words were even more so. He showered Auren with such poetic words, such honest and vulnerable declarations that Auren was constantly flushed. Elias called him gorgeous, *ethereal*, even. That his scales caught the light like tempered glass, shifting color with every breath. That he couldn't look away.

Elias held his gaze without shyness or shame. Told Auren that his eyes didn't shine...they *struck*. He told him his hair looked like it had been dyed in the essence of roses. And when Auren looked confused by the statement, Elias brought him the flower the next day.

"It's the closest I could find. But it still doesn't compare to your beauty." Elias said, and tucked the delicate petals behind Auren's ear.

Auren shivered. The closeness, the subtle brush of fingertips over the shell of his ear. It was overpowering. Then Elias's enraptured gaze roamed up and down the contours of Auren's body, and the Merman had to look away, abashed by the awe in the human's eyes.

"Even the lines of you," Elias murmured, "don't make sense.

You weren't made for symmetry. You were made to be *perfectly imperfect*."

Auren didn't know how to accept such praise. Didn't know where to place it inside himself. The look in Elias's eyes was too much. Auren shifted, the weight of being seen pressing hot against his skin. Not like a prince. Not like a nuisance. But like he was a story worth telling.

"Some people pray to stars," Elias whispered. "But I think I'll start praying to the sea. Because it gave me you."

He told Auren he'd studied marine life his whole life, hoping that one day, a creature like him would exist.

He studies the sea as I study the land.

Auren shivered at the possibilities. Of what they could learn from each other. How they could enrich each other's lives.

"You're the answer to a question I've been asking since I was a boy," Elias said. "And now that I've found you... I don't think I could ever stop asking for more."

Auren's heart had thundered so hard he thought it might burst.

One night, Auren surfaced to find Elias sitting cross-legged on the deck of the *Windless*, a hollow wooden instrument in his lap. When his fingers plucked the strings, a sound Auren had never heard before filled the air.

Soft. Melodic. Wrapping around him like an embrace. And then... Elias began to sing.

Auren was so captivated by the song—by the voice, by the sound—that he didn't realize how long he'd been above the waves until his gills burned and his mind went fuzzy. He panicked, wheezing, and flung himself back into the water.

The next night, Elias had a new song. And the next. And the next.

Auren never tired of them.

But, save for the night with the rose, he never let Elias get too close. Instinct and years of warnings kept him cautious. But Elias never seemed to mind. Never tried to touch. Just watched him like he was something worth seeing. And for once, Auren let himself believe it.

Then the first snow came. The docks froze. And when Auren surfaced, the *Windless* was gone.

Panic consumed him.

He dove and scoured the bay, heart cracking with every wave. Had he been discarded again? Then he spotted it. Just beneath the surface, caught on a rock where the ship had docked. A glint of glass.

A bottle.

Inside was a message, inked on tanned animal hide.

I'll be back for you in the spring, my darling. Please wait for me.

Auren made a startled sound at the words, causing Iska to flinch and then chatter indignantly beside him.

My darling.

My.

He read the words over and over, heart fluttering wildly. *Feeling* that single word. The word of possession. Of wanting Auren enough to claim him as *his*.

So he waited. With gladness, he waited. Because Elias had waited for him, and this time, Auren would not turn away.

Spring bloomed beneath the melting snow, and the sun returned from its journey through the cold. Winter had passed quietly in Atlantis—without Elias to visit, Auren had little reason to sneak away and, to the Kraken's quiet satisfaction, stayed put within the palace walls. By the time the ice thawed and the tides began to turn, months of good behavior had pushed him to the back of Ulric's mind, making it easier than ever to slip away unnoticed.

And on the first night the ships returned to port, Auren was there, hidden beneath the dock, heart pounding. The *Windless* led the convoy, and when the lanterns were snuffed and the crew disembarked, he hauled himself onto the deck, eager as a seal pup.

Elias was already there—like he'd known Auren would come. Immaculately dressed, his shirt crisp and open at the collar, Auren's seashell necklace lying delicately against his chest. He looked radiant. Alive. And so, so beautiful. Elias turned and smiled as though he'd waited all winter for this moment.

"My sea-born angel," he whispered, rushing toward the edge of the deck. He slowed at the last moment. His voice gentled. "May I come closer?"

Auren's instincts screamed. To run. To flee. To dive.

But he didn't.

He stayed and nodded.

Elias stepped forward, careful and slow, before kneeling in the pool of water beside Auren's tail. His fingers reached up, brushing the damp strands of hair clinging to Auren's shoulders, until he found the silver silk braided there.

"You kept this," Elias said softly. "I'm honored."

Auren nodded, a shy smile tugging at his lips.

"Then you shall have another," Elias whispered. "Wait here."

He darted below deck and returned seconds later, holding a golden silk ribbon.

"For you, my sweet. Now you'll have them in both colors."

Auren took the gift with shaking fingers. Their hands brushed, and he froze. Elias's hand was... just like his. Five fingers. A palm. Calloused and warm. Not the same. But so close. So very close.

Elias didn't push. But he was breathing harder now, eyes bright and wide with joy shining behind them.

"I know you can't speak," Elias said, voice raw. "I don't even know your name. But I have to tell you..." He dropped to his knees again, so that they were eye level. "I have completely fallen for you."

Auren's heart jolted.

"I haven't stopped thinking about you since the moment I saw you. This winter, without you, it was torture. I... I missed you more than I thought it was possible to miss someone."

He reached, then stopped. "May I touch you?"

Auren's chest tightened, gills aching—but he nodded. Elias leaned forward until they were nose to nose, water dripping between them. He paused again, waiting for any sign of resistance. Waiting for an objection.

Auren didn't give one. He only closed his eyes and allowed himself to exist in the moment. He felt Elias close the distance between them and...

And kissed him.

The world stopped.

Auren's first kiss... was with a human. And it was warm.

When they pulled apart, Elias pressed their foreheads together, voice shaking.

"Go," he whispered. "Go now, before you suffocate."

Auren hesitated.

"Come back tomorrow," Elias said, voice so full of devotion it cracked. "Please. For now that I've tasted the salt on your lips... I will starve without them."

Auren dove into the sea, heart blazing, arms shaking. He was seen. He was wanted. He'd found a place where he *belonged*.

Atlantis never needed him. Never wanted him. And Ulric left him broken.

But Elias...

Elias made him feel whole.

Auren swam for home with the gold silk clutched tight in his palm. And this time, he didn't feel alone. This time... he felt loved.

Chapter Six

Ulric

Ulric sank deeper than he'd ever dared before. Past the darkest trenches. Past the ancient bones of long-fallen leviathans. Into the chasms where even the sea itself grew quiet. It should have brought peace. The pressure, the cold, the blessed silence. But nothing eased the ache in his chest or the fire in his veins.

He had run.

The runes inked into his skin pulsed with quiet rage. What began as a whisper turned into a burn. A flare of warning beneath his flesh. As if the sea itself was screaming—*You are not finished.*

And he wasn't.

He wished for the god of time to play his tricks again. That days, weeks, months, would flow like the tide, leaving a chasm of *years* between him and Auren. That when he returned, Auren would have taken a mate, grown bored of the surface, found a future that didn't involve Ulric at all. That he'd forget Ulric ever existed.

But of course, the games of time never worked in his favor. When the burning magic forced him upward, he found that only a season had passed. The winter months had come and gone, and spring bloomed.

The reef outside Atlantis bustled with new life. Bright swaths of coral stretched like paint across the rock. Tiny fish darted in spirals, their scales fresh and jewel-bright. Seaweed unfurled in slow, lazy coils, kissed by sun-warmed currents. Everywhere he looked, there was color, motion, life.

And still... his chest ached. It ached like a slow, expanding void was growing where his heart should've been.

Ulric hesitated outside the city gates. Shame wound tight in his gut. He had nothing to say. No apology good enough. And yet the pull of the court, of his duty, left no choice. Ulric returned. When he entered the Hall of Currents, it was like nothing had changed. The queen offered him the barest welcome, then it was back to business as usual.

Now he floated to the right of Queen Tritheya's throne, where a Court Sorcerer belonged—arms clasped behind his back, tentacles swaying loosely to keep him in place, his hair pulled back and fastened with whalebone.

As though nothing had changed.

He'd just finished assisting the Council of Agricultural Tithes with a proposed tonic to accelerate the growth of reef-grain. Ulric gave his final recommendation, which seemed to appease the council; their thanks were genuine as they left the courtroom.

The Queen did not look at him. But her voice carried the

authority of one who saw more than she said. "Thank you, Court Sorcerer. Your absence was noted this winter. I am glad to see you back."

He inclined his head, a spark of pride lighting his face at the formal recognition.

This is my duty. To help the people of Atlantis. To serve Her Majesty.

As the Council filed out, Ulric turned his focus toward the next matter on the docket. Something about noblewomen requesting stronger sleeping draughts—likely another passing court trend. He adjusted his stance, ready to receive them.

And then the doors opened.

And flame swam inside. Red hair blazed like the magma of underwater eruptions and with just as much destructive power.

Auren.

Ulric's breath caught. He straightened without meaning to, bracing like a wave had struck him. And Auren—gods, Auren— looked like he'd been struck too. Shock froze his features, his body rigid. But the shock was fleeting. It turned to ice. Rage sharpened every beautiful angle of his face. Auren barely remembered to bow to the Queen, rushing to kneel on the marble floors. His movements were stiff, brittle. Then he turned toward her, voice sharp. "What is *he* doing here?"

The Queen arched a brow. "He is the Court Sorcerer. Does he not belong?"

A muscle twitched in Auren's jaw. "I thought he would be away longer."

The words landed like knives. Ulric kept his gaze forward, unmoving. But his chest bled with each syllable. Auren didn't even look at him. As if he weren't there. As if Ulric had become another shadow in the hall. It should've been easier that way.

But it wasn't.

"Auren," the Queen said, firm. "I summoned you to commend your recent conduct. Your renewed dedication to council matters has not gone unnoticed." Auren shifted on the floor, clearly uncomfortable. "Your presence in court has been more frequent. More engaged," she added. "It speaks well of your maturity. And your future."

Auren gave a tight nod, but remained silent.

"I look forward to what you have to offer this court in the future," the Queen said by way of dismissal with a gentle wave of her hand.

He was gone like a flash light that blinded the sky, storming from the chamber before the guards had fully opened the doors.

Ulric didn't wait for permission. He followed. Down the gilded corridors, through the glass archways, past startled nobles and curious guards. He followed the furious trail Auren left in his wake, catching up to him in a secluded outer courtyard. This particular garden was overgrown with moonberry thickets. Silvery-blue shrubs with arching branches that curled like sea serpent horns. Their translucent berries glowed in clusters, casting the whole space in a hush of pale luminance. The thickets formed a dense canopy overhead, creating the illusion of a private chamber. The current slowed here. The world felt smaller. Quieter. No one else would hear them.

"Auren—"

"Don't."

Ulric surged in front of him, cutting off his path. "You can't swim away from this."

Auren's voice was venom. "Oh, you mean like you did? Just watch me."

"Auren," Ulric said quietly, as though trying to calm an agitated eelhound.

Auren didn't turn, but the shake in his shoulders was unmistakable. "You have a lot of nerve showing up like nothing happened."

Ulric drifted closer, careful not to breach the space between them. "I didn't mean for things to happen like they did."

Auren let out a bitter laugh. "What part, exactly? The way you held—" his voice cut off, unable to finish that intimate sentence. "Or the part where you vanished afterward?"

"I—" Ulric's voice faltered. "It wasn't supposed to go that far."

Auren spun to face him, eyes burning. "One second, you looked at me like I was... And the next, like you couldn't leave fast enough."

Ulric's throat worked around a thousand things he couldn't say. "I had to go," he said at last.

"You ran."

"I *had* to," Ulric growled, pain bleeding into every word. "You don't understand what would've happened if I hadn't left."

"No," Auren spat, "because you never gave me the chance to understand."

Silence flared between them like a wound torn open. A moment passed, and Ulric's gaze dropped. His eyes landed on the braid in Auren's hair. Not silver. Gold. Ulric's jaw clenched. He tried to breathe slowly, to keep his voice even. But the words came sharp anyway. "That silk," he said, nodding toward Auren's braid, "that's new. It used to be silver."

Auren froze, just for a moment. Then he looked away. Ulric didn't need an answer. The truth was already unraveling.

"That human gave it to you," he said quietly. "Didn't he?"

Auren's only response was a tick in the muscle lining his jaw.

Ulric couldn't keep the bitterness from his voice. "Your mother just praised your renewed dedication. She actually believed you'd let go of this surface nonsense. So did I. I thought you were done chasing illusions." His eyes locked on the silk. "And then you appear wearing that."

Auren didn't deny it—and that alone sent dark, angry thoughts spiraling through Ulric's body. His tentacles flexed of their own accord, coiling with restless agitation, as if seeking to purge the irritation from his skin.

"The one studying the sea," Ulric continued, jaw tight. "The one your mother is worried about. The one drawing ships too close to our waters. That's the human you're seeing."

Auren still wouldn't look at him, but his hand lifted to touch the golden silk. A quiet act of defiance. A reminder of the choice he'd made, and the promise he no longer intended to keep.

"You can't go to him again," Ulric snapped, wishing to tear that silk from Auren's head. "You're being manipulated. Whatever promises that human made, they're lies."

That shattered the silence, and when Auren rounded on him, there was a glassiness in his eyes. "I want someone to *choose* me!" Auren exploded. "Is that so hard to understand?"

Ulric reeled.

Auren's fins flared, magic pulsing faintly from his skin. His tail lashed behind him, powerful and wild. His face flushed, radiant with rage. "You think I don't know the risks?" Auren yelled. "You left. You *ran*! You don't get to come back and tell me who I can love."

Ulric recoiled, physically pushed back by the word.

Love?

"Auren I—"

"You don't understand what it's like to be left behind," he snapped. "I waited for you. I *wanted* you. And you vanished like I was nothing."

Ulric felt like he was being torn in two. Everything inside him begged to reach out. To hold Auren. To apologize. To explain. But the prince wasn't done.

"I looked to the surface because when you left, it felt like all I had left was the sun," Auren said. "Something warm. Something that *stayed*."

When Ulric finally spoke, his voice was controlled.

"I've seen the surface, Auren. More times than I can count. Most of the ingredients for my potions grow there. I've walked their shores. I've spoken with their traders." His eyes locked with Auren's. "I've seen what they do to the things they desire."

Auren's expression showed only the faintest hint of surprise before hardening again. "You're not afraid of the human," he said. "You're afraid of anyone else wanting me."

Ulric flinched. Because it wasn't a lie, it was the deepest truth. He was afraid. Afraid of how beautiful Auren had become. Of how that fierce, fiery heart made him ache in ways magic couldn't fix. Afraid of how badly he wanted to break every vow inked in his skin.

But he couldn't.

So he stayed frozen. Watched Auren's gaze fall one last time, filled with hurt and betrayal.

"If you ever cared, even a little, then you'll leave me alone."

He left, and this time, Ulric didn't follow. He hovered in the water, trembling. The burning runes on his arms pulsed, stinging with a reminder of his forbidden desires. His magic was older than the kingdom. He possessed knowledge of the world above and below, and carried enough power to command storms.

But right now, none of it meant a damn thing.

"You have no idea what I'd do to keep you safe," he whispered to the empty courtyard. "Even if it means protecting you... from me."

Chapter Seven

Auren

How stupid could he be?

Auren dragged a palm across his face, scrubbing away the stubborn tears that clung to his lashes. His chest still heaved from the confrontation, from the sharpness in Ulric's voice, from the sheer audacity of the Kraken to show up after everything. After the silence, after abandoning him without so much as a breath of explanation.

"I can't believe I just did that," he muttered.

He cracked open like a shell beneath Ulric's tentacles and spilled everything. All the longing, all the fear, all the stupid hope. And for what? For Ulric to flinch away like he'd been scalded. Again.

His jaw clenched so tight it hurt. "Just pour your heart out to the one person who'll never want it," he whispered bitterly. "That's smart."

He should've known better. He'd told himself not to fall. Told himself Ulric was just a protector, a mentor, a stubborn wall between him and the world. But that wall had looked so warm in the bloomlight. Had looked so much like something Auren could lean on. Something he could hold onto.

His fingers rose to the silk braided into his hair. It still carried Elias's scent. Sun-warmed linen, sea breeze over sand. Human. Auren breathed in. Elias didn't turn away. He didn't flinch when Auren got too close. Didn't recoil when affection bloomed. Elias never made Auren feel like he was too much.

And Ulric? Ulric had run.

"I'm done," Auren hissed through his teeth. "Done hurting for someone who doesn't want me."

The sea was dark and hushed when Auren surfaced. The wind carried the sharp scent of lantern oil and brine. The lights along *The Windless* were extinguished, sails slack in the evening lull, rocking side to side like a creature at rest. He moved beneath the waves, inspecting her like he always did. The hull was solid wood, treated and tarred. Cracks sealed with pitch. The ship creaked with each shift of the tide, breathing with the ocean.

No lights. No movement.

Perfect.

Auren pulled himself over the rail with a strong thrust of his tail, dragging himself silently across the damp deck, careful not to slip. The wood beneath him was warm from the day's sun, smelling of varnish and smoke.

"You've come earlier than usual, my dear," came a voice like velvet.

Auren startled—and then smiled. Elias stepped from his hiding place beneath the helm and into the moonlight. And gods, he was beautiful. All long lines and soft angles.

"Though I admit, I sent my men to bed early in case you would," Elias said, and then crossed the deck in a few strides.

Before Auren could think, Elias cupped his face and pressed a kiss to his cheek. Another to his jaw. His lips were warm—startlingly warm—and sent a shiver through Auren's whole frame. When Elias pulled back, his gaze had darkened.

"Do you know how long I've waited to see you again?" he murmured. "To touch you like this?" He sat on the wooden deck beside Auren, eye level and mesmerizing.

Auren's heart was thudding like thunder in his ears, his gills fluttering with the need to pull in water. Elias's hands slid down to his neck, then lower, exploring the strange seam where scale met skin. His thumb brushed the curve of Auren's waist, just before the tail began, and he let out a breathless sound.

"This," he whispered, "is extraordinary."

Auren swallowed hard.

"Does it hurt?" Elias asked. "To stay so long in the air?"

Auren shook his head.

Elias ran a hand over the seam again, eyes glittering. "Have you ever wondered what it's like for us? How different we are beneath it all?" He leaned closer, breath feathering Auren's ear. "Would you like to see?"

Auren nodded, maybe a little too emphatically.

Elias smiled and leaned back, slowly undoing the last buttons of his tunic. The fabric slipped from his shoulders, revealing smooth, lean muscle and pale skin dusted with the faintest freckles. His chest was bare, flat, sculpted. Auren stared, eyes wide.

"Do I meet expectations?" Elias teased.

Auren's face flushed, heat flooding his cheeks and chest. He nodded once, quick and shy.

"You can touch," Elias invited.

Auren reached out, fingertips grazing along Elias's side. His skin was warm. Firm. Unfamiliar. Auren trailed down to Elias's stomach, memorizing every ridge. He dared move lower, to where human and Mer began to differ. His exploration stopped at the cold brush of Elias's metal buckle.

Elias exhaled, breath stuttering, lips still exploring the curve of Auren's neck. His voice dipped into a hush, soft as velvet.

"Would you like to know more?"

Auren didn't move. Couldn't. He was boneless for this man.

"Come now, surely you're curious. Do you want to explore more of me, darling?"

Ever so slowly, Auren nodded, then his mouth opened in a silent, breathless gasp when Elias's tongue ran down the length of his neck.

"Tomorrow, my sweet," he gasped into the crook of Auren's jawbone. "Come to me tomorrow and I shall sate that incredible curiosity all night long."

Auren's breath caught. He couldn't move, couldn't think. He only nodded, dazed and warm and pulsing with sensation.

He slipped over the edge of the ship like a falling star. His heart was a drum. His mind buzzed with thoughts he couldn't hold still long enough to name. He was flushed, shaking, high on the heat of Elias's touch and the echo of his words. He barely noticed when Iska fell in beside him, her huge body cutting the water with practiced ease.

She pulled him through the sea with eager urgency, but Auren hardly registered the speed. He didn't feel how fast they moved. Didn't hear the agitated trill Iska let out as they approached the reefline. Didn't see the way her head dipped, twitching uneasily. And when he slipped from her side, too dizzy with desire to even say goodnight, he didn't notice how she lingered. Watching. Warning.

If he had... he might've been prepared for the figure waiting in the dark.

Tentacles sprawled across the stone. A shadow in the center of everything. Ulric didn't rise. He just looked at him. Steady. Cold.

"I see," the Kraken said. "So my assumptions were correct."

Auren's spine went rigid.

"I shouldn't be surprised," Ulric said. "You've shown your disregard for rules plenty of times."

"You have no right to lecture me," Auren snapped, dragging himself into the cave and keeping a wide berth. "Not after what you did."

"I left to protect you."

"You left," Auren said. "Again. Without a word. Without a thought. And now you're here, in my space, talking like I'm the one who broke something."

Ulric's tentacles twitched. Then his face twisted. His voice dropped, curling sharp like a hook. "I can scent that human all over you." His nose wrinkled in disgust. "Did you let him rub his oily body across your skin like some kind of beast in heat?"

Auren flushed, rage detonating in his chest. "He touches me because he *can*," he snapped. "Because I want him to. He's beautiful. And warm. And not covered in cold, slimy limbs that reek of regret."

Auren's heart dropped to his stomach even as the words escaped. He tried desperately to force away the memory. Of being wrapped in those tentacles. The way they'd curled around him. The way they'd made him feel safe. Whole.

Never again, he told himself. *Don't be that fool again.*

But his chest still ached with the weight of it.

"You smother everything with all that bitterness you carry," Auren added, voice quieter, but no less venomous. "You twist everything that touches you. I'd rather be loved by a human than pitied by you."

Ulric flinched.

Good. Let it sting.

"You think I wanted to care?" Auren snarled. "You think I wanted to feel anything for you after the way you treated me? I was stupid. But I won't be making that mistake again." His voice cracked. "You're just a bitter, old Kraken who doesn't know how to love anything he can't control."

Ulric's jaw clenched, his gaze locked on the floor. Silent.

"You may have the Queen's ear. But you don't have mine," Auren said with finality. "You can't tell me who I can and can't love."

Ulric opened his mouth—but Auren cut him off.

This conversation, and all future conversations, were over.

"You're not welcome here, Kraken. I never want to see you in my cave again."

The cave echoed with silence. Ulric's throat bobbed once. He nodded stiffly, eyes far away. "If that is your decision... then so be it." He turned and vanished into the water, a shadow pulled by the tide.

Auren shook in the wake of his absence. The water in the cave felt colder. The edges of his treasures dulled. The elation Elias had filled him with drained like blood from an open wound.

"Fuck you, Ulric," he whispered.

But the tears welled anyway. And this time, he let them fall.

Chapter Eight

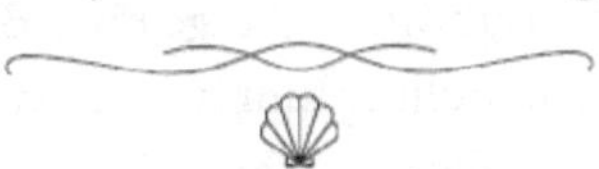

Auren

Auren clung to Elias's words like they were his last morsels of sustenance. Like they were the only thing keeping him alive from one moment to the next.

"You're more beautiful than the legends. I wish I could etch you onto canvas so I'd never forget the shape of you."

"Every night, I come back here and hope. And every time you appear, I forget how to breathe."

"What are you made of, my beauty of the sea? Salt and silk? How can you be real and not wreck me?"

They echoed in his mind, soothing the ache Ulric left behind.

As Auren completed his duties in the palace, anticipation thrummed through him. The promise of "more" from Elias ignited a flush on his cheeks that wouldn't go away through the long court proceedings. When he finally slipped away, his heart was pounding so hard he thought he might be able to use it to break through the wall of the city. He pressed his palm to the hidden stone on the outer wall.

Nothing happened.

"Damn it, Ulric," Auren muttered, realizing the sorcerer had blocked the passage. Undeterred, he navigated his old tunnel, scraping himself as he went, cursing Ulric with every sting. He hoped Elias wouldn't mind a few extra bruises.

Emerging near the coast, he prepared to whistle for Iska when a pulse of water vibrated behind him. Auren darted into a hidden alcove, pressing against the rock, waiting for the patrol to pass. The Deepguard passed, none the wiser to Auren's presence.

But something loomed behind him in the darkness. It stretched on all sides, as though to cage him. Before he could react, a tentacle seized his tail, pulling him further into the shadows.

Auren didn't have time to scream.

One moment he was alone in the water, and the next, his back slammed into stone, the impact knocking the breath from his gills. Tentacles wrapped around him in an instant, like coiling serpents. One clamped tightly around his torso, trapping his arms at his sides. Another looped around his throat—not enough to choke, but enough to hold. A third slithered up his chest and latched around his hips with an unforgiving grip.

Auren lost track of how many limbs gripped him. As he was about to cry out, another wrapped over his mouth, thick and rubbery. The suction cups clung to his skin, pinching, pulling, as if the strength of the coils wasn't enough.

He thrashed wildly, tail whipping against the rock. But the grip didn't loosen. It only held him tighter. Then the darkness shifted, and a face materialized from the inky gloom.

Ulric.

His eyes glowed like volcanic glass still cooling. It was powerful and furious and... Auren went still as he named the uncharacteristic glint in those eyes, the angle of his thick brows.

It was desperation.

Auren's breath heaved against the tentacle across his mouth. Heart pounding like a war drum, strong enough that he knew Ulric must feel it. The sorcerer glared down at him, jaw clenched so tightly a muscle jumped in his cheek. The sharp line of his beard framed a mouth drawn in a grim line. His hair was partially pulled back, the rest loose in dark waves. Moonlight from above filtered through the cracks in the rock, dappling his face with shifting light.

Fury tightened every line of him, but underneath that? A hunger Auren dared not acknowledge. He couldn't.

Ulric's body was taut to the point of snapping—a weapon held at bay by a single strand of snail-silk. And yet the way his tentacles wrapped around Auren told a different story. It was tight, yes, but not painful.

The tentacles looped around him again and again. It wasn't necessary—Auren couldn't have moved if he tried—but Ulric still wrapped more of himself around Auren's shape. Possessively. Like some part of him couldn't help it. Slick and strong, curling with the kind of strength that could crush pearls or snap bones.

But they didn't.

And for a maddening moment, Auren didn't want to escape. Not yet. Not when it felt like Ulric's very soul was unraveling between them. Not when he could feel every inch of heat between their bodies. The sorcerer's skin against his. The strength in his tentacles. The thrum of a Kraken's magic. It called to the magic still dormant in his blood.

Ulric didn't speak, but he was so close Auren could feel the shake in his breath as it ghosted across his cheek, making the small hairs on his jaw rise. His scent was everywhere—black water and volcanic stone. Heat and brine. Familiarity and... *want*.

There it was, curling at the base of his spine and betraying him.

Ulric was too close. So close, Auren could see the uneven line where his beard faded toward his neck. Could see the glimmer of a scar just under his collarbone.

And gods help him... Auren wanted to be even closer.

He wanted to lean in just a little and feel the scratch of Ulric's beard against his cheek. To feel those powerful arms—not tentacles —wrap around him and never let go. His stupid, traitorous heart still ached for what had been denied.

"You have to stop this," Ulric growled. His voice was hoarse, scraped raw. "I've let it go on too long. You're taking too many risks."

Auren struggled, and the grip on his body eased enough for him to shove free. He smacked away the appendages.

"So now you care?" Auren snapped. "Now, after all this time?"

Ulric's expression twisted. "I never stopped."

"Then why did you leave?"

"I had to. I had to get away before—"

"Before what?" Auren interrupted, eyes burning. "Before your reputation was tarnished? Before I embarrass you by existing?"

Ulric's eyes darkened. "You don't understand—"

"No, *you* don't understand!" Auren shouted. "You don't get to wrap yourself around me like I'm yours and then vanish into the black. You don't get to show up after all those nights I waited for you and act like I'm the one who's wrong!"

Ulric's eyes flashed. "You have no idea what this is doing to me."

His voice was rough and frayed at the edges. Then, he moved. No more shouting. No more anger. Just the sound of their breathing in the water. He closed the space like someone approaching a wounded creature—aching to touch, terrified to be bitten.

Auren's chest rose and fell with shallow, panicked gulps of water, gills fluttering. His body screamed to back away, but he didn't.

And Ulric's hands found him.

One slid up the curve of Auren's spine, a light touch gliding on skin, until it reached the nape of his neck. Fingers slipped gently into his hair, curling around the roots, thumb brushing against the soft place just behind his ear. The other hand pressed to the small of his back, pulling him close.

Auren's mouth parted in a shaky breath. He didn't understand this—this gentleness. The shift between them was seismic, but Ulric's touch was so agonizingly careful. Ulric leaned in until their foreheads touched, breath ghosting over Auren's lips.

Ulric closed his eyes.

Auren did too.

And for a moment, there was no war between them. No anger. Just skin and silence, and a heartbeat shared between bodies.

"Forget everything that happened. Forget those moments. Forget *me*." Ulric whispered, voice so soft Auren barely heard it, "I'm begging you... Stop this."

Auren couldn't breathe, overwhelmed by the proximity, the scent, the memories.

He didn't mean to.

But before he even realized what he was doing, his arms lifted and wrapped around Ulric's waist. It was instinct. A reflex from some aching, unguarded part of him that had never stopped wanting this. *Needing* it. His fingers pressed into the firm muscle at Ulric's back, his cheek brushing the Kraken's stubbled jaw. And for the briefest moment, Auren let himself fall. Let himself lean into the warmth and weight of that embrace. He let the fear slip. Let the bitterness go.

And then—

Ulric shoved him.

Hard.

Auren's body jolted, crashing into the alcove wall with a dull thud. The side of his head cracked against the stone, and his vision went white. He blinked, stunned, and lifted a hand to rub his skull, fingers coming back with dissipating whisps of blood.

"Auren, I... I'm sorry I didn't mean to...." Ulric was panting, his tattoos flashing rapidly, his face twisted in agony.

The tears welled before Auren could stop them. His voice trembled as he spoke. "You'll never choose me," he said, each word like a blade between his ribs. "Elias did."

Ulric flinched as though he were the one bleeding, but the shock faded quickly, features hardening into a fathomless cold.

"You leave me no choice, then," he said, and the glow in his tattoos went out. His voice dropped to a low, aching rasp. "Hate me," he said, eyes unreadable. "Hate me for what I must do."

And he vanished into the dark. Leaving Auren alone in the alcove. Shaking. Ashamed. And bleeding. But the worst of the pain came from a wound nobody could see.

Auren's entire body ached with the ghost of an embrace that had almost meant something, before shattering his heart again. He blinked away the tears now flowing freely to join the sea. He drew in a shaking breath and whistled, calling for the one soul who could take him where he needed to go. He needed Elias. Desperately. Needed to feel arms around him that didn't recoil. Needed to hear words that didn't twist like knives in his ribs. Needed someone to love the hurt out of him like a sickness.

But no sound answered. No familiar shape broke the gloom. Auren waited. He whistled again, more frantic this time. The sound echoed off the stone and drifted into the dark, but there was no response. No distant chitter. No thrum of water. No dorsal fin slicing through the sea.

Iska didn't come.

Auren's throat clenched. Tears spilling in earnest. His shoulders curled in as the truth settled heavy in his gut. She wasn't coming. Ulric had done this. He'd sent her away. Or blocked her.

Or taken her far enough from the outer reefs that she couldn't hear him. Without her... without her speed, Auren would never reach the harbor before dawn. Tonight was lost.

He crumpled to the sand floor of the alcove, curling in on himself, arms wrapped tight around his middle. His tail lay limp in the silt.

"Fuck you, Ulric," Auren sobbed into the sand. "Fuck you."

He stayed there a long time, shivering in the quiet, his body wrung out from rage and grief alike. But as the first rays of light touched the reef far above, Auren lifted his head.

He wouldn't lose another night.

Even if it meant swimming the long distance on his own, he'd do it. Because nothing, *nothing* was going to stop him from seeing the only person who ever saw him back.

Not his mother.

Not tradition.

And not a bitter old Kraken drowning in his own skewed sense of obligation.

Auren wiped his tears with the back of his wrist, squared his shoulders, and faced the distant glow of sunrise.

Tomorrow night, he'd be in Elias's arms. And nothing was going to stop him.

Chapter Nine

Ulric

"There, that should keep you happy for a while," Ulric murmured as he scattered strips of eel meat and halibut into the water. Iska trilled happily, her sleek body twisting with delight, none the wiser that right about now her companion would be calling for her.

"You're a good beast," he said, patting her side. His gaze lingered for a moment, admiring the craftsmanship along her body —proof of Auren's work, and the second chance at life he'd given her.

He left her to her spoils and ducked into the palace. He swam down the familiar corridors, moving like a shadow through the current, until he reached his quarters.

Ulric floated perfectly still in the center of his apothecary, arms folded behind his back, jaw tight.

The room was quiet, anticipatory. As though the stone walls were also holding their breath. Waiting.

Hollowed into the seafloor and lit with suspended orbs of bioluminescence, the room shimmered with an eerie, otherworldly glow. Melted sand mirrors lined the far wall, crafted from lightning-struck beaches and volcanic glass. Each shelf was carved directly into the stone and cradled dozens of potions and tinctures. Delicate vials held fluids that shimmered in unnatural colors, swirling with enchantments that could calm fever, cure blindness, mend broken fins, or banish grief. They were sealed with stoppers Ulric designed himself, infused with a binding spell to prevent seawater from tainting the contents. Even the deepest trenches couldn't ruin their effects.

Every inch of this place was an example of study and precision. Of the honor he carried as a magic wielder. The pride he took in his craft.

And tonight, he would break it.

A commotion outside jarred his thoughts. A chorus of shouting. A struggle. Then the guards burst into the cave, dragging someone between them.

Auren.

Ulric's heart clenched.

"What is the meaning of this?!" Auren cried out in a panic. He thrashed in their grip, red hair wild, face flushed, muscles straining beneath shimmering green scales. To the prince's credit, two guards were having trouble subduing him, with a third trailing behind just in case.

Ulric wanted to tear the guards off him. To pull the prince close, whisper apologies, touch his face, and swear he didn't mean for this to happen—but he couldn't. He had no choice.

"By order of the Queen," Ulric said, voice like ice, "you are to receive the potion that will restrict your depth. You are not to breach the surface again."

The words echoed like a death sentence.

Auren froze in the guards' grip. His eyes snapped to Ulric, wide with disbelief, his face draining of color.

"You told my mother?" His voice cracked, high and furious.

Ulric didn't answer immediately, already mourning for the flame he was about to snuff out. Auren was always beautiful, but tonight, somehow, he was even more radiant. His long red hair was woven into intricate, ceremonial knots, adorned with tiny shells and smoothed black pearls. His scales shimmered with fresh polish, catching the light like jewels. But what stopped Ulric's heart was what adorned his braid. Both tokens from the human were woven together—a braided cord of silver and gold.

Ulric's gut twisted.

He's done all this to look nice for the human. He intends to meet him. Tonight.

Ulric wanted to ask if the human had dared to touch Auren. If those greedy hands had traced the ridges of his spine. If his lips had tasted the slope of Auren's throat. The thought made his magic stir, and a foul taste coated Ulric's tongue.

But of course, he didn't ask. Not in front of the guards. Not with his pride clinging to him like armor.

"I let it go on," Ulric said stiffly, "hoping you'd stop on your own. But it became clear you wouldn't."

His mind supplied him with the words he could never say.

I was terrified for the night you wouldn't return.

Terrified that those humans would see you and choose not to give you back.

Back to me.

Auren's eyes burned with betrayal. "You had no right."

"I had duty."

"Don't lie. You did it because you can't stand to see someone else choose me."

"You're reckless," Ulric said, voice detached. "You've put the city at risk. I've told you time and time again what the surface world does to creatures it finds beautiful. They don't love. They claim and cage."

"Like you," Auren spat.

"Call me whatever you want," Ulric said, "but I am only your jailor because of your own actions."

Auren's tail lashed, restrained by the guards' grip. "You think this is protection?"

Ulric's jaw tightened. "You've forgotten what danger looks like."

"I know exactly what danger looks like," Auren hissed. "It looks like control disguised as care."

Ulric leaned forward despite himself, and his tentacles flared. "It looks like a city that loses its prince because he mistook human greed for desire."

Auren's eyes flashed. "No," he snarled. "It looks like *you*. The one who left me drowning."

"I was protecting you," Ulric growled.

"You don't dictate who sees me!" Auren shouted, struggling harder now. "I'm not yours to protect!"

Ulric's mouth opened, then closed. His fists clenched.

You are. You always have been.

But he couldn't say it.

He couldn't say anything except, "The Queen has made her decree."

Auren shook his head, trembling. "You coward."

"Auren—"

"You could've come to me," Auren whispered, voice ragged. "You could've told me what you were feeling. What you were afraid of. But you ran. You always run."

Ulric's throat bobbed. "And *you* chase the first hand that reaches to soothe your blatant need to be wanted."

That struck harder than he meant it to.

Auren recoiled like he'd been slapped.

"I hate you," he said, his voice breaking on the last syllable. And it cracked something in Ulric's bones. His insides roiled, begging him to undo this. To move forward. To say anything that could make it right. But the guards held Auren too tight, and pride held Ulric tighter still.

So he said nothing.

And watched as the prince was held down, and subdued to his cruelty.

"Hold him," Ulric commanded.

Auren fought them. His tail whipped, crashing into shelves. Vials tumbled and shattered. The scent of crushed herbs and magic burst into the water like blood. Ancient ink hissed as instruments scattered across the floor.

"Enough!" Ulric roared.

The water shook. His tentacles shot out like whips, coiling around Auren's arms and waist. With his other hand, Ulric reached for the decanter—the one filled with the iridescent blue potion that shimmered with regret.

He held it to Auren's mouth. The prince's jaw clamped shut, eyes blazing. Ulric lowered his voice, leaning in, speaking just above a whisper so the guards couldn't hear.

"Please..." he begged. "Don't make me force you to drink this."

But Auren stared him down, unmoving.

And so Ulric did what he never wanted to do. Touch those full lips with violence and cruelty, instead of lavishing them with tenderness. He pried Auren's mouth open and poured the liquid past clenched teeth, holding him until it was swallowed. When it was over, Auren choked and sputtered. The guards released him.

Ulric stared straight ahead, heart so heavy it might sink him.

"It is done," he said, though his voice barely carried. The

silence afterward was jagged. Auren's hands trembled at his sides. He looked at Ulric like he couldn't recognize him. Like he'd become a monster.

When Ulric dismissed the guards, he expected Auren to leave. But he didn't.

"So that's it? You trap me in the depths. Keep me close—only where *you* can see me?"

Ulric didn't answer.

"You won't love me," Auren continued, voice shaking. "But you won't let me go either."

He was right.

Ulric couldn't speak. His throat had closed around the words he'd never be allowed to say.

I want you. Gods help me, I love you. But if I touch you, I'll burn. The magic will destroy me.

Already, the ink beneath his skin was thrumming. One of the runes on his wrist flashed dangerously, threatening a flare.

"Leave," Ulric said, hoarse.

"I've been trying to," Auren replied.

And then—he was gone.

The moment the water stilled, Ulric collapsed to the far end of the apothecary. His tentacles curled in around him like armor. He almost wished they would turn on him, wrap tight around his throat, and choke the grief out of him. But the guilt was already doing that, granting him a long, slow death right through the heart. He pressed his forehead to the stone wall, watching his shattered instruments drift through the water like a shipwreck.

The scent of magic and broken herbs filled the space. Bitter. Ashy. Wrong.

He curled tighter. Disgusted with what he'd done.

And unable to stop wanting the Mer he had shackled.

Chapter Ten

Auren

He was alone now. Alone with the ache. Alone in a cage Ulric wrapped around him in the name of protection.

When Auren first tried to rise—just high enough to feel the sun's warmth kiss his skin—his body stopped responding. And then, like a weight was tied around his fins, he was yanked downward with brutal force. The magic gripped tight, slamming him into the sand. His tail locked up, muscles spasming. It felt like gravity had multiplied tenfold, pressing in on his ears, like the ocean grew teeth and was dragging him back into its belly.

It punished him.

Every time he swam upward, pressure surged through his limbs until his vision blurred. He couldn't breathe. Not when it was light he craved and couldn't have. Not when the surface was so close yet out of reach. He couldn't even rise high enough to feel the warmth of the sun.

The realization broke something inside him.

Auren collapsed into a seagrass field, body trembling with exhaustion and rage. The tall, rippling blades swayed. Tiny bubbles curled through the water from his gills, rising to nowhere. Sea turtles grazed nearby, their wide jaws grinding on the soft fronds. One blinked blankly at him, then returned to chewing.

It was quiet here. Peaceful, even.

He hated it.

"I don't belong down here," he whispered hoarsely into the sand. "I never did."

Tears stung his eyes and trailed upward through the water. He pressed his face into the earth, curling into himself.

Elias wouldn't have done this.

Elias looked at him with wonder, not caution. He'd smiled without guilt. Touched Auren's cheek like he mattered. Like he meant something.

He saw me. He saw me.

Ulric didn't see him. Not really. Or worse—he *did* and still chose duty over him. Maybe Auren was never meant to be sea-born. Maybe he belonged on the land. With Elias. Auren was angry. Angry at his own helplessness. At the pathetic way he could do nothing.

"I'm so sorry, Elias. I'm sorry."

He whispered into the fronds of grass, miserable as a passing crustacean nibbled at his tail. He flicked it away with an irritated jerk. What Auren would give to feel the sun. To be free of this burden and never have to return to the water—

His heart stopped, and a powerful jolt sent shockwaves

through his body as though he'd been struck by an electric eel. He sat up in the grass, his mind buzzing with clarity.

"How could I be so stupid?"

Hadn't that bastard given him the answer? Ulric said he'd been to the surface. Seen the greed of humans. He'd meant to use that information to fight Auren, but the bitter Kraken had given Auren exactly what he needed. Ulric had gills, same as any Merfolk. He couldn't breathe air.

There is a way.

Auren realized. If Ulric was spending hours, even days, on the surface, there was a way to do it. A way he transformed his gills to tolerate human air. Or perhaps a potion that stopped the need for breath altogether? Auren didn't know; all he knew was that he would find it.

And take it.

Grief was swept aside by purpose. Hope surged through him like a breaking wave. He would talk to Elias. Tell him everything. *Be* with him, in all the ways two beings of flesh and blood could.

Auren knew what he had to do.

Elias, wait for me.

He waited over a week.

No word from Ulric. No summons from his mother. The guards thinned, pulled away by the Queen's command. There was a political summit between courts, an emergency gathering of magical delegates.

Perfect.

Auren bided his time. He smiled at the right nobles, nodded when spoken to, and feigned the interest expected of a prince. But tonight, as the tides receded and the palace sank into its usual ebb and flow of courtly pomp and posturing, he slipped away.

The path to Ulric's apothecary was darker than usual, the blue bubble flames dimming to barely a glimmer. The private quarters in the palace were almost completely unguarded. Almost.

Two eelhounds patrolled the mouth of the apothecary. Grotesque things with coiled, rippling bodies like undulating sea snakes. Their underbites protruded viciously, exposing rows of serrated teeth.

They hissed low in their throats, sensing him immediately.

Shit.

Auren ducked behind a statue of Poseidon, racking his brain.

Think, dammit.

He dug through the pouch at his side and pulled free a few strips of sea-urchin nuggets. He thanked his lucky stars for having grabbed a few morsels from the feast in the ballroom. Auren tossed the bits of flesh to the left of the corridor entrance, where they caught in a drifting current and tumbled down the hall. The eelhounds snapped their heads toward it instantly, their serpentine bodies streaking after the scent, all slashing teeth and whip-like speed.

Auren slipped inside the apothecary, closing the door behind him just as the beasts vanished into the darkness. His pulse roared in his ears. But he was in. And no one was going to stop him now.

The air was thick with crushed herbs, burnt coral, salt, and something more arcane, like magic ozone. Vials floated on shelves made of driftwood and stone. Tinctures glowed in shades of blue and green, bobbing up and down in the soft current.

It was all very hypnotic.

Okay... think. You know what you're looking for. Sort of.

There were too many bottles. Too many labels in languages he didn't understand. He moved deeper, searching for something, anything, that looked secret or well-hidden. Ulric wouldn't want access to the land to be so easily discovered.

Then he saw it.

Tucked behind a curtain of seaweed was a mirror. Not one of the practical ones. Not a caster's tool.

This mirror was hand-carved, delicate, with tiny seabirds etched into the edges. They circled the frame like they were caught in flight. Auren's heart skipped.

The shape of the bird's beak, the span of its wings. These carvings were modeled almost identically to the sculpture in his cave. Had Ulric sponsored a court statue maker for this? Auren didn't know what to make of it, but didn't allow his mind to ponder. He reached for the beautiful art piece, searching. His fingers curled around the frame, and he gave it a light tug.

A soft click echoed.

A hidden alcove shifted open behind the wall. Auren's heart slammed into his ribs. Inside was a single decanter, glowing violet. Stoppered tight. Etched with runes so old even the water around it shimmered with resistance. He had almost missed it.

But the birds brought me here.

Auren stared at the vial for a long moment, reconsidering his actions. But just as quickly as it came, he shook off the thought and took it.

No going back now.

Auren exited the room, dashing as fast as he could away from the palace. There wasn't time to exit the city entirely, not when he could be discovered at any second. He had to surface. Now. No time to wait and swim to shallower waters. He pointed himself towards the sky and swam. He swam higher than he'd dared since the sinking potion. When the pressure stopped him—when the magic seized his limbs and anchored him there—he took the vial from the pouch tied to his belt.

He unstoppered it. The scent hit him in a wave of algae and sulfur. He raised it in shaking hands.

For freedom. For air. For Elias.

He drank.

The liquid was thick, like gooey kelp and crushed pearl, strangely sweet at first, then bitter as rot. It coated his tongue, clinging like syrup, and the moment it slid down his throat— Pain exploded through him.

His tail convulsed. His spine arched. Muscles locked, and his skin felt as if it were being flayed with volcanic rock, scraped raw until there was nothing sea-born left. The water turned white. Then red. He screamed, but no sound came. Only bubbles and the soundless pressure of a world trying to tear him apart.

He was being pulled upward.

Dragged by a force so strong it fractured his thoughts.

The last thing he felt was fire in his bones.

And then—nothing.

Chapter Eleven

Auren

The magic clung to his tongue with the residual taste of metal, like iron ore and copper. Auren grimaced, trying to work some moisture into his mouth. He stirred and lifted his head. Sand coated his lashes as he blinked at the unforgiving light. He took a large pull through his gills.

Wait.

No— he *inhaled*.

Lungs expanded in his chest, and Auren snapped to full wakefulness, hands flying to his neck. Smooth skin met his fingertips. No gills. It had worked.

Oh, my gods. It worked. It actually worked!

The world came into focus. He was lying on warm, white sand, the breeze caressing his skin. The scent of the sea lingered, familiar. But now, it mingled with the smell of sunlight, pollen, the distant hint of woodsmoke, and... human cookfires?

Auren closed his eyes and tilted his head toward the sun.

The *sun*. The only constant in his life. The thing that had always been there, waiting above. Now, he could feel it without the ocean's barrier. Without the weight of Poseidon's power pulling him back. He sank his fingers into the sand, feeling every grain sift through his palms.

"I can't believe it. I made it."

He tried to roll over, to drag himself through the sand, only for two separate appendages to kick out from beneath him. He flinched, heart stuttering. Then looked down.

Holy shit.

Where his tail had been, there were now legs. Actual, human legs. He wiggled his toes experimentally.

Oh my gods. Oh my gods, oh my gods—

This was happening. This was real. He bent one knee, then the other. His skin was smooth. No scales, no fins. But also no hair. His body was hairless, unlike the men he'd glimpsed from beneath the waves. His eyes traveled upward, taking in every unfamiliar detail of his new form. Then he reached the apex of his thighs—

Oh. So that's what it looks like.

He'd imagined it, of course. Wondered. The anatomy of mammals, of humans. If he was honest with himself, he hadn't stopped thinking about it since Elias had offered him a viewing. But it had all been speculation. Humans rarely stripped fully when near the sea. He'd never seen one bare like this. Now, the proof was... undeniably attached to him.

"Well. That's that, then," he thought with finality, cheeks flushing at his own nudity. He'd need something to wear. He'd

seen humans bare-chested, but *never* without covering their lower halves.

Pushing up on shaky arms, Auren used the nearby cliffside to steady himself and stand. His center of gravity was completely wrong. He swayed, limbs uncertain.

A puff of water burst in the distance. Then came the familiar, arcing rise of an orca's back. The flash of that makeshift leather dorsal fin told Auren exactly who it was.

"Iska!" he shouted, voice hoarse.

She answered with a chirping whistle. Of course, she'd brought him here. He'd drunk the potion directly above Atlantis—too far from the beach. If not for his friend, he likely would've drowned right there, his body left to sink and settle on the palace roof.

He waved both arms overhead, showing her he was alright. Iska clicked again, louder this time, then vanished into the waves with a powerful flick of her tail. Auren stood there for a moment, chest aching. How long had she stayed near the shore, waiting? He'd saved her once. And now she'd saved him. His heart warmed.

A flash of white caught his eye. A washed-up tarp lay tangled in old lead lines where the waves lapped at the shore. He grabbed it, fashioning a makeshift skirt. His right hip was still exposed, but the delicate bits were covered. It would have to do.

Now all he had to do was...what?

I didn't think I'd get this far.

His heart pounded with the weight of what came next. Elias. He had to find him. He wiped windblown hair from his face, blinking into the breeze.

Go to the port. Ask for directions. Someone has to know a human named Elias—

"Um. Are you lost?"

Auren spun around, startled. A human was approaching and...

Oh my gods. I can't believe it. He found me.

Elias.

He stood a short distance away, barefoot on the sand, more

casually dressed than Auren had ever seen him. His dark hair was messy in the breeze. He wasn't as tall as he'd appeared while Auren was on the deck of *The Windless*. He was an inch or two shorter than Auren, though Auren had absolutely no reference for how tall *he* was, now that he stood on two legs. Elias wasn't rugged like some of the sailors Auren watched. He was gorgeous, like a painting brought to life.

It might have been a coincidence. Or maybe Elias finding him was a sign from the gods. An omen that this is where Auren was meant to be.

Auren's heart launched into his throat. Elias stared, frozen in place, recognition blooming in his eyes.

Auren opened his mouth to speak, to finally introduce himself but—

But nothing came out. He frowned. Cleared his throat. Tried again.

Still nothing.

No. No, no, no!

Some potions had side effects. He knew that. But *this*?! Now, when he was so close?! Tears welled in his eyes, stinging hot against the sun. He stared helplessly at the human of his dreams, tongue useless, voice gone. Elias took a few slow steps forward, eyes wide.

"I'm sorry," he said softly. "You just... you look like someone I —" He swallowed. "Someone I know."

Closer still. And with him came scent; sunlight on linen and ... something else.

"I'm sorry, are you..." Elias trailed off again, uncertain.

Then Auren saw it. A faint glimmer beneath Elias's shirt collar. He reached, fingers trembling. Elias didn't pull away. Auren pulled the necklace free—a string of smooth seashells. *His* necklace. The one he'd given Elias all those weeks ago.

Auren traced the familiar shape, eyes brimming with tears.

He met Elias's gaze—sky blue locked with ocean deep—and

touched the necklace, then his own chest. Then back to the necklace.

"You're saying..." Elias whispered. "You're the one who gave me this?"

Auren nodded enthusiastically. He pointed to his legs, then back up at Elias with a hopeful, half-panicked look.

"Yes, I can see that," Elias said, laughing—and gods, that *laugh*. It was the sound of waves against a warm shore. Auren wanted to settle deep in its softness.

He reached out, resting his hand on the necklace and, by extension, on Elias's exposed skin. The warmth of him. The rhythm of his heart. Elias gently took his hand in his own, calloused and real.

"I can't believe you're here," he murmured. "My beauty of the sea."

Then, like a storybook prince, he lifted Auren's hand to his lips and pressed a soft kiss to his knuckles.

"Will you...," he hesitated. "Will you come with me? Can I show you my world?"

Auren nodded, eyes shining. He didn't recoil when their fingers intertwined. He leaned into it. This was everything he wanted. Someone who saw him. Who chose him. Who loved him. The side effects of the potion would wear off eventually. Then they could talk about anything and everything. Then they could be together completely.

The breeze shifted, fluttering Elias's dark hair and sending his scent into Auren's nose again.

Salt. Sweat. Sunlit warmth. And— something else. Something trying to stay hidden. Sharp and wrong and rotten.

Decay.

Auren coughed lightly, trying to clear it from his throat. A dead fish, maybe. Washed up nearby and carried on the wind. He wasn't going to let it ruin this. Not now. Not when everything he ever wanted was finally within reach. This was his moment. His perfect world. The one he had the bravery to claim for himself.

Chapter Twelve

Ulric

The court proceedings dragged on long into the night. Nobles and emissaries hovered like swarms of brightly colored reef fish, spinning eloquent nonsense between sips of fermented kelp wine and bites of moon-snail canapés.

Ulric played his part. He smiled and wove a tapestry of flattering sentences and meaningless pleasantries. All the things a Court Sorcerer was supposed to say. The Queen's children swam through the festivities like constellations brought to life. They shimmered in bralettes of pearls, their throats adorned with carved shell jewelry. They were radiant. Regal. And yet— One spark was missing.

Ulric hadn't seen a flash of red hair all night.

Where is he?

The thought gnawed at the back of his mind.

Did he retire early?

Auren should have been here. He was usually hovering around the ballroom's perimeter, talking to the guards, not bothering to hide his annoyance.

Rude, yes. With a clear disregard for his position as a prince? Absolutely.

But present.

His absence sent eels slithering down Ulric's spine as he pressed his lips into a thin line. After bidding Queen Tritheya goodnight, he excused himself and swam with urgency. Auren wasn't in his chambers. Ulric checked the coral gardens next. Then the terrace overlooking the city.

Nothing.

Ulric tried to reason with himself. The potion should have kept Auren tethered to the depths. There was no way he could reach the surface. But the worry sank into his gut like a stone. By the time he reached the apothecary, it was nearly dawn.

"Hey, boys," he murmured, greeting the two eelhounds lounging by the entrance.

They chirred in response, their long, sinuous bodies quivering at his presence. He tossed them a slab of fresh mahi. They shredded it to ribbons in seconds.

The apothecary remained unchanged. Quiet and dimly lit. But the unease inside him only grew. Ulric swam deeper, through the rows of glowing tinctures and dried herbs, past his personal wards, and into his study.

Nothing was out of place. He almost turned to leave. But then, from the corner of his eye, he noticed something wrong. The mirror. The one with seabirds etched in a delicate circle as though frozen mid-flight. It was ajar.

Ulric surged forward, panic cascading into him with violent force. He reached behind the mirror, heart already thundering. The alcove was empty. The potion was gone.

"Damn it!" he snarled, tearing through the room, checking and rechecking. But there was no denying it. The potion that allowed him to walk the surface world was missing.

Which meant—

"Stupid, stupid prince!" Ulric roared, throwing a fist against the marble wall and shaking the palace.

He didn't know how the sinking magic would react when combined with the potion. That tonic was designed specifically for him—for a Kraken. A creature with entirely different biology. Would it tear Auren apart? Would it kill him? The thought turned his stomach inside out.

Ulric scrambled to assemble a parcel of vials and salves. He packed anything and everything he thought might fix this. Might give Auren a fighting chance. His hands shook as he rushed, grabbing vials at random, praying to the gods that one of them would be enough. That one of them would save Auren's life. Fear clawed up his throat like a second heartbeat.

He burst from the palace in a surge of magic, tearing through the open sea toward the human coast.

By the time he arrived at the shore, the sun was already high in the sky, spilling waves of heat across the surface. He identified Auren's favorite ship, the *Windless*, rocking at anchor near the port. He'd start there.

Ulric reached for the second vial of the violet potion—a backup. His fingers brushed the glass and—

Fire *exploded* through his wrist.

"Gahh!" he shouted, wrenching his hand back.

The runes inked into his skin seared with white-hot agony. The mark of Poseidon flared across his arm like lightning come alive. Ulric clenched his jaw, tried again. More pain. Blinding, ricocheting all the way up his shoulder.

"I am the Court Sorcerer!" He roared into the ocean. "He is a Prince of Atlantis, son of Queen Tritheya!"

The sea didn't answer. But the pain spoke volumes. Each time he reached for the potion, the magic burned him. It was not his duty. It was not his role. No one had ordered him to save Auren.

And yet he couldn't stop.

His chest heaved as he sank to the seafloor, shaking.

"I know why," he whispered, eyes closed.

"I love him."

He laughed. Hysterical and broken.

"I love him!" he shouted with morbid defiance.

The ink along his ribs buzzed violently, searing his skin in a warning. He looked at the marks. At the vows carved into his flesh like chains. If he listened—if he obeyed—he would never see those deep blue eyes again. Never touch that impossible red hair. Never know what it felt like to kiss him. To *choose* him.

Ulric clenched his fists and lifted his face to the sky.

"Let me save him!" he shouted into the sea. "Grant me this one wish! Let me save him, and I'll pay the price. Take my magic. Take everything. Take my life if you must. But let me save him."

His voice echoed through the water, vibrating with timeless fury.

This was who Ulric had become— and he was ready to let it all go.

Silence followed.

Ulric reached for the potion one more time. He braced, waiting for the punishment. But it never came.

No pain.

His hand closed around the vial like an answered prayer. He raised it to his lips.

The ocean trembled, as though the very water knew what was about to happen, and already mourned the loss.

"I accept the price," he whispered.

And drank.

Chapter Thirteen

Auren

THE SURFACE WAS EVERYTHING HE'D IMAGINED IT TO be. Sun-drenched and waiting for him like he belonged there all along.

Soft linens, warm breezes, the taste of honeysuckle in every breath. Elias took him in without hesitation, without question, as though he'd been waiting for Auren's arrival all his life.

The first thing Elias did was dress him. Light cotton shirts that clung to his shoulders and opened loosely at his sternum. Breeches that hugged his hips, stitched in navy and cream, the buttons carved from polished bone. The tailor's eyes darted curiously over

Auren's body, but her hands were skilled and kind. Elias stood nearby, watching with a smile that made Auren's skin buzz.

"Perfect," Elias murmured. "You look like something from my dreams."

Then came the servant girls, chattering in lilting voices as they fussed over his hair, braiding it into intricate patterns and weaving in soft blue beads.

"Weave these as well. He likes them." Elias ordered, nodding to the silver and gold silks.

"Yes, Sir."

Auren's chest warmed under Elias's attention. The girl's fingers were nimble and practiced, and when they finished, Elias approached, eyes gleaming.

"Breathtaking," he said, reaching out to tuck a loose strand behind Auren's ear. His fingers brushed skin and lingered a beat longer. "They don't make beauty like yours on land."

Auren's cheeks burned. He ducked his head, smiling despite himself. He couldn't speak, but his face said enough. Elias offered his hand, and Auren took it without hesitation.

They spent the day roaming the city.

It was alive with color, sound, and scent. It was nothing like the solemn quiet of the sea. Vendors shouted over one another in a dozen different tongues, peddling fruits in all shapes and shades. Spices clung to the air. Cinnamon and clove, firepepper and sugar. Roasted meats turned on open flames, their smoke rising in savory ribbons. The taste of the world was as wild as its scent. Auren devoured soft bread smeared with jam, sucked the juice of honey-orange slices from his fingers, and let Elias feed him bite after bite of something he called *lamb*. It melted on Auren's tongue like butter.

"You like that?" Elias chuckled, brushing his thumb over Auren's lower lip. "There's more where that came from. Anything you want—just ask."

Coins passed hands all day. Shiny metallic pieces that Auren had only ever seen rusting in shipwrecks. Elias gave them freely, slipping them to merchants, performers, and servers with easy charm. All the while, he held Auren's hand. Guiding him. Welcoming him. *Choosing* him.

Even though Auren couldn't speak, they found ways to talk. Gestures. Smiles. Pointed looks and over-the-top expressions. Auren mimed frustration more than once, dramatically flailing his hands and pointing at his throat.

Elias laughed, grabbing his hand and pressing a kiss to the knuckles.

"I don't need words to know what you're thinking," he said. "I've been dreaming of you too long for that."

Auren didn't know how his heart didn't float right out of his chest.

They passed street musicians and tavern bands. Fiddles and flutes layered harmonies that clashed and danced and spun through the air like magic. Auren had never heard anything like it. The haunting hymns of the Merfolk in Atlantis couldn't even compare.

This music was wild. Joyful. *Human.*

Elias led him into one of the largest taverns as the sun dipped beyond the horizon, the whole world washed in soft amber. The room was a riot of sound and movement. People danced, laughed, and drank freely. Flames danced in hanging lanterns, and candles clustered on long tables.

Auren's wide eyes must've shown too much.

Elias leaned in, whispering, "This is the best tavern in town. And now, with you here, the night is absolutely perfect."

They danced.

Auren was *terrible* at it.

He tripped over his feet, stomped on Elias's toes twice, and spun the wrong way so hard he knocked into a nearby server. But Elias only laughed, cradling Auren's waist, steadying him.

"You're adorable," he said. "If you weren't already mine, I'd fall for you all over again just watching you try."

Auren bit his lip to hold back a grin, pressing his forehead to the crook of Elias's neck as they swayed gently, even after the music ended. When they finally sat, Auren's legs ached in the best possible way. Elias handed him a goblet filled with something dark and sweet.

"Berry wine," he said. "You'll love it."

The wine was thick and luxurious, the sweetness clinging to Auren's tongue. He took another sip. Then another. The warmth hit, spreading through his stomach and down to his limbs. The firelight blurred into orange whisps. The music softened into a steady hum, a heartbeat beneath the world. He leaned into Elias's side, eyelids heavy. The room swayed, as if he were back underwater.

"You alright, darling?" Elias asked, brushing fingers along his jaw. "Getting sleepy?"

Auren nuzzled his face into Elias's neck with a blissful sigh. Gods, he loved it when Elias called him *darling*. Loved how tenderly he touched him. How he made him feel like the most precious thing in the world.

"Let's get you somewhere comfortable to sleep."

Elias's voice was a lullaby, and Auren let himself be led. The feel of the linen shirt beneath his cheek was soft, comforting. His limbs were slow, heavy with wine. There was a thickness to his thoughts. A warmth that slid too deep, too fast.

Still, he didn't care.

The scent of Elias clung to him. Oil. Smoke. Linen.

And there it was again, hanging at the edges of Auren's fading consciousness.

Decay.

He coughed once, a light breath. Maybe it was the wine. Or a breeze carrying the smell of rotting fish from the docks. He didn't let himself dwell.

He was wanted. Chosen. This was what he'd always longed for. And he'd come this far to claim it.

The last thing Auren remembered was the hum of tavern music, the clatter of tankards on old wood, and the steady pulse of Elias's hand wrapped around his.

He was in bliss.

Chapter Fourteen

Ulric

THE MOMENT HIS LEGS HIT THE SHORE, ULRIC EXHALED a heavy breath. It burned in his lungs. The air up here was always too dry.

He moved quickly. The sand stuck to his bare skin, clinging in wet streaks as he walked through the grass-tangled path. His cabin was remote and practical. Nothing fancy and far enough from the city to give him privacy, but close enough to conduct business. He often required extended time on land to harvest rare herbs and minerals. Drinking the transformation potion too frequently took a toll, even on *his* body.

It was a temporary location. Now, it felt like the last place he might ever see. He pushed the thought aside. If it meant Auren was safe, it was a grave he'd gladly lie in. Ulric changed, his robes hanging where he'd left them. He dressed in layers of navy and onyx black. The fabrics clung to his frame like night poured over bone. The outer robe was long, split at the sides for movement, embroidered with thin lines of dark silver thread that caught the light only when it wanted to. High collar. Folded cuffs. A wide leather belt that secured a swath of knives.

Not royalty or nobility. But no one would mistake him for a common peddler either. His presence carried enough weight to avoid questions—and that was all he needed. Just enough presence to deter predators. Just enough anonymity to move like a ghost.

The city was already buzzing when he entered. Carts creaked. Vendors barked. Smoke rose in spirals from meat fires, casting a haze through the narrow alleys. Ulric started there. The salt-crusted docks. The roadside stalls that stank of brine and blood. He offered coin with every question.

"Do you know a human biologist called Elias?"

He got nothing but blank stares and shrugged shoulders.

"Bi-what?" one grizzled man barked. "Speak proper. Don't bring that rubbish in here."

Another scoffed and waved him off. "Try the royal quarter if you're lookin' for bookworms. This ain't the place."

Ulric moved on. His frustration simmered hotter by the minute. He entered higher establishments. Places where the tile gleamed, and the smoke smelled of rare herbs instead of ash. Where the coin mattered more than the man.

Finally, a breakthrough. A brothel—one of the more extravagant ones. The sign outside read "The Garden of Wonders", and from the inside, it was clear why. The women lounged on embroidered cushions, bare-chested and painted in rosy swirls. The men wore perfume and kohl and little else. And the madam—no, the *Duchess,* as she called herself—lounged like a cat draped in silks.

"Elias?" she asked, eyes sparkling. "Oh yes. One of my most loyal customers." Her painted mouth curled. "Always asks for the prettiest young men."

Ulric's jaw ticked, and his spine straightened.

"And I suppose you know where I might find him?" he asked, calm as a sheathed blade.

The Duchess tilted her head, appraising him now with a different kind of curiosity. Her eyes dragged down the length of him, taking in the long lines of his frame, the ink curling just beneath his collar.

"Mm. You're quite the specimen yourself," she murmured. "It's a shame you've come here hunting. You ought to be hunted, darling."

Ulric said nothing.

She leaned forward, voice syrupy. "Why not take a break from your chase? Spend the night with one of my wonders. A man like you shouldn't have to walk away alone."

He offered the smallest of smiles. "Tempting," he said, "but I don't pay for distractions. Not tonight."

Her laugh was light and knowing. "Pity. But you'll find that information is like fine silk. Rare and expensive."

Ulric didn't blink. He slid a pouch of coin across the table. It clinked with a weight that made her eyes gleam. She tapped it once, then leaned in.

"He has a private study. Sponsored by the crown, no less. A few streets up from the palace wall, tucked behind the archives. Has his own key. Keeps to himself." Her voice dropped, and the atmosphere shifted. "I'd be careful if I were you," she purred. "He doesn't like being interrupted. His smile is sweet, but there's a wicked streak under that charm. One of my boys once brought him a rare bird, still alive. A gift for his patronage. He laughed and snapped its neck as if it were a flower stem. Said he needed the bones for dissection."

Ulric's stomach twisted. His fists clenched at his side, and it was all he could do to keep from reaching for the knives.

"He's cold," she went on. "Doesn't see people. Only specimens. Doesn't care what he hurts, so long as he can cut it open and study what's inside." Her smile returned. "I thought you might like to know the sort of man you're chasing."

He stood, thanked her, and exited her Garden of Wonders. The moment he stepped outside, the city was muffled. Dim, compared to the roaring in his ears. His robes swept over the cobblestones in a whisper of the violence to come. Every step tightened the coil inside him—wound by fear, by love, and by the weight of his broken vow.

The magic hadn't tried to stop him again. He was unhindered. Allowed to fulfill every selfish desire of his heart.

His prayer was heard.

And now—

Now, he would find Auren.

Whatever consequences came after, he would face them gladly.

Ulric pressed a hand to the inked runes on his forearm. Still warm, still alive, but flickering at the edges, like a flame nearing its final breath.

Let me be too late, he thought, *and I'll emerge as the creature the gods sealed in the pits of the earth. A nightmare even Olympus dare not name.*

Because if Elias touched even a hair on Auren's head—

The gods would weep at the monster Ulric would become.

Chapter Fifteen

Auren

THE WORLD WAS TOO BRIGHT.

Firelight throbbed against his eyelids, searing into his skull. His body was heavy—unnaturally so. Every limb dragged, as if filled with stones. His spine ached fiercely as he shifted on an unforgiving, flat surface.

He tried to roll over. But as he did, something snapped taut and bit into the delicate skin around his wrist.

Rope.

Auren's eyes flew open. And the stench hit him like a wave.

It was the same rotting scent he'd caught on the wind back on the beach— it was everywhere. It clung to the air, soaked the walls, crawled into his mouth, and gagged him.

Auren turned his head and retched, but there was nowhere to go. Nothing in his stomach. His throat seized, his body twitching weakly against the restraints.

He was tied down, his arms and legs strapped to four corners of a wooden table, each limb stretched and fixed tight with coarse rope. A thick leather collar dug into the skin of his throat, buckled around his neck, and secured to the table below. He wore nothing but the thinnest pair of shorts—barely more than a strip of fabric clinging to his waist. His chest was bare, exposed to the chill of the room. The frigid air bit at every inch of exposed skin, and it wasn't long before Auren was shivering.

Panic seized him. Gripping around his lungs, locking his joints, making his breath stutter in shallow, useless bursts. His head swam as he blinked away the haze, trying to make sense of the room.

This was no bedroom. No sanctuary.

The walls were stone, slick, and sweating. Shelves lined the perimeter, filled with glass jars—some fogged, some translucent. And inside each one...

Gods.

Floating organs. Coiled intestines. Pale, bloated eyes that stared without blinking. A jar of white teeth sat open on the counter, crusted in brown. Everything bobbed in a thick, yellowish fluid that burned Auren's eyes and filled the room with fumes. It was chemical, like stomach acid soaked in rot. Instruments gleamed from wall racks. Blades, needles, bone saws. Some were clean. Most were not.

What is this place?

It was the opposite of Ulric's apothecary—where every vial shimmered, where herbs hung in fragrant bundles, and mirrors caught the glint of light like magic. That place was full of wonder and life.

This place oozed with death.

The door creaked open.

"Oh, you're awake, darling," came that soft, velvety voice.

Elias.

Auren's heart stuttered. He turned his head enough to see Elias step into the firelight, calm and smiling, sleeves rolled to his elbows, hands scrubbed clean. The voice that once made Auren feel safe, seen—now sounded like it belonged to a stranger. Too soft. Too casual. Completely out of place in this room of horrors.

"I was worried I gave you a little too much," Elias said cheerfully. "You slept like a rock." He walked to the table and reached for something behind Auren's head. "I hope you won't take this personally. I *am* thrilled you're here. Really, I am." He chuckled, rolling something small between his fingers. "You just made it so easy. Walking up to me like that on the beach—saved me the trouble of setting another trap on the deck. It was a good trap, too. I designed it specifically to take you alive without wounding you too much. But alas, you never came. After a week, I thought I'd lost my chance. That you'd slipped away forever." He leaned in, eyes bright with fascination. "And lo and behold, you walk right into my arms. Walk! Of all the things I imagined you capable of, I must say you still managed to surprise me. This transformation... *how* did you manage it?"

His hand slid up Auren's leg—clinical at first, until it passed his thigh and crept too high. Too close.

"I must say, I've had many specimens on this table. But you're the first to tempt me. The first to make me want to... partake."

Auren recoiled, jerking against the ropes. He tried to kick— tried to scream—but the collar held fast, and no sound escaped his throat.

Elias sighed. "Now, now. Don't struggle. It makes this so much harder than it needs to be." He turned away, selecting a scalpel from a tray with a practiced hand. The metal gleamed as he examined its edge, utterly unfazed by Auren's panic. "I don't mean to frighten you. I simply need to know. You're incredible. Your body

—your biology—it's beyond anything I've studied. I could spend a lifetime trying to understand it. And I intend to."

He walked with heavy boots, blade in hand, trailing the tip across Auren's bare stomach. The cool metal kissed his skin. Elias paused, standing over him, gazing down Auren's exposed form.

"Beautiful," he murmured, almost to himself. "You really are something else. And so quiet, too. That's a blessing. Saves me the trouble of a gag." Elias smiled as he crouched down, eye level with Auren's abdomen. "Poor unfortunate soul. You're not going to like this part."

Then he cut.

It was deep. Clean. Measured. The scalpel slid through his skin like fruit flesh. Auren arched off the table, body straining against the restraints as a white-hot blaze erupted across his belly. It felt like being flayed alive. He *was* being flayed alive. His body convulsed—and yet, no scream came. His mouth opened in a soundless wail, but there was nothing. No release. No voice.

Only the silent pooling of blood down his side.

He trembled, gasping in silence. The pain didn't stop. It spread, blooming in nerve endings he hadn't known existed. And through it all, Elias hummed to himself, dabbing away the blood with a pristine cloth as though wiping down a dinner spill.

"I'll keep you alive, of course," Elias murmured, his tone still conversational. "I want to see how everything works. How it all connects. We'll go slow—section by section. That way, I can make the most of our time together."

His voice softened, but the gleam in his eyes was cruel.

Sadistic.

Auren screamed inside his mind. The blade bit in. He arched in agony as the scalpel cut into the skin below his navel. Tears streamed down his face as fire spread through his belly. He thrashed uselessly against the ropes. His voice—gods, why couldn't he scream?

How did I let this happen?

How could I have been so stupid?

He'd been so in love with a fantasy that he didn't see the monster behind the smile. Ulric warned him. Again and again. Told him humans consume beauty.

And now...

Now, he was a science experiment. A curiosity to be sliced apart and studied.

Auren sobbed as Elias wiped the blood with a linen cloth, humming a sickeningly cheerful tune. His short gasping breaths and tear-filled eyes did nothing to slow Elias's examination.

"There, there now, my beauty. It'll fade. Or you'll get used to it. Regardless, the first time is the worst. Take heart in the fact that the more I learn, the less I'll have to cut."

Auren grit his teeth so hard his ears rang.

He thought of Ulric. Thought of his voice. His eyes. His inked skin and the way he'd looked at Auren as though he were in pain.

I should've listened.

If he had his voice—if he could speak one word—he wouldn't scream.

He would beg Elias to end it. To slit his throat and be done with it. Because this wasn't life. This was punishment.

And he was a fool.

Auren didn't know how long he had been unconscious. Only that he woke in bursts. Pain was the tide that carried him through the waves of torture—dragging him under and spitting him back out.

Each time his eyes opened, the firelight blurred and spun. His thoughts were fleeting and stripped to just sensation. He couldn't tell if it had been hours or days. If Elias ever left. If he was still... himself.

The next time he woke, something burned along the side of his ribcage. His vision cleared enough to see the gleam of neat stitches —black thread pulled taut over angry, raw skin. He was sewn shut. Fresh panic clawed at his chest. What had Elias done? What had he taken? His head lolled to the side. Glass jars lined the shelf like trophies. One was filled with a faintly blueish tissue.

Is that mine?

The next time, his eyelids fluttered open to the cold kiss of metal against his collarbone. A sharp pinch. Another cut. A tug. The smell of blood filled the room again. Auren wanted to thrash, to scream, to die—but his body wouldn't obey. He whimpered before blacking out again.

When he woke next, he was colder.

Lighter.

His whole midsection ached like he'd been gutted and stitched back together. He didn't know how much was gone. He didn't want to know. The pain was constant now. Barbed around the edges, dull in the center. There was a sick kind of rhythm to it. His body pulsed in time with the pain. His breath. His heart. All of it synced to agony.

Elias's voice was the only thing that broke the stillness.

"The elixirs I'll make from this..." he mused aloud, scribbling into a leather-bound journal with one ink-stained hand. The other held a vial—Auren's blood, thick and red and glowing beneath the firelight. "I'll need to increase your iron intake. You're running a little dry, sweetheart. Don't worry—we'll fatten you up again. I have so many more jars to fill."

He didn't look at Auren as he spoke. Just talked around him, like he was already dead.

A specimen.

Auren stared blankly at the rafters above. They swam in and out of focus. Was that supposed to be comforting? That Elias would keep him alive? That he wouldn't take enough to kill him? Auren wasn't sure anymore. Death felt less frightening than this slow unraveling. At least death would end. Maybe if Elias slipped, he'd cut too deep. Sever an artery. Let the blood run free until the world finally went dark for good.

Auren prayed for it. For mercy.

But Elias's hands never faltered.

Time twisted. Collapsed in on itself. Auren was losing track of who he was. What he'd been. Just another piece of flesh on a table. Another wild thing caught in the net.

Dark hair swayed with the tide, and eyes darker still—like they had swallowed the ocean depths whole. A place where light didn't reach. Ulric's reluctant smile. His wicked smirk, sharper than his teeth. The way his onyx-black tentacles had held Auren so gently, with more care than any human touch. Arms that wrapped around him like they were made to fit.

Why now, of all times, did those memories rise to the surface? How much more was he meant to suffer? To regret?

The memories came one after another, but not the way he wanted, not wrapped in warmth or fondness. It felt like pressing on a bruise, like a hook buried deep in his ribs.

Ulric's voice, rough as waves against stone. His scent, like obsidian warmed by underwater vents. And his eyes... black as trench water, where sunlight dared not touch.

Auren tried to banish the memories. Because those memories, growing more vivid with each passing heartbeat, kept him tethered.

Even now, with his blood in jars and his body in pieces, something in him held on. Wouldn't let go.

But Auren was ready to let go.

He longed to fall into madness. To let go of thought, of memory, of pain. To drift away into the black where nothing could hurt him anymore.

But Ulric's voice echoed through the dark recesses of his mind. Just loud enough to keep him from disappearing completely.

"Fight it, Spriteling. Fight it for me."

It was cruel, the way hope worked. Worse than the scalpel. Because hope meant maybe. Hope meant what if. And in this place, hope was the most exquisite torture of all.

But I left him.

Auren clenched his eyes shut, but it didn't stop the voice in his head. If anything, it made it louder.

I left him, and now he'll never come looking.

Auren's chest tightened, particularly on his left side, until it felt like he might snap in half. His wrists strained weakly at the ropes again, but there was no strength left in them. No strength to fight. No strength to scream. Only the voice in his head, crueler than anything Elias could ever do to him.

You had someone who loved you.

And you chose the lie instead.

Tears slipped down his cheeks. Ulric had tried. And Auren had thrown it away for a smile and a promise wrapped in pretty words. For a man with soft hands and sharp knives. Now, all he had was pain. And silence. And the memory of a voice that would never call his name again.

"Auren."

Elias scribbled a few more notes before setting the blood-filled vial into a rack alongside others. Ten now. Maybe twelve. Auren lost count. He couldn't cry anymore. The pain ate all his tears.

He was so tired.

But the worst part was that his body clung to life.

And Elias knew it.

The human brushed a hand over Auren's shoulder as he passed, almost fondly. "You're doing so well. You're a marvel."

Auren wanted to tell him to go to hell. Instead, his vision blurred again. The firelight smeared into amber streaks. And he sank once more into the dark.

Chapter Sixteen

Ulric

THE GUARDS WEREN'T READY FOR IT. FOR THE MONSTER that descended the stairs. For the storm that filled the halls with black smoke and silenced them without ever drawing a blade. Ulric didn't give them time to react.

Three men now lay in broken heaps behind the corridor walls, limp and unconscious. One might not wake again. Ulric stepped over them without pause, boots silent on the stone floor. The deeper into the dungeon labs he moved, the worse the smell became.

Formaldehyde. Blood. Brine. And something far worse.

Pain.

Ulric lived long enough to know that pain carried a scent. It was acidic, like spoiled milk and rusted metal. It stung the nostrils and settled heavy on the tongue. The air in Elias's lab reeked of it —pain layered upon pain, caked into the walls and soaked into the floorboards.

It was everywhere.

Yet underneath it all was the fading trace of Auren's scent. Sea salt and coral. The sweetness of crushed pearls and the purity of spring.

It was faint.

Ulric stopped at the final door, pressing an ear to the small iron-barred opening at its center. At first he heard nothing, only the steady drip of water echoing through the dank halls. Then a small shuffle. Of movement. Of struggle. And a whimper.

It slipped beneath the doorframe. Not a scream, not even a cry, just a wet hitch of air, like something trying not to choke.

Ice sliced through Ulric's veins.

Auren.

Then came a second sound. The human, Elias. His voice was smooth, as if he were proud of his cruelty.

"You're doing so well, sweetheart. There now, look how the muscle twitches when I peel it back. It's like you're performing for me. I'll admit, I was hoping to save this for later and give you more time to heal. But your body begs to be explored."

Another faint sound of a struggle, but weak... so weak.

"Now, now, love... don't wriggle so much. You'll ruin the stitching." A pause. A quiet chuckle. "Though with legs like yours, perhaps you'd look better ruined."

Ulric's fist shattered the door. It didn't swing open—it cracked clean off the hinges. And for a moment, Ulric questioned whether he'd stepped into the vilest pit of the underworld.

Auren lay spread across a heavy wood table, his skin pale as bone, a patchwork of stitches carved along his chest, his arms, his sides. Some fresh, some crusted in blood. One leg twitched reflexively—nerves misfiring. His lips were a ghostly shade of blue. His crimson hair was plastered to the surface with rust-colored clots. His eyes were open, but dull. Dry. Like he'd stopped blinking regularly.

Ulric's sweet, wild prince looked hollow. Wounded and emptied of life.

Elias didn't even flinch. He adjusted the magnifying lenses strapped across his eyes and continued digging into the exposed muscle in Auren's bicep. Surgical hooks held the skin apart as he inspected the sinew and flexor tendons beneath.

"Oh," Elias said mildly, as if commenting on a guest's unexpected arrival. "I expected someone to come and collect."

Ulric didn't speak, just blinked in stunned shock. At the human's words. At the scene before him. In all his centuries...

Elias gave a light, pleased chuckle. "I should've guessed. A face like his?" He gestured toward Auren's motionless form. "Of course, he'd be the whore of the sea. Probably expensive too."

Ulric's eyes darkened, but his voice, when it came, was calm. Calm as the sky with a hurricane on the horizon. Calm as the waves before the tsunami brings destruction.

"Do you even know what you've done?"

Elias tilted his head, as though puzzled by the question. "I preserved him. Studied him. If anything, he should thank me."

"You...you..." Ulric could hardly speak through the rage smashing the inside of his skull. "You broke him."

"I've studied him," Elias said coolly, wiping blood from his fingers with a cloth. "And I think you've arrived just in time to strike a deal. That's what you sea monsters do, isn't it? Trade, bargain, barter." He smiled like a man holding all the cards. "So name your price. I know how this works. The sea demands tribute. Coin. Flesh. Secrets. Name it, and I'll pay. Or the royal court will. I can assure you, they'll be generous."

Ulric stared at the human for a long, terrible moment. Then he smiled. Not the smile of a man. The smile of something long past morality. Past reason. A smile carved from rage and grief. It wasn't human. It wasn't a creature. It was a weapon. And it was awake.

"You think there exists compensation for what you've done?"

Elias's fingers twitched, and he removed the magnifying lenses from his eyes. He looked confused. "Well, of course. Everything has a price."

"I have lived through the birth and drowning of kingdoms. I've bartered with storms and wrestled gods. You think you have something I want?"

A rumble of thunder shook the walls as he moved closer, a cloud of black mist seeping in, covering the floors and climbing the walls. And when the Kraken spoke, it was as if the abyss had found voice.

"I want your silence. I want your screams. I want to peel back every layer of that twisted mind and see how you whimper when you're laid bare."

Elias finally stepped back, and Ulric's lips curled, revealing his serrated shark's teeth.

"Good," he whispered. "Now you understand."

He bit down. The capsule cracked between his molars like glass. Pain bloomed under his tongue as the potion spilled down his throat, and in seconds, the magic took him. Power flooded his body like a black tide breaking free. Bones twisted. Muscles surged. Flesh rippled and tore as obsidian skin replaced legs. Nine monstrous limbs erupted from beneath his cloak, curling with liquid fury.

Elias screamed.

Too late.

Ulric moved like a wave as his mass flooded the small space. Tentacles crashed through glass and steel, sweeping aside tables, smashing jars, sending vials shattering against stone. Blood and formaldehyde painted the walls. Every sample, every artifact Elias had ripped from Auren's body, was lost in the maelstrom.

Ulric didn't stop.

He lunged—one slick tendril curling around Elias's arm, another locking around his torso, hoisting him into the air like a doll.

"You wanted to see how things work?" Ulric growled, snatching a jagged scalpel off the floor. "Let me give you a lesson in anatomy."

Then he gutted him.

The blade sank in deep, through the belly and beneath the ribs, carving upward. Elias's scream broke into a gurgle as his intestines spilled in warm, wet ropes down the front of his legs. Blood sprayed. Ulric didn't flinch. He seized a long, rust-speckled autopsy hook from the surgical tray—a grotesque thing with a curve like a butcher's smile. It sank into Elias's side with a wet crunch, punched between bone and muscle, and drove deep into the stone wall.

Ulric twisted the hook just to hear his cry.

"Rot, you filth."

He finished pinning Elias like a specimen on display. His mouth bubbled with blood the color of wine as his body sagged and spasmed, still very much alive. But he wasn't long for this world; let his final minutes be spent in agony.

The world went still, save for the steady stream of human insides hitting stone floors.

Then, the potion's effect faded.

Ulric stumbled back a step, his breath ragged as the monstrous limbs retracted into flesh and bone. He gasped, sucking in air with lungs newly reformed. The transformation was short, a small dose of potion intended to give him an advantage in case of a fight. Long enough to overpower his opponent. But with the addition of his Kraken form came gills that stuttered uselessly in the air. He stumbled, light-headed from breath held too long. His tunic hung loose, barely covering him, and his cloak hung awkwardly over his shoulders. But modesty was the farthest thing from his mind.

Ulric stumbled to the table, bare feet slick on blood-soaked stone. His throat burned raw from the transformation, lungs still struggling. He braced himself on the edge and stared at the fragile, ruined form before him.

"Auren..." he rasped.

No response.

Auren's eyes were half open, dull and unfocused. His lips had gone a bluish-gray, cracked, and still. He wasn't blinking.

He wasn't breathing.

"No, no—come on, my sweet sea-sprite. Please." Ulric's voice broke as he knelt beside the table, brushing blood-matted hair from Auren's clammy forehead. "I'm here. I'm here, Auren. You're safe now. Just... open your eyes. Gods, please, say something."

But there was nothing.

Panic hit fast and hard, shattering through Ulric's composure. He ripped his satchel open, fingers fumbling past bandages and vials until he found the slender bottle—glowing a soft, sea-glass green. A healing draught. He unstoppered it with his teeth and tilted it into Auren's mouth.

It dribbled down his chin.

"Dammit—breathe, love. Please. Don't you dare give up. Don't leave me."

Ulric brought the bottle to his lips and drank—the potion burned in his mouth, leaving frost in its wake. Cradling Auren's broken face in both hands, he pressed their mouths together, funneling the magic between their lips. He repeated the process two more times, each time carefully pressing his mouth to Auren's, each time passing him more of the potion. When the bottle was empty, Ulric leaned back, mouth tingling.

For a long, terrible moment, nothing happened.

Auren lay still, cold, untouched by the miracle Ulric had poured into him. The room was too quiet. No breath. No twitch. No life.

And then—

A sharp inhale.

Auren's chest rose the slightest fraction, and his eyes fluttered.

Ulric nearly collapsed with the force of his relief, forehead pressing to Auren's as he held him close. "There you are," he whispered, voice cracking under the weight of it all. "There you are, my sweet prince. My beautiful, foolish heart." He kissed Auren's temple, his brow, his bloodied knuckles. "I'm sorry. I should've come sooner. I should've known. I've got you now. I swear it."

Ulric wrapped Auren's limp body in his cloak, holding him close, shielding him from the nightmare surrounding them. Elias hung from the wall like some macabre portrait, blood trailing in thin, glistening streams—Ulric turned away.

He carried the prince of the sea out of that place of ruin and rot, out of death's waiting hands, and into the dark embrace of his arms.

Chapter Seventeen

Auren

AUREN EXPECTED THE PAIN TO GREET HIM. BUT HIS awareness of the world came first through scent.

Pine and linen. Smoke and sea-brine. It was comfortable. Warm. Then another scent, one that rivalled all the others. That sparked understanding in his brain like the pop of a woodfire.

A wild scent. Deeply familiar. Boiling tides over volcanic stone. The chill of the blackest ocean canyon. It was the scent of the deep, here to run a salve over his wounds.

It crawled into his lungs, coating them in a healing balm.

For a moment, Auren thought perhaps he was dead. Maybe

this was Poseidon's mercy after all. A final kindness—a phantom scent to carry him gently into the dark. Auren thought it fitting that his last memory be the scent of *him*. Of Ulric. Of his sweetest regret.

But it didn't fade. And neither did Auren.

He breathed easier. Warmth spread through his limbs. The ache remained, but it no longer swallowed him whole. Slowly, he blinked, focusing enough to catch the sway of sea foam curtains rustled by a breeze. A window cracked open, welcoming in the cry of gulls and the crashing lull of waves.

Auren lay on a proper bed. Not a table. No cold iron and tight restraints. Thick blankets covered him, tucked tight around his battered frame. A hearth crackled nearby, radiating a gentle heat that sank into his bones.

He didn't dare speak, didn't dare break what had to be an illusion created by his own delirious mind.

What is this place?

A door creaked behind him. Boots on wooden floors. Auren didn't have the strength to turn, but when the figure stepped into view, his breath caught.

Black linen trousers, worn leather boots, and a loose dark shirt unbuttoned to reveal a torso of swirling tattoos. His hair was damp, curling wild and loose. And his eyes, those deep, dark eyes, were fixed on Auren.

Ulric.

No. That's not possible.

His mind reeled.

I'm dead. This is a trick of my dying brain. One last memory of him before I slip away.

Because surely, no vision, no memory, could conjure the shine of tears in Ulric's eyes.

Tears in his eyes... for me.

The illusion didn't vanish.

"You're awake. Welcome back, young prince."

And at the sound of his voice, the tears finally escaped the confines of Auren's eyes and fell freely. This wasn't a dream. This wasn't the illusion of death.

He's here. He came back for me.

Ulric crossed the room in three long strides. He dropped to his knees beside the bed and took Auren's limp hand in both of his.

Warm. Solid. Real.

"You're awake," Ulric breathed. His hands tightened around Auren's, the tremble in them unmistakable. "Gods, you're awake. I thought—I thought I'd lost you."

The dam broke with a shudder. Auren sobbed, his whole body shaking with the effort. Not from pain, but from release. From the overwhelming, impossible reality of being alive.

Ulric climbed into the bed beside him, boots tossed to the floor, coat shrugged off to settle around both of them like a second blanket. His arms curled around Auren with so much ease; it was as though he'd pictured holding Auren this way a thousand times.

"I've got you," Ulric whispered, voice rough as waves on stone. "I've got you. You're safe now. It's all over."

Auren was so overcome, it took him a moment to realize Ulric was kissing him.

A kiss to his forehead. Then his temple. Then Ulric tucked his face into Auren's hair, the bristle of his beard scraping gently against his skin as he exhaled a shaking breath.

He's kissing me. He's touching me. He... he is here.

And for some reason, that only made Auren sob harder.

He clung to Ulric with everything he had, curling into him like a drowning creature latching onto driftwood. He clung until his knuckles went white against Ulric's chest. Still, no sound escaped him—only the ragged, wheezing breath of a broken creature.

"Drink this," he murmured. "It'll counter the side effects of the potion. You'll be able to speak again."

He held out a small decanter of clear liquid. Auren lifted his hand to take it, but trembled so violently the bottle nearly slipped to the floor. Ulric stopped him. He took Auren's hand in his, weaving their fingers together.

"Let me," he whispered.

Ulric shifted, propping Auren more securely against his chest, one arm wrapped around his back, the other carefully guiding the decanter to his lips.

The first drop was warm, soft as down feathers, and strangely familiar. Like *karsa-root broth*—the warm, briny Merfolk stew the palace servants used to feed him as a child when he was ill. A comfort food from simpler days.

The familiar taste shattered him.

A fresh wave of sobs wracked through him, body hitching uncontrollably. He choked on the first sip and turned away, unable to hold it in. Ulric didn't flinch. He shifted the bottle away, curled his arms tighter around him, and held him through it. No scolding. No impatience. Only a steady strength anchoring Auren in place.

Three times, Ulric tried again.

And on the third, Auren finally stilled enough to drink the rest.

All the while, Ulric remained there, closer than he had ever been. Holding him not like a sorcerer, not like a guardian. Something Auren dared not name.

A shield.

A harbor.

Auren stilled in the safety of that presence. The crackle of the fire, the scent of Ulric's skin, the steady thump of his heart—it wrapped around Auren until the storm inside went quiet. It didn't erase the pain. But it gave it shape. It gave it reason. It gave it a place to rest.

And as the tears ran dry and his breathing slowed, Auren whispered. His voice was cracked, but finally free from chains.

"...Don't let go," he rasped.

Ulric's arms pulled him tighter.

"Never, my prince."

Auren only managed to stand once. Just long enough to stumble to the basin while Ulric held him steady, and that alone left his limbs trembling. The rest of the time, he remained tucked beneath thick quilts in Ulric's cabin, resting on a bed that smelled of cedar.

It was modest. Lived in. The shelves were lined with dried herbs, driftwood carvings, and worn books with softened corners. A fireplace crackled at the far end of the room, casting shadows across the walls. Outside, the ocean hissed against the cliffs.

And Ulric was always there.

The Kraken didn't leave his side—not once in the five days Auren remained bed-bound. He was either perched on the edge of the bed with a book resting on his knee, or seated in a wooden chair beside the hearth, watching the flames with distant eyes. And when Auren stirred from fevered dreams, nightmares soaked in jars and blood and metal, Ulric was beside him, arms waiting.

"Gentle, my sweet prince," he murmured, gathering Auren close. "You're okay. I'm here."

And gods, how those words stopped the nightmares.

They wove around Auren like silk. That voice could've called back the tide. Could've commanded storms to still and the earth itself to quiet. It carried the weight of oceans and the hush of sand.

It felt as though Ulric's words could stop the very sun from rising, if only to let Auren rest a little longer in that safety. Wrapped in Ulric's arms, his mind finally let go of the horrors— the blood, the jars, the knives—and returned to the one thing that still made sense.

Ulric.

Auren spent too long just... watching him.

Ulric's human form was unfamiliar, and in the quiet intimacy of the cabin, Auren was given an unobstructed chance to observe. His top half looked much the same—broad shoulders, arms dusted with ink, his scars and sharp lines exactly as Auren remembered. But lower down...

His legs were sturdy, long, and powerful. Muscle shaped the curve of his thighs, the solid line of his calves. Auren flushed the first time he caught himself staring when Ulric bent low to tend the fire. The hem of his tunic shifted just enough to reveal the sharp lines of his back and, lower still, the firm curve of his ass.

Auren buried his face in the blankets and groaned. "Unfair," he muttered into the pillow.

"You said something?" Ulric called over his shoulder, glancing back.

"Nope. Nothing. Sleep-talking."

Ulric gave a suspicious hum but said nothing more.

The next day, Auren woke, and as they talked over a breakfast of fresh fish Ulric caught that morning, he asked, "How... am I still human?"

Ulric glanced up from his plate, his expression softening. "Once you're strong enough, I'll give you the transformation tonic, and you can return home. You're too weak to survive the transformation right now, or I would have given it to you already."

Auren nodded, swallowing against the lump of guilt.

"Oh." His gaze dropped to the blankets curled around his legs —whole now, healed. The horrible places where Elias had cut into him were nothing but faint pink scars, like echoes on his skin. He didn't deserve to feel whole. Didn't deserve Ulric tending to him for days, all because of his own stupidity.

"I'm so sorry," Auren blurted out. It was the first time he'd managed the words in all the days spent in the house. "I stole the potion. I thought I knew better. I didn't know what I was walking into. You tried to stop me, and I—I should've listened."

Ulric didn't look surprised. He nodded, like he'd been waiting for this moment. He set his plate on the coffee table before the hearth, but the food was only half finished.

"The blame isn't with you alone," he said quietly. "I bear half the blame. I took your freedom, tried to cage you, and when I did that... I made you desperate. It should never have happened the way it did. *I* shouldn't have allowed it to happen."

He sighed, dragging a hand down his face, rising from his chair and pacing the small room.

"Ulric, you can't truly believe—"

"What happened to you," Ulric's voice rose in volume. "It should never have... What you had to—I could have—"

It was the first time Auren saw the Kraken at a loss for words. For once, the weight of centuries offered him no answer. And in that pause, Auren saw not the Court Sorcerer, not the Kraken, not the legend... but a man who suddenly didn't know what to say.

Ulric stomped heavily to the edge of the bed and sat hard, head falling into his hands. "I thought I was protecting you. That I was following orders. The Queen wanted you close, and I... I wanted that too. I told myself it was duty. But I would be lying if I said there weren't other motives. It was selfish."

Auren leaned forward, crawling closer until he was within reach. He brushed a lock of dark hair from Ulric's face.

"You were doing your job," he said. "And I was being stupid."

"There were other ways to serve the Queen," Ulric muttered, not looking at him. "But I didn't take them. Because I wanted to keep you close. I wanted to pull you into the deep..."

His voice dropped to a whisper.

"...with me."

Auren's heart stumbled in his chest.

Ulric couldn't be saying what... what Auren thought he was saying.

He rested a tentative hand on Ulric's knee, the heat of his palm settling them both. Ulric exhaled slowly. His hand dragged through his dark hair, shoulders hunched forward.

"I've pushed you away for years," he said finally. "Watched you from the shadows but never let myself get close."

He hesitated, fingers curling into the fabric of his trousers. A tremor ghosted through his knuckles.

"When I saw you begin to drift from me," Ulric continued, not looking at him, "when I thought I was losing you…"

He rubbed at his mouth with the back of his hand, as though trying to smother the admission. His foot tapped against the wood floor, restless.

"I panicked. I tried tying you to me. Tried dragging you down into the black deep. Into the only world I've ever known how to exist in."

His eyes lifted then, meeting Auren's with raw and bottomless vulnerability.

"I should've realized… I couldn't harness someone as brilliant as the sun, and never expect them to look to the sky."

Ulric clasped his hands together, his head dropping to them as though in prayer.

"Forgive me, Auren. This… your pain. It's my fault. If I'd been more forthcoming, if I'd revealed what I knew of the surface world, this all could have been avoided."

The silence that followed was thick with everything unspoken. The steady pulse of the sea beyond the window. The crackle of the fire. And the aching beat of Auren's heart. The rapid rush of blood in his veins.

He moved without thinking. Sidling across the mattress, his knee brushing Ulric's thigh, eyes never leaving the older man's face. He was trembling—not from fear, not this time. From want. From everything that was buried for so long, it took root in his bones.

"I thought for the longest time I'd only be the 'young prince' to you," Auren whispered. "That you'd never see me. Never see me for who I am." His cheeks flushed. Heat crept up his neck, but he didn't stop. "I wanted you to see me so badly."

Ulric didn't move, the tips of his thumbs pressing into his brow as his eyes closed tight as though he were in pain.

"I saw you, Auren," Ulric whispered. "I've always seen you." His voice fractured like sea glass underfoot. "And in four centuries, nobody has ever tempted me to break my vow—"

He stopped short, jaw tightening.

Ulric sat up on a gasp, reaching out, cupping Auren's cheek in his palm. His thumb brushed along the ridge of Auren's cheekbone, feather-light. He tipped his face up with a tenderness that made Auren's breath hitch.

"Nobody has ever left me so utterly helpless. So completely at their mercy as you have, Auren. My spriteling."

Auren's breath caught. He searched Ulric's face, saw the war behind his dark eyes. Guilt battling desire.

"I let duty keep me from you," Ulric said at last. "Then I let my own selfishness shackle you to the seafloor."

His forehead touched Auren's.

"I'm so sorry."

Auren pulled back—just enough to search those eyes. Those fathomless, storm-dark eyes that saw too much. He searched for regret. For restraint. For the glimmer of warning that usually came when Ulric got too close.

But there was nothing.

No push. No rejection.

Just Ulric, watching him with an intensity that made the world quiet.

Auren's breath stuttered. "Kiss me," he whispered.

The shock in Ulric's gaze made Auren think he'd said the wrong thing. That, once again, he was going to be pushed away. But that only lasted a second. And, as though waiting for permission, Ulric closed the space between them until their mouths met.

It started slow—lips brushing lips, breaths mingling—but the moment they touched, something inside Auren broke open.

A dam. A floodgate. A lifetime of need.

Tears sprang to his eyes and ran down either side of his face. Overcome by the sheer *relief* of it. The crashing, soul-deep relief of being *wanted*—openly, freely, without rules or shame. Every breath he hadn't allowed himself to take, every whisper of longing he'd tried to drown, surged to the surface in that one, trembling second.

Ulric let out a sigh, and it was as though the seafloor itself had fractured.

Auren held that sigh in his mouth, and it tasted like years.

Years of restraint.

Of aching denial.

Of loneliness wrapped in duty, now unraveling in the warmth of Auren's lips.

And gods help him, Auren let it all in.

A kiss written in tears. Ulric's hand tangled in his hair, the other holding him firm, and Auren gasped against his mouth, reeling. He didn't know a kiss could feel like this. Like forgiveness. Like gravity. Like coming home.

The glide of Ulric's lips, the gentle brush of his tongue, asking permission to taste. To explore.

To love.

Ulric guided Auren back onto the bed, lowering him to the cushions. The Kraken settled his weight over him, not heavy but enough that Auren's body was on fire with the weight of the man on top of him. Their mouths met again in a greedy kiss, tasting, taking, giving. Auren's hands roamed upward, slipping beneath Ulric's tunic, tracing along his broad back, over the contours of muscle and damp skin. Ulric's fingers ghosted over Auren's waist, his ribs, the place where scale had once met flesh.

With every touch, they grew braver.

Fingertips to palms. Lips to throat. Breath to breath.

And then, Ulric pulled back, just enough to rest their foreheads together. Both of them were panting, chests rising and falling in sync. The air between them thick with exhales and sweat.

"Never…" Ulric murmured, voice hoarse, "In all my years has anyone… anything… made me…"

He trailed off, shaking his head. Damp strands of his dark hair fell forward, brushing Auren's cheek. But there was a smile there. Shy and a little stunned. Like it wasn't meant to exist but had broken through anyway.

"I do not know myself like this," Ulric admitted.

Auren reached up, pushing the hair from Ulric's face. His fingers were deliberate as he cupped the side of his jaw, searching those ink-dark eyes—and finding something new.

Not sorrow.

Not shame.

But joy. Quiet and nervous, tucked behind thick lashes.

"I want to know you like this," Auren said softly. "In all the ways you exist. All the things you hide. I want… you."

Ulric's hand came to rest on his cheek, the pad of his thumb stroking beneath Auren's eye. He leaned in, pressing a kiss there, then another at the corner of his mouth.

"My spriteling…" he murmured. "You don't know this. But you've had me all this time." He sighed, breath heavy on Auren's neck, voice tight. "Until now, I couldn't allow myself to feel this. Have this."

Auren squeezed his eyes shut, overwhelmed. "My pride blinded me," he whispered. "I kept trying to prove I was strong enough. That I knew what I was doing. I was a fool." Auren opened his eyes, and when he did, found Ulric already staring at him. "But… if I'm broken, if I'm stubborn and cut up and used… will you still have me, Kraken?"

Ulric's expression shattered.

"Auren," he breathed, as though the question itself wounded him. He lowered himself until their bodies touched chest to chest, one hand slipping behind Auren's neck to hold him steady. "There is nothing you could become that would make me turn away from you."

Auren's eyes sparkled with sea-salt tears. "Nothing?"

Ulric pressed his forehead against his.

"Nothing."

Auren let out a shaky breath, his voice breaking into a tender whisper.

"I would cross any ocean for you."

Ulric smiled and leaned in, inhaling deeply as though to drug himself on Auren's scent.

"For you," Ulric said softly, "I would drain them."

Auren shivered beneath him.

"The world has asked many things of me. You are the first thing I have ever wanted to keep for myself. For all my time in this realm," Ulric said, voice barely more than a breath, "I am yours."

Auren wrapped his arms around Ulric's ribs and whispered into the space between their mouths.

"Then I am yours."

They lay like that, wrapped in warmth, the last flickers of fire-light dimming around them. Ulric's lips pressed a lingering kiss to Auren's temple, then to his hair. And that was the last thing Auren remembered. Falling asleep in arms that didn't let go. Held through the hush of night. Kissed into a peace he had never known.

Chapter Eighteen

Ulric

AUREN WAS WELL ENOUGH TO WALK NOW.

He moved slower than he used to, still favoring the side of his body where the wounds hadn't cut as deeply. But the light returned to his eyes. That fire. That insatiable spark of curiosity Ulric feared the humans had smothered for good.

But no. It was still there.

Just that morning, Ulric found him wandering the beach, crouched in the sand with his head bent, marveling at a tarnished piece of silverware. Its four prongs glinted as Auren pulled it from the sand.

Auren turned the fork over in his hands, eyes narrowed in that adorably concentrated way of his. Ulric opened his mouth to explain its purpose—only for Auren to tilt his head and begin combing his hair.

A swell of adoration rose so suddenly in Ulric's chest that he didn't have the heart to correct him. He watched as Auren dragged the cutlery through his red locks.

"You look lovely," Ulric complimented, pursing his lips to keep from smiling too broadly.

Auren hummed, visibly pleased with himself. When he was finished, he turned the silver fork in his hands without really seeing it. His mind was elsewhere, and by the haunted look in his eyes, Ulric could guess where it had gone.

"What happened?" Auren asked.

Ulric tilted his head, brows knitting together.

Auren took a shuddering breath. "To him. To Elias. I... I don't remember much."

Of course, he didn't. He'd been so tightly wrapped in death's embrace that Ulric had to pry those cold, dead fingers from his skin. He barely got Auren back.

"Do you want to know the answer?" Ulric asked, his voice low.

Auren flinched. "I guess I just want to know... if he... if I'm..."

"You're safe," Ulric said with certainty. "He is gone, my prince. But again, I ask you not to force me to reveal the manner in which he departed this world."

Auren nodded, understanding. And even though he was still visibly shaken, some of the tension in his shoulders eased. He didn't have to worry about that monster touching him ever again.

He resumed his exploration of the beach, a lightness returning to his steps.

Auren was still Auren. Still hungry for knowledge and full of wonder. Still made of mischief and magic, held together by sheer stubbornness. The horrors he'd endured hadn't broken him. And

Ulric, who had stood witness to every battle in the sea, every storm, every sacred rite, felt small in the face of it.

So Ulric answered him without hesitation. Every question Auren asked, he met with truth. He would hide nothing anymore. Not what he'd seen. Not what he knew. For what little time he had left in this realm... he would give Auren everything.

A pit sank in his stomach, but Ulric brushed it away—not when this beautiful man stood before him with shining eyes and red hair whipping in the wind.

For all the time I have left... I am yours.

Ulric dressed Auren in a simple tunic and soft, worn trousers. Plain but dignified, the kind of thing a man might wear on a festival day. Auren looked oddly princely in it, even with the hem rolled up at the ankles and his hair still messy from the wind.

"You're taller than most humans," Ulric noted as he adjusted the collar.

Auren smirked. "I suppose then that must make you a giant."

"Maybe that is why I've never been mugged before," Ulric said, lips quirked. He was a good head taller than Auren, who wasn't a small man by any measure.

No—Auren was anything but small.

Even in his human form, his body bore the unmistakable marks of excellence. The grace of a swimmer combined with the strength of a fighter. Not the bulky build of a warrior, but something more fluid, sleek, and agile. Auren's shoulders rolled with quiet command, his torso tapering to a narrow waist. His thighs, powerful from a lifetime of pushing through the ocean's weight, now filled out his pants in a way that drove Ulric mad.

The tunic Auren wore clung in places where he was more defined. It outlined the planes of his chest, clinging to each curve of sinew and skin. When he moved, the fabric shifted with him, revealing flashes of hip bone, the contours of his abdomen, and the hollow where neck met shoulder.

And Ulric, damn him, saw it all.

He was painfully aware of how the sun painted gold into Auren's red hair, how it caught in the delicate curve of his jaw, the proud line of his throat. His lips—always expressive, always ready with a cutting remark—seemed perpetually kiss-bruised.

The prince walked at Ulric's side with a kind of ease that came from knowing someone as long as they had. Laughing. Pointing. Looking up at the world with bright, curious eyes as though he hadn't been caged and broken only days before. There was still light in him. And Ulric wanted to press it to his chest and keep it there, safe, even as desire twisted molten through his veins.

He tried to be decent. Tried not to stare too long at the way Auren's shirt dipped at the collar, revealing the slope of collarbones he ached to kiss. He tried not to let his gaze drag down the lines of Auren's back or linger on the faint dip of his spine when he bent to examine something.

But it was impossible.

Because Auren—flushed from excitement, sunlight glossing his skin, breathless with joy—was the most beautiful thing Ulric had ever seen.

And all Ulric could think was: *Don't push. Don't ruin this. Don't be greedy.*

Not when Auren had just come back to life.

Not when he was here, laughing at Ulric's side, walking through a world he never thought he'd get to touch.

Ulric curled his fists at his sides and breathed through the ache. He didn't know how much time he had. But he would not spend it chasing pleasure at the expense of Auren's peace. Not now. Not ever.

Still, every time Auren leaned into him, brushing their shoulders, grinning at some new delight, wide-eyed and radiant, Ulric's restraint burned a little more.

And gods help him... he didn't want to stop burning.

They went into town together, Auren beside him, walking freely on legs that had once been tail. Ulric kept a half-step behind him at first, watching. Ready, in case the crowds overwhelmed him. But Auren surprised him again.

He didn't shrink back. He leaned in.

The scents were the first to hit—roasted nuts, grilled meat, something sugary and fried, thick with spice. The whole world smelled like indulgence. Rich oils and fresh bread, flower garlands drying in the sun, tobacco from the pipes of lounging old men who tipped their hats in Ulric's direction with vague familiarity.

The colors dazzled next. Canopies stretched between wooden beams, bright fruit piled high in woven baskets, painted signs swinging in the breeze. Children darted past, laughing, shrieking. Someone played a fiddle near the bakery. Auren's mouth parted, his eyes wide and tracking every detail.

And then—

"Ulric!" Auren shouted so suddenly that Ulric's hand was halfway to his belt when Auren tugged at his tunic in frantic excitement. "Ulric, look! Look over there! Do you see it? Do you think we can get closer?"

It was a horse.

A broad-chested bay with a thick black mane and white-blazed nose came striding past them at the edge of a small paddock.

Ulric smiled. "Would you like me to introduce you?"

Auren nodded too quickly, excitement buzzing like someone meeting a beloved celebrity. Ulric couldn't suppress a chuckle.

He's so damned cute.

"Wait here."

Ulric approached the rider, spoke briefly, and passed him a coin. The man dismounted and handed over the reins. When he returned, Auren was in full-blown jitters.

"His name is Casco," Ulric said, holding the reins. "His owner says he's gentle. We have the pleasure of his company for a few minutes."

Auren stared in awe. "He's beautiful."

Ulric watched as Auren stepped close, one hand out. Casco

snorted, nudged his palm, and Auren laughed—a delighted, wind-chime sound. He ran his hand over the horse's muzzle.

"It's softer than I expected," Auren said in wonder.

"Would you like to ride him?"

"Can I?"

"Of course," Ulric said. Auren hesitated for a moment before nodding sheepishly.

Ulric didn't give him the reins—he wasn't suicidal—but he helped Auren into the saddle, hands firm at his waist. Auren was warm beneath his hands, soft in places, but still lean and strong. When he was seated, Ulric led Casco in slow circles around the paddock.

Auren spoke to the horse as if it were an old friend.

"You're so strong. Do you know that?" he whispered. "Your eyes are like glass. You understand everything, don't you? I bet you and Iska would be friends."

Ulric watched, his chest aching with feelings both sharp and sweet.

By the time they returned the horse, Auren's face was flushed with contentment.

"That was incredible."

"There's more to see. Would you like me to show you?" Ulric offered.

"Yes," Auren said instantly. "All of it."

So Ulric took him to the food stalls, guiding him with one hand on his back. He kept it to light, fleeting touches. He guided Auren to foods he would likely enjoy—shellfish grilled in lemon and herbs, and sweet cakes made with black currant syrup. They sat on a warm stone wall and ate with their fingers, and Auren made small, delighted sounds at every new bite.

"This one," he said, holding up a dumpling. "This tastes like seafoam."

Ulric chuckled. "You always did have a poetic palate."

Auren popped the rest into his mouth and chewed thoughtfully. "No, really. It's light. A little salty. Like... the bubbles that cling to your lips after diving too fast."

Ulric arched a brow. "Is that a compliment or a complaint?"

Auren grinned. "I haven't decided yet."

Ulric shook his head. "Remind me never to cook for you. I'm not sure my pride could survive the verdict."

Auren stuck his tongue out at him.

"You better put that away, or I'll put it to work."

And Ulric couldn't help but chuckle deep in his chest at how quickly Auren's cheeks matched his hair.

They wandered on. Near the center of town stood a tavern, and Ulric was about to suggest they enter when he noticed the way Auren tensed. His steps slowed, and his lips pressed thin. Without a word, Ulric changed course. He led him instead to the open-air pavilion, where musicians and acrobats were setting up to perform under the stars.

It was a wise choice.

Auren's delight returned in full force. He clapped quietly for jugglers. Laughed aloud at a child doing handstands. And when a group of dancers rode past on horses wearing jingling ribbons and embroidered blankets, Auren looked like he might cry from joy.

Ulric didn't care if anyone stared. He was too busy watching Auren glow.

The performance concluded with a musical number, a love song that filled the twilight air with a poignant feeling. The lyrics were brazen, full of longing and heated devotion. The words were unapologetic, suggestive even. Ulric glanced over. Auren was blushing.

"You don't hear words like that in the hymns of Atlantis," Ulric commented.

"No. I suppose you don't," Auren said, then added, "But I like it."

Ulric's heart stuttered. He reached down, gently taking Auren's hand.

"Would you like to go home?"Auren made a disconcerted face, and Ulric added, "I promise to bring you back as many times as you want. But let's rest for today."

Reassured, Auren nodded, his heavy lids betraying his weariness.

They walked through the cooling streets, hand in hand, and all Ulric could think about was the way Auren's fingers fit in his.

He didn't know how long he had. He didn't know what the next day would bring.

But Auren was beside him, smiling, alive.

And for now, that was enough.

Even if his thoughts couldn't stop circling back to the kiss. To how Auren had tasted. To how much more he wanted. How his body ached to press closer, to ask for more—

But he wouldn't.

Not tonight.

Because the most beautiful creature he had ever known was still learning how to live again. Still healing. And Ulric would not ruin that by being greedy.

So he walked on, beside his not-quite lover, carrying a hunger in his chest as vast as the sea.

And somehow, it felt like joy.

Chapter Nineteen

Ulric

THEY RETURNED TO THE CABIN UNDER A QUIET SKY, THE air tinged with the warm suggestion of summer. Auren was still smiling as he kicked off his boots by the door; windblown, flushed from laughter, eyes tired but alight with everything he'd seen.

Ulric wasn't sure if that smile would still remain once the fire was out. He could tell Auren was restless as he wandered the house, trailing fingers along the mantle and window ledges, before poking through the fruit basket and stealing a pear.

He likely fears more nightmares.

And now, with night falling and the fire crackling low, Ulric wasn't sure where he belonged.

They'd shared the bed out of necessity before—when Auren's body had been weak and his spirit shattered. When holding him through the shakes was the only way Ulric knew to anchor him.

But now... Auren was healing. He was walking. Breathing. Laughing.

Ulric didn't want to presume that his presence was still necessary. Or welcome.

So he laid out spare blankets near the hearth, folding them into something vaguely resembling a cot. It wouldn't be comfortable, but it would suffice. The last thing he wanted was to crowd the prince. Not now. Not when Auren had just begun to stretch his limbs again and smile without flinching.

"You can go to sleep first," Ulric offered as he sat on the floor by the fireplace. "I'll read for a while."

Auren hesitated. "Oh. Okay."

There was something uncertain in the way he slid under the covers with a hint of reluctance. But he didn't argue.

Hopefully, he will sleep without a terror waking him.

Ulric would remain awake long enough to ensure Auren was in a deep slumber before retiring himself. He pulled a worn book from the shelf—an old sea-bound journal of arcane tides—and settled before the fire. The cabin was quiet, save for the crackling wood and the faint rustle of sheets.

He'd read only a few pages when a silent hand lowered the book.

Ulric blinked up in surprise.

Auren stood over him. Shirtless. Only the soft cotton of his loose trousers hung from his hips. His hair tumbled over his shoulders as though the fire had leaped from the hearth and made its home atop his head. His cheeks were flushed, and his lips parted as though he might say something, but the words never came.

"Auren," Ulric said slowly, his heart taking up a frantic rhythm. "What are you doing up? Do you need something?"

Auren stepped closer, eyes half-lidded.

"Are you hungry? I can fetch you—"

Ulric's words cut off as Auren took the book from his hands and let it fall onto the floor. Then he straddled Ulric's lap, knees settling to either side and framing his thighs.

Ulric inhaled sharply.

His hands found Auren's hips without thinking, fingertips brushing the indent of bone, the hard sculpt of trained muscle. This body, born of magic and sea, was strong. Beautiful. Perfect.

"Auren..." he rasped. "You need to rest."

But his voice lacked conviction.

Auren still hadn't said a word. Just looked with an intensity that made Ulric forget his name. And then he was leaning in, and Ulric lost himself.

Their mouths met.

The kiss exploded between them. Ulric kissed him back like he'd been starving for it. He gripped Auren's hips possessively, anchoring their bodies.

Their tongues danced, tasting, teasing, testing. And when Auren broke away to suck at the hollow of Ulric's throat, the Kraken groaned low in his chest—a sound so deep it vibrated the bones in his ribs.

He couldn't help it.

His hips rolled upward, grinding against Auren's. Auren gasped and did the same, and suddenly they were moving together, hungry, bodies aligned in perfect rhythm.

Their arousals strained against fabric, barely contained. Ulric's head dropped back as Auren's hips rocked again, and a tremor ran through him.

He was seconds from losing control.

His hands slid lower, dipping beneath the hem of Auren's

trousers, cupping the prince's ass—firm and sculpted, like it had been made to fit in his palms.

But just as his fingers flexed, ready to take more, a bolt of clarity hit him, like the cold spray of water.

No.

He tore his hands away, gasping.

"Auren," he panted. "We can't. You're still healing. I won't take advantage of you like this."

Auren blinked, lips swollen from kissing, chest heaving. A trace of sadness touched his face as he sat back.

"This body is new to me," he whispered.

He touched his upper arm, below the shoulder, where Elias had once split his skin open to poke and prod at the muscle beneath. The mark was faint now, but still there. Still a scar that no magic could fully erase.

"All I've ever known in this form is pain," Auren whispered. "I want to forget it. And... and when I'm with you, like this, it feels... good." Auren looked away as he said it, cheeks flushed. "I want to forget the pain. I want to erase it and replace it with... you."

Ulric couldn't bear it.

He surged forward and pulled Auren into a fierce embrace, pressing his lips to his temple.

"If that is what you want," he said, voice shaking, "then I will banish those memories. I will carve away every scar with pleasure. I'll replace them with something you won't want to forget. And it will all belong to you." He cupped Auren's cheek and pulled back, eyes searching. "Is that what you want of me, my prince?"

Auren nodded.

And the fire roared hotter.

They kissed again, hungrier this time. Messier. Ulric lifted him easily, carrying him to the bed without breaking contact. He lay Auren on the pillows, worshiping him with every brush of his lips.

Ulric undid the laces of his pants, sliding them from his smooth legs, until Auren lay beneath him in nothing but firelight. And gods... he was breathtaking. His manhood was long, thick, flushed, and perfect. Ulric had never seen anything so divine. So powerful. So tender all at once. He knelt between Auren's legs and wrapped a hand around him—marveling at the way Auren cried out, head tipping back, body arching into the touch.

"Does that feel good, my prince?"

Auren's mouth remained open, gasping at the new sensation.

"It-it's very sensitive. I... it looks different now," he said, struggling to find words as Ulric continued to touch him.

"Yes, an interesting part of the human body. It hardens when aroused, and by the looks of it, you're very aroused, spriteling. Are you not?"

Auren nodded.

"Would you like me to continue? I know a great deal about the human body."

"Please," Auren begged, fists clenching and unclenching.

"You're stunning like this," Ulric whispered, holding back the words he could not say.

I will carve myself into your memory, so that even when I am gone, you will remember the echoes of my touch.

Ulric stroked him with deliberate motions. Learned every ridge. Every breath. Every gasp and bite of lips. Auren's hands tangled in the sheets, his mouth parted in desperate moans as Ulric brought him to the edge. He increased the speed of his strokes, squeezing tighter.

"Ulric-Ulric!" Auren said in a hurried panic.

"Don't fight it. Let go, my prince. I'll be here to catch you."

And with a final motion of his wrist, Ulric coaxed Auren over the edge.

He came with a cry, spilling across his stomach in hot, white ribbons.

Ulric leaned forward and kissed him through his orgasm, tasting every moan, sharing in his pleasure. When the member in his hand stopped pulsing, Ulric released him, giving him a moment to return to himself.

"Are you alright spriteling?"

Auren took a moment to respond.

"I-I think so."

"Are you in any pain?"

Auren shook his head, but looked troubled.

"What is it?" Ulric asked, alarms ringing in his ears.

"Does that... is that a one-time thing for humans? You feel it once, then it's gone?" He looked so sad as he asked it.

Ulric laughed and pressed a heavy kiss to Auren's lips.

"Oh no, my prince. I can make you come like that a million more times if you'd like."

Auren smiled and nodded, "I'd like that."

Afterward, they lay together, tangled in sheets.

"I didn't know this body could feel so good," Auren murmured sleepily. He turned his head, blinking at him. "You make me feel that way."

Ulric kissed his forehead. "Always."

And as the fire dwindled to embers, they drifted into sleep, limbs entwined, hearts steady.

Ulric was running out of time. He could feel it. Could sense the magic ebbing away from him day by day. Hour by hour. But as long as this mortal realm would have him, Ulric would stay. He would live in the moment... because in this moment, he had everything he ever wanted resting in his arms.

Chapter Twenty

Auren

THE TOWN SQUARE BUSTLED WITH LATE MORNING LIFE, and Ulric's coin passed freely. Auren supposed that was the reward for centuries spent scavenging treasures from shipwrecks.

The merchants were delighted to see Ulric. They clapped him on the back and whispered good-natured gossip with a kind of familiarity that struck Auren deep.

He's been here before. Often.

There was a depth of knowledge that Ulric had hidden from Auren. But they were free now, and Auren didn't hold back. He asked about anything and everything—the odd way humans preserved food with salt or why some hats were shaped so outrageously tall. And every time, Ulric had an answer, never laughing at his questions (well, maybe a little bit), and offering informative answers.

The sheer amount of information left Auren dazed. He was sure that he'd asked the same question twice, but Ulric never acted annoyed. He answered with the same calm patience every time. And the look in his eyes as he answered them... It made Auren's knees weak with need.

And yet, through it all, Auren's mind kept wandering. Kept slipping back to the night before—the feel of Ulric's hands on his body, his calloused touch, the shared heat of their skin.

How badly he wanted to feel that again.

Still, a part of him remained suspicious. Normally Ulric, practical to a fault, would have insisted they return home by now. After all, if Auren was well enough to walk the bustling streets, surely he was well enough to endure the transformation potion and swim back to Atlantis. To fill his role as prince, and Ulric his station as Court Sorcerer. The thought of them returning to the cold, touchless way they'd been before made Auren want to grind his teeth in frustration.

But Ulric said nothing.

If anything, he seemed as reluctant to leave as Auren was. And Auren, selfishly, wasn't about to question it. If the Fates were kind enough to grant him more time, he would hoard it.

He would make it last forever.

Their wandering took them past stalls of baked goods, salted meats, and colorful woven cloths. A burst of childish laughter snagged his attention. There, in the square, a puppet theater was in the middle of a show. Small children sat cross-legged on the cobblestones, their faces alight with glee as they watched tiny wooden figures dance across a miniature stage. Bright colors. Clanging swords. Wooden dragons breathing ribbons of smoke.

Auren hovered on the edge, enchanted. When a puppet

vanquished another with a clumsy wooden sword, Auren lowered himself onto an empty stump among the children, utterly rapt.

He didn't even notice Ulric standing back, arms crossed and smiling faintly.

The entire performance passed in a blur of wonder—heroes and dragons, evil wizards and princesses cleverer than the kings who ruled them. And when it ended, Auren was almost reluctant to rise, blinking as if waking from a dream.

Ulric pressed coins into the performers' palms as they packed up their tiny stage.

"You enjoyed that," Ulric said, a note of pleasant surprise in his voice.

Auren flushed. "Maybe a little."

Ulric chuckled low in his chest. "Good. That gives me an idea."

Auren perked up. "What idea?"

But Ulric only leaned in, his breath hot against Auren's ear, sending a shiver racing down his arms.

"It's a surprise, spriteling."

That night, they dined under the stars in an open-air pavilion strung with lanterns. The food was hearty and strange—soups thick with root vegetables and spices Auren couldn't name but devoured without question. His body was starved, not just for nourishment, but for life.

But he was distracted, and it wasn't by the soup.

Ulric sat across from him, relaxed in a linen shirt open at the throat, revealing the broad, bronzed expanse of his chest dusted with dark hair. His strong jaw was shadowed by scruff, and his long black hair was tied back with his signature whalebone clasp, a few strands falling free to frame his face.

Auren was so taken by the sight of him that he kept dropping his spoon into the soup and had to stick his fingers in to fish it out. The lanternlight painted Ulric's skin in deep, honeyed tones, and Auren knew that the heat pooling low in his belly had absolutely nothing to do with the stew. He had to take several deep, calming breaths before they rose to leave to avoid embarrassing himself.

The walk back to the house was a blur. Neither of them spoke. Tension crackled between them, like pine nuts popping in a fire. All of it came to a rapid crescendo the second they reached the door.

They barely made it inside.

The door slammed shut behind them, and—

Ulric's mouth was on him.

Dragging across his jaw, down the column of his throat. The Kraken's stubble scraped against Auren's sensitive skin, setting every nerve on fire. Ulric kissed a spot, just behind Auren's ear, and licked the curve of his ear lobe. Auren gasped, clutching his shoulders as warmth flooded him so fast it was dizzying.

Ulric pulled back enough to rasp, "Sensitive there?"

Auren blushed. "I-I think so."

"Good." Ulric's wicked smile promised delights Auren was not ready for.

Ulric's hands moved over him, undoing the buttons of his shirt one by one, sliding his broad palm up his belly to rest against his bare chest.

"Is this okay?" he murmured.

Auren nodded, breathless.

"Does this feel good?"

"Yes—gods, yes."

Ulric's thumb brushed his nipple, and Auren jolted, rattling the door on its hinges as pleasure sparked across his skin.

"Too much?"

"No," Auren panted. "It's—It's good."

Ulric continued, pinching Auren's nipple hard enough to send a quick spark of sensation all the way down to his toes. Auren arched into the touch, the door cool against his spine and Ulric hot everywhere else.

Before he could catch his breath, Ulric leaned in, voice rough against his ear.

"Let me show you more."

Yes. Gods yes. Show me more. Show me everything.

But Auren was too breathless for words and only managed a quick nod.

He watched, aching, as Ulric leaned back and shed his own shirt. The firelight kissed every inch of inked skin and muscle, from the thick ridges of his abdomen to the ancient glyphs spiraling over his ribs.

"You can touch me," Ulric said, voice thick. "Anything you want. My body is yours to explore."

Auren did. He let his eyes wander over every ridge. Every inch of skin pulled taught over muscle. He counted the sigils inked there. Wait... were they always so faded? Several of them had an unfinished look. Unfinished— or disappearing. But before Auren could inspect further, his thoughts were interrupted by Ulric's hand grabbing him by the neck, forcing his chin up.

Ulric kissed him—harder this time—then spun their bodies and walked them backward, lips never leaving Auren's as they stumbled toward the bed. When the back of Auren's knees hit the edge, he let himself fall onto the mattress, dragging Ulric down with him.

Auren's hands slid up Ulric's torso again, exploring every line, every curve, everything that marked Ulric as powerful. Auren wanted to leave marks of his own. He pressed his lips to the crook of Ulric's neck, sucking skin into his mouth. Ulric made a low rumbling sound, and when Auren pulled away, he was delighted to see a red spot blooming there.

He's mine, Auren thought with a rush that went straight to his groin.

Auren licked the side of Ulric's neck, right where he could see the frantic pulse of his vein. He went lower, and when he reached Ulric's chest, he paused. Instead of mimicking what Ulric had done, Auren leaned down and gave one pink nipple a slow, languid lick with his tongue.

Ulric jerked, but then resumed his statuesque pose above him, braced on his knees, hands gripping the bed sheets as though clinging for dear life.

He's holding back.

Auren relaxed into the pillow, staring into those bottomless eyes. "I want to explore more of you. *All* of you," Auren clarified, and to be sure the message landed, he reached between them. His fingers found the worn leather of Ulric's belt. The clasps gave with a satisfying *clink,* and the sound of sliding leather might as well have been thunder in his ears.

Ulric's breath hitched, his body turning to stone—but he didn't stop him.

Carefully, Auren pried Ulric's white-knuckled hands from the bedding and guided them to his waist.

"Don't hold back now," Auren whispered, voice shaking. "My monster of the deep."

Ulric broke.

In a rush of desperate heat, he grabbed Auren and kissed him with a hunger that stole the air from his lungs. Their hips rolled together. Auren's whole body pulsed with need, desperate to be closer.

He barely noticed the shifting fabric as Ulric kicked off what remained of his pants.

"You can touch me," Ulric whispered, the words gasped as though he'd been holding his breath all this time. "Take whatever you want."

He didn't wait for permission to be granted a third time.

Auren slid his hands down the trail of hair, over the definition of Ulric's abdomen. He felt down the hard lines of his hips, finding coarse hair and trembling thighs. And then he reached the core of Ulric's pleasure and couldn't help the small gasp as his hands wrapped around the thick shaft. It pulsed in his grip, so hot it might scorch him.

Ulric stuttered as Auren explored the sheer size of his girth, leaving no place untouched. He let out a low, guttural curse.

"Fuck."

The slip of Ulric's composure emboldened Auren. Made him want more. Somehow, with one dose, he was addicted to hearing sultry words fall from those lips. He stroked carefully, marveling at the way Ulric's body responded to every movement.

When a bead of liquid welled at Ulric's tip, Auren's heart raced —and before he could think better of it, he brought his fingers to his lips and licked it clean.

The result was instant.

Ulric let out a feral sound, stripping Auren of what remained of his clothes, eyes wild and black with need.

"You have no idea what you've just done," he growled.

He yanked down Auren's trousers, baring him to the air. Auren gasped, but Ulric was already on him, stroking, teasing, worshiping with hands and mouth, and whispered praise.

"Oh gods—oh gods—" Auren gasped.

"No gods tonight," Ulric said darkly. "Only me."

It was too much. Too good. Auren whimpered under Ulric's relentless ministrations, his body straining toward climax.

He wanted to give Ulric the same. Wanted to taste him, to touch him, to make him lose himself the same way.

But Ulric wouldn't let him.

Every time Auren reached, Ulric guided his hand away with a kiss and renewed his efforts until Auren was seeing stars.

"Tonight is for you, my prince," Ulric breathed against his skin. "Only you."

It frustrated Auren—this stubborn devotion.

"I-I want to feel you too," Auren pleaded. "I want you to feel it too. With me."

Those seemed to be the magic words because Ulric responded by moving his hips forward and wrapping both their shafts together in one powerful hand. Auren let out a moan that filled the room. His back arched, and his toes curled. He was unraveling, heat flooding his skin, pleasure coiling hot and fast in his belly.

With blurred vision, Auren looked up at Ulric.

And in the middle of it all, it hit him.

The way Ulric saw him. Touched him. The way he whispered his name with ruddy desperation.

I'm in love with him. I've always loved him.

He'd loved Ulric for years. He just hadn't had the words for it. Not then. But now, feeling Ulric's hands, Ulric's breath, Ulric's body trembling with need against his—he knew. He was completely, helplessly, beautifully in love with him.

And it was terrifying.

He gasped, body jerking as pleasure surged up through him like a riptide.

"Ulric—careful—I'm—"

"I've got you," Ulric gasped, working them both.

Auren let go, moaning the Kraken's name as he came hard between them. A heartbeat later, Ulric followed, hips stuttering, a growl of pleasure breaking from his throat as his hand tightened around them, drawing out their orgasm.

They collapsed together in a tangle of sweat-slicked limbs and panting mouths. It was a few minutes before either was ready to move. Ulric was the first to regain his senses, finding a cloth and cleaning them both. When he slid back in bed, his body was still hot. Still naked. Still fit against Auren's own, like the two pieces of a shell.

"You're perfect," Ulric murmured, pressing kiss after kiss to Auren's brow, his cheeks, his lips.

Auren didn't speak at first, but when he did, a rush of emotion struck him so hard that tears welled up in the corners of his eyes. He clung to Ulric like a shipwrecked man.

"I'll have you, Ulric. From the sky to the blackest depths of the sea, I'll have you. All I ask is that you take me in return."

Ulric's answering kiss was gentle.

"Always, my prince," he whispered. "Always."

And Auren—full of love and warmth and the man he'd waited a lifetime for—let himself believe it.

He let himself hope.

And he didn't let go.

Chapter Twenty One

Ulric

THE BATHHOUSE DOOR SLID OPEN, RELEASING A WAVE of heat and the sharp, clean scent of eucalyptus oil. Their little cabin by the sea had a small basin fed by cool well water. Good enough for washing the grime from hands and face, but nothing like the true luxury of a real soak.

And Ulric needed it. If he were to be honest with himself, Ulric was aching.

Not in the way men ached after long days, but deep in his bones, deep in his roots. Holding onto his magic these past weeks was like gripping the handle of a water bucket while the gods poured more and more weight into it. Every minute, another drop. Every hour, heavier. His hands were slipping. His grip was failing.

And he knew it.

Tonight, he needed to feel renewed. To scrub away the sweat, the dead skin, the creeping weight of the inevitable. Even if just for a little while.

The bathhouse owner took one look at Ulric and Auren and perked up when Ulric pressed a coin pouch into his palm.

"Private use for the evening," Ulric murmured.

The man tucked the coins away with a wink. "Take your time, my Lord. Everything's prepared."

Ulric nodded and turned toward Auren, who was already looking around wide-eyed. Steam curled through the air, softening the stone walls and wooden beams. Off to one side, low stools and gleaming basins stood ready for scrubbing. Beyond them stretched a tiled pool, filled with steaming, scented water, while lanterns threw rippling light across the surface.

"This is too big to be just for a single person," Auren commented, noting the row of stools.

"It's a bathhouse. Meant for many men at once, the women have one next door."

"This is fancy."

"I brought us to the upper ring of the city. Common coin will get you a bathhouse beside a farm where they use the same water as the pigs."

Auren wrinkled his nose. "I appreciate the worth of your coin more and more each day."

Ulric laughed. "Yes. There are many pirate treasures being passed around town these past few days."

Auren glided to the center, bare feet sliding on damp tile. He spun in the dimly lit space like a dancer, the faint trickle of water his music.

"You paid for all this?" Auren asked. "I'm not shy, we could have kept it public."

Ulric shrugged a little stiffly.

Auren smirked. "What? Shy, old man?"

Ulric gave him a deadpan look. "I'm not shy. I've visited more bathhouses than you have hairs on your head, sea-sprite."

"Then why bribe the owner?" Auren teased, sidling closer, mischief in every line of him.

"I don't want anyone gawking at you."

Auren stopped short, blinking. "Gawking at me?"

"There might be... questions," Ulric muttered, rubbing the back of his neck. "You're—" He gestured vaguely. "Very smooth. Most would notice."

"Oh, come now. The sight of a man with no hair on his body can't possibly be that much of a novelty."

Ulric's lips quirked despite himself. "You want the truth?"

Auren pressed close, the steamed air already hot, but his presence made it suffocating.

"The truth, spriteling, is if anyone else so much as looked at you, the whole city would quickly become acquainted with the bottom of the sea."

Auren flushed scarlet and turned away, but not before Ulric caught the pleased lilt in his lips.

They stripped down together, wrapping thin cotton towels low around their waists. The steam clung to their skin, making them glisten under the lanterns.

At the edge of the pool, Auren hesitated. He glanced uneasily at the water, one hand fisting the towel tighter at his hips. "Will this... will this make me—?"

"You won't transform," Ulric said, resting a hand on Auren's shoulder. "The potion holds until you touch the true sea. This doesn't count."

To prove it, Ulric slid into the bath first, sinking low into the heat with a contented sigh that wrung the ache from his muscles.

Gods, I needed this.

The water loosened him, peeled the tightness from his joints, quieted the terrible buzzing under his skin.

"See?" he said, stretching his arms along the smooth stone edge, body half-floating. "Still very human."

Auren grinned and dipped a toe, eyebrows lifting at the heat, before sliding in and settling beside Ulric. The water lapped around their waists, their towels billowing between them. Steam curled and blurred the bathhouse in a comfortable haze.

They sat on a tiled seat built into the bath, letting the heat melt the weight off their bodies. Ulric tipped his head back against the stone, closed his eyes, and for once—for only a moment—let himself drift.

When he cracked one eye open again, he found Auren watching him. Watching him the same way he inspected a new human artifact. Studying. Learning.

Ulric's stomach tightened. "You're staring," he murmured, his voice rougher than intended.

Auren tilted his head, unbothered. "You're different when you're relaxed."

"Am I?"

Auren nodded, a smile curving his lips. "Softer. I like it."

Ulric huffed a quiet laugh. "Don't get used to it."

"Always such a grouch," he said with fondness. Then he narrowed his eyes and beckoned Ulric closer. "Come here."

"Why?"

"Just do it."

Ulric eyed him suspiciously but obeyed.

"Turn around."

The Kraken rolled his eyes but did so. The moment he was within reach, Auren's hands disappeared into his hair.

Ulric froze.

Before he could ask what he was doing, Auren slipped the whale-bone hairpin free. Dark strands spilled over Ulric's shoulders and down his back.

"There it is," Auren murmured.

"There what is?"

"The source of all your brooding."

Ulric snorted.

Auren threaded his fingers through the damp black strands.

"There are knots in here."

"I am aware."

"Clearly not aware enough. This is a mess."

His fingers continued their work, dragging slowly through wet black hair. Untangling. Separating. Combing the strands with nothing but his hands. Ulric wondered how many times he'd taken care of his own hair this way.

Steam curled around them as Auren hummed quietly to himself, entirely focused on the task.

And Ulric... fell into a trance.

No one had ever done this for him.

Not when he was a child. Not when he became a guardian. Not in all the centuries that followed.

Touch meant obligation. Healing. Violence. Magic. Duty.

Never this. Never hands moving through his hair simply because someone wanted to care for him.

Ulric swallowed, his throat tight and his eyes stinging. A strange pressure gathered behind his ribs.

Auren remained blissfully unaware of the devastation he was causing.

He worked free another knot, smiling to himself in satisfaction.

"There."

He gathered the dark strands, repinning them with the whale bone clasp, the way Ulric liked.

"Much better."

"Thank you," he said quietly.

"It's just hair," Auren said flippantly, moving to tend to his own long red strands.

But oh, how wrong he was. It was... so much more than that. A hundred more things. Things Ulric didn't have enough time to say.

So instead of saying them, he watched as Auren reached for a lavender soapstone resting at the edge of the pool. The scent was heady in the steam as he lathered it between his palms, working it into a soft, fragrant foam.

Ulric remained still. Helpless. Rapt. Forced numb by the enchantment of watching Auren wash. Watching him slowly drag his hands over his chest, up the strong lines of his arms, the hollow of his throat. Soap and water slid down his body in shimmering trails. His muscles flexed and shifted with every pass of his hands, strong yet graceful, a natural elegance that no court tutor could have taught him.

Then Auren tilted his head back.

The tendons of his throat stretched, water sluicing down his skin as he dipped himself backward into the bath. His hair fanned out like red seaweed before he emerged again with a toss of his head, droplets spraying like a halo of mist around him.

It was a dance. A siren's call.

And Ulric, poor fool that he was, was already drowning.

Auren's eyes fluttered closed for a moment, lost in the simple pleasure of the heat, the scent, the cleansing touch of his own hands.

He moved through the water like a creature born of it. Every ripple, every gliding motion of his hands, seduced without a single word spoken. Ulric's hands itched to reach out, to drag Auren into his arms and kiss him until neither of them remembered how to breathe.

He was beautiful.

And Ulric's heart beat out a single, insistent rhythm.

Touch him. Touch him. Touch him.

Auren shifted closer through the misted bath, the steam

curling around his shoulders. Ulric noticed his towel coming loose beneath the water.

"Feels weird," Auren said, words echoing slightly in the tiled room, "to be in the water like this. With legs."

"You're adapting well. Your balance is impressive, all things considered."

"I'll still never get over how sore my thighs are after walking all day. No one warned me about that. After all the treks in and out of town, this feels nice."

"Oh, believe me," Ulric murmured, fingers drifting along the curve of Auren's hip, teasing the already loose tie of his towel. "I could show you a hundred reasons your thighs might ache by morning."

Ulric was losing the battle with his free will. The siren's call stripped him of reason, of the ability to hold himself back.

Auren flushed scarlet, tucking a strand of hair behind his ear. "You're the worst."

Ulric chuckled and pressed a kiss to his hair.

I love you, my prince.

But he didn't say it.

The words hovered, aching behind his teeth, but remained caged. Maybe he didn't want to burden Auren with his confession. Maybe he didn't want to expose the last bit of his heart. But no matter how he delayed things, every step Auren took, every symbol that disappeared from Ulric's skin, brought them closer to the end.

Closer to the moment Ulric would cease to exist.

And Auren didn't know.

He didn't know Ulric could have returned him to his sea-born shape days ago. The potion's effects lingered only because Ulric was using his precious stores of magic to keep them here. To keep them in this human form.

Because the moment Auren returned to the sea, the moment Ulric's purpose was fulfilled—the gods would owe him nothing.

And Ulric owed them everything.

Their blessing would leave him. Strip him of his magic and leave time to rapidly take back what Ulric had stolen from it. He'd dissolve into the sand. Forgotten by time. Buried, like all things the sea no longer wanted.

"You're thinking too hard," Auren said, gliding through the water until their knees brushed. He pressed an index finger to the furrow in Ulric's brow. "Stop it."

Ulric laughed. "Maybe I need a distraction?"

Auren leaned closer, water trickling from his hair. "I was hoping you'd come to that conclusion. I don't think we've finished my lessons. There is more to this body I have yet to learn."

Ulric took Auren by the arm, guiding him through the water until the prince was on his lap, his towel slipping loose as he settled, ass bare and perfect. Auren leaned into the embrace, his back to Ulric's front. Ulric wanted to grip him, claim him, crush him close.

"There's more than one place I can touch you," Ulric whispered, lips brushing Auren's ear, "to make you come undone."

Auren shivered. "Show me."

Ulric started slow. He kissed his way down Auren's neck, his shoulder. His hands roaming lower still, until Auren gasped as Ulric's fingers teased the inner apex of his thighs.

"Spread your legs for me, darling."

Auren hesitated, his breath stuck in his chest. But a moment later, he obeyed, relinquishing control. And that submission made Ulric throb, tenting his towel, pushing against Auren's back.

"Do you trust me?" Ulric breathed.

"Y-yes," Aurent said, already breathy though Ulric had hardly touched him.

In one swift motion, the Kraken lifted him and spun, setting Auren on the edge of the bath. His legs still dangled in the water, and streams ran from his soaked scarlet hair.

"What are you doing!?"

"Hush," Ulric commanded.

Ulric kneeled in the bath facing the edge, his mouth inches from Auren's parted legs. The Kraken's mouth watered. His prince was hairless here too, but it didn't make him look bare—if anything, it drew more attention to the sharp lines of muscle running down his stomach, leading straight to his proud length. Ulric was done waiting. He descended, taking Auren into his mouth with a wicked stroke of his tongue.

"Mmmm~!" Auren's head fell back as Ulric worshiped him.

Ulric tortured him. Up and down in languid licks, flattening his tongue to taste more, until pearlescent drops gathered at the tip. He teased the slit, savoring the musky tang. But he didn't stop there. Ulric's tongue slid between Auren's thighs, lower, lower— grazing places that had never been touched before.

The muscles along Auren's thighs trembled. But never once did he close his legs. Never once did he restrict Ulric's access. It made Ulric shiver. He grabbed hold of Auren's waist, tilting his hips, forcing Auren to lean back, exposing more of himself. He pressed a kiss to the curve of that magnificent ass, then nipped it playfully. Auren jerked at the contact of teeth, but didn't shove Ulric away. His body was a coil of tensed muscles and electric nerves. Ulric couldn't have possibly imagined a more beautiful sight.

"I'm going to make your new body feel so good, spriteling," Ulric growled. "I'm going to make it writhe—"

He kissed the sensitive skin of Auren's inner thigh.

"—shiver—"

A kiss on the other side.

"—and sing for me."

Auren whimpered, the sound echoing off the bathhouse tiles.

Ulric dipped lower and teased that delicate perineum, drawing out a choked sound from Auren's throat.

Then—lower still.

With both hands, he spread Auren's ass open, extracting every last drop of pleasure, memorizing the way the tight crevice squeezed his tongue. Auren's hands repeatedly flexed on the tiles, as though looking to grab something, to anchor himself as he floated into delirious bliss.

"Hold on, spriteling."

It was all the warning he gave before diving into that crevice, his tongue finding the sensitive hole. Ulric growled as his tongue traced the clenched, circular ridges.

Auren cried out.

"Ulric—what—oh—"

"You're alright," Ulric murmured, tongue moving again, licking gently as Auren moaned against him. "Just relax. Let me take care of you."

Auren was panting, head tipped back, face flushed and wild.

Ulric tongued him open, until Auren was writhing beneath him, whimpering his name.

Begging.

"I told you, there are many ways I can make you squirm, my prince."

Ulric withdrew a breath. Then, with one slicked finger, pushed carefully at that rosy bud.

Auren gasped. "That feels—gods, what is that—?"

"Your body," Ulric whispered, "is learning how to sing."

He pushed further. Past that tight ring, until he was knuckle deep. Ulric rotated the joint and curved it forward at—

Just

The

Right

Spot.

Auren *screamed*.

Ulric's cock ached, but he didn't care. Not yet. He kissed Auren's trembling thighs, his hips, and whispered, "You're so beautiful like this. Let me see you fall apart." He crooked his finger again, finding that perfect place. That button to bring Auren crashing into oblivion.

And crash he did.

Auren cried so loud his voice echoed off the tile walls. His eyes rolled back, moaning Ulric's name, body writhing as his pleasure spilled free. Ulric held him through it, murmuring sweet things, lovely things, things he had no right to say.

Because this couldn't last.

He knew it.

But still, he whispered, "Mine."

And Auren gasped through heaving breaths, "Yours."

Chapter Twenty Two

Auren

SOMETHING WAS WRONG WITH ULRIC.

And whatever it was, it was creeping closer. The hesitation in the Kraken's stride, the faint hitch in his movements. It was so subtle at first that Auren convinced himself he imagined it.

But now... now there was no denying it.

The tattoos along Ulric's body were fading. Some had disappeared entirely, while others dimmed from inky black to a wispy gray. The thick glyphs over his chest, the ones Auren had traced with searching fingers, looked worn thin.

Auren tried to explain it away. It must be the toll of being away from the sea for too long. Ulric's magic was draining. His body straining to hold its shape above the waves. But if that were the case, why wasn't Auren feeling it? If anything, he felt *better* than ever. Buzzing with energy. Alive in ways he hadn't known were possible.

And still, every time he tried to ask the Kraken, Ulric always found some new way to pull his attention elsewhere. He led Auren to sprawling stables where horses in every imaginable color—coal black, pearl gray, flame red—snorted and stamped their hooves against the dust. To a sun-drenched garden market where sweet-meats, roasted nuts, and jewel-bright fruits perfumed the air. To a dockside artisan's square where glassblowers shaped molten fire into delicate baubles that caught the light and glittered like stars in the palm of Auren's hand.

Beautiful distractions. But distractions all the same.

It gnawed at him. A knot of worry in the pit of his stomach.

That morning, it all came to a head.

Auren woke, groggy from the wine they'd indulged in the night before, but otherwise rested. The fire had long since died, leaving the room cool and blue in the pre-dawn light. Ulric lay beside him, warm and strong, his face turned toward the window, the light gilding the lines of his jaw.

Auren smiled to himself and slid his hand under the covers, running his fingers through the thick hair on Ulric's chest.

"Can I interest you in a little breakfast, Kraken?" he teased, voice still rough with sleep, waiting for the gruff, amused remark that usually followed. Something about overeager spritelings or the scandal of being propositioned so early in the morning.

But none came.

Auren's fingers hesitated. Truthfully, it had been several days since they'd indulged in each other's bodies. Ulric had been so insistent on showing him everything. Every horse, every market, every garden, every sunset. Dragging Auren from wonder to wonder until he collapsed into bed, too exhausted to do more than kiss Ulric goodnight. It was wonderful. It was perfect.

But it wasn't enough.

Auren suspected Ulric was doing it on purpose. Holding himself back. Afraid of hurting him somehow.

Don't hide from me. I want all of you, my monster of the deep.

Auren grinned against his chest, already plotting how he might rectify that. He tilted his head, bumping his elbow against Ulric's shoulder.

"Did the wine carry you to such a deep sleep? Here I thought you could hold your drink better than I."

Still nothing.

Ulric breathed, a faint rise and fall of his ribs. There was a steady throb of his pulse in the hollow of his throat. But he didn't stir. Didn't even twitch.

Auren's own pulse picked up. "Ulric," he said, sharper now. He shook him once, twice. "Ulric. Wake up."

No response.

His blood coursed with ice. Auren scrambled on top of him, pressing his ear against Ulric's chest, desperate to hear the familiar, steady beat. It was there, but so faint. So *weak.*

"Ulric—Ulric!" Auren was shouting now, shaking his shoulders. "What is going on? What's happening?"

And right before his eyes, one of Ulric's runes, a sailfish etched beneath his ear, the one Auren knew by taste, flickered... and *vanished.*

"Oh no," Auren choked. "No, no, no—Don't do this. Ulric, please!"

Another shake, this one harsh enough to send Ulric's head lolling. And finally, Ulric groaned. His eyelids fluttered open, his mouth parting in a quick gasp. Auren let out a choked sound and collapsed against him, burying his face against Ulric's neck.

"What the hell was that?" he breathed, shaken. "Don't you ever do that again!"

Ulric stirred, sluggish. Sluggish like something that had remained still for too long. He managed to lift a hand, clumsily patting Auren's back.

"I'm fine," Ulric mumbled, voice slurred. "Just... too much wine."

Auren pulled back, mouth set in a firm line. "No, you're not fine," he said fiercely. "You can't keep brushing this off. You can't keep lying to me. Something's wrong."

Ulric's eyelids fell closed for a long moment, as if the very weight of them was too much.

When he opened them again, he managed a faint smile. "You're worrying too much, spriteling."

"I'm not," Auren insisted, heart pounding painfully in his chest. "Your tattoos are disappearing. You're getting weaker. Don't think I haven't noticed."

Ulric didn't answer. Didn't deny it. Just reached up and brushed the back of his knuckles along Auren's cheek, a gesture so tender it sent fear racing down his spine.

Why does his every move feel like a goodbye?

Auren blinked back tears and whispered, "Ulric... if we must return to Atlantis, we can. Who says we can't come back here, once you're strong again? Being away from the sea is taking a toll on you. Please don't do this for me."

Ulric averted his eyes, hand dropping to the blankets, jaw chewing on words unspoken. Auren's heart twisted painfully because he knew what that silence meant.

It meant the moment they returned to the sea, everything would change, or rather, would go back to what it used to be. Ulric would become the Court Sorcerer again. Bound by duty. Bound by oaths. Bound by everything that had kept them apart for so long.

And Auren would lose him.

He would swim the same corridors, but Auren would not be allowed to touch him. Not as he had here. Auren would carry the memory of Ulric's kiss, the feel of his arms, the taste of his breath —but he would carry it in silence.

He would know the secret weight of Ulric's love while the rest of the world only saw the cold, dutiful sorcerer. He would know the warmth of him, the wonder of him, the softness he showed no one else—

And yet be unable to touch.

Unable to call Ulric *his* anywhere but in the secret places of his heart.

Ulric must have seen the fear in his eyes because he pulled Auren close again, pressing a lingering kiss to his brow.

"Let's not dwell on what comes after," Ulric said quietly. His arms wrapped around Auren, so similar to the weight of his tentacles below the waves. "I'm here. We still have time."

Auren squeezed his eyes shut, willing himself to believe it.

"Okay," he whispered, even though it hurt. Even though it tasted like lying to himself.

Ulric kissed him again, slower this time. Full of sorrow and heat and a kind of love that burned even as it bloomed.

Auren kissed him back, clinging to him like he could keep him from slipping away.

For now, it was enough.

But somewhere deep inside, a clock started ticking.

And Auren didn't know how much time they had left.

The day passed in a strange sort of haze.

Auren tried to push the morning's fear aside, tried to pretend it hadn't happened, but the image of Ulric lying so still haunted him. He *should* have pressed. Should have demanded answers. But one look at Ulric's weary smile, one lingering kiss pressed to his hairline, and all Auren could do was cling to the precious present they still had.

So he followed Ulric out into the world again, their footsteps winding through the now-familiar town.

Ulric's coin flowed as freely as ever, the merchants calling greetings, pressing treats and trinkets into Auren's hands. They walked, talked, and still Auren watched. Watched the way Ulric's steps faltered every so often. The way his smile dimmed when he thought Auren wasn't looking. The way there was no color in his cheeks.

Something was wrong.

And it was getting worse.

He opened his mouth once, twice, to say something. To demand Ulric *tell him*—

But each time, Ulric would catch his hand, spin him into a new adventure.

"This way," he'd say. "You'll love this."

And damn it, Auren *did*.

The day passed in a haze of simple pleasures, until Ulric pulled Auren aside just as they were leaving the market.

"Don't think I've forgotten the *surprise* you're owed," he said with a smirk.

Before Auren could ask, Ulric led him deeper into the town, toward luxurious streets closer to the city's heart. The storefronts became grander here, lined in carved wood and polished brass, colorful awnings stretching overhead like banners.

They stopped before an extravagant shop of silks and linens, and Auren's mouth fell open. Mannequins dressed in shimmering suits and gowns stood proudly in the windows. Embroidery glinted in the afternoon sun.

"Come," Ulric said, taking Auren's hand warmly. "It's time you were dressed properly."

Inside, tailors swarmed the moment they entered. Auren barely had time to stammer a protest before he was swept into a whirlwind of measuring tapes and bolts of fabric. He was dressed first in a shirt of impossibly fine linen—cool cream, tailored to perfection, clinging like poured water. But it was the piece that followed that stole Auren's breath.

The corset.

Rich emerald, the exact hue of his scales. It gleamed in the light, threaded with subtle metallic accents that caught and shifted with his every breath. It looped over one shoulder only, the opposite side tucked beneath his arm in a clever asymmetry that made it feel more like armor than fashion. Heavy ropes bound it to his body, crossing in intricate knots along his ribs, while polished metal clasps bit into the thick material, holding it firm. The weight of it surprised Auren, another testament to the rich quality of the cloth. Auren ran his hand over the fabric, half in awe. The color. The feel. It was like wearing a memory. Like his past self was stitched into the seams and tied around him.

Auren flushed as he caught Ulric's gaze lingering *a little too long* at his hips, a look so openly hungry it made Auren's knees threaten to buckle.

And Ulric—

Fucking gods have mercy

Ulric was dressed in all black, fitted to every hard inch of his powerful body. The high collar and silver fastenings only made him look more dangerous, more untouchable.

And Auren wanted very much to *touch*.

As they were about to leave, Ulric said, "Wait. One more thing."

Auren turned, and Ulric pulled the whalebone pin from his hair, letting the black waves tumble around his broad shoulders. He stepped forward and gently pinned it in Auren's hair instead, his fingers brushing the back of Auren's neck.

"I like to see you in something of mine," Ulric murmured, inspecting him with a sweep of his dark eyes. "It's not as nice as... well, the other gift you've worn. But I hope you'll wear it."

The vulnerability in those black eyes, as though Ulric didn't know if Auren would accept such a humble gift, made his heart squeeze. Auren leaned in, standing on tip-toe to place a chaste kiss on the Kraken's cheek.

"I'll cherish it."

They made their way further into the city, and as the buildings grew more elaborate, Auren's excitement mounted. Marble facades, high sweeping arches, intricate carvings of horses, gods, and sea creatures twined around stone pillars. It faintly reminded him of home.

Finally, they reached a grand structure, its entrance flanked by tall statues of muses draped in flowing robes.

The Royal Theater.

They queued in line behind a scattering of elegantly dressed couples, Auren craning his neck to take it all in. The wide velvet banners, the way music floated from inside.

But Ulric shifted, dropping Auren's hand.

"I'll be back in a moment. Stay here," he said, suddenly stepping away and disappearing into the crowd. His hand grabbed the satchel at his waist, and Auren's stomach twisted at the shake in his fingers. Ulric looked ready to be sick as he dashed behind a corner, shoving a few passersby out of the way.

Auren frowned, noting the bout of dizziness. It was the second time that day. Ulric was going to take another one of his tonics to ease the discomfort and didn't want Auren to see. Auren fought the urge to follow, regardless of Ulric and his stubborn pride. But he kept his feet planted, stepping forward as the queue grew shorter.

A few moments later, Auren sensed a presence step behind him. A man in a velvet coat sauntered up, far too close, his smile oily.

"Well," the man drawled, raking his eyes over Auren with a lasciviousness that made his skin crawl. "Aren't you a sight? You a

performer tonight, pretty thing? I'd *very much* like to see you...
perform."

Auren blinked, confused. "I'm just watching," he said
carefully.

"Oh, shame," the man murmured. "Still, the night is young.
Perhaps after the show, you'd like a private stage? I'm very accom-
modating."

Before Auren could respond, a shadow fell over them both.

The Kraken's hand slid around Auren's waist, pulling him
possessively close, his fingers splaying over the curve of his back
where the corset cinched him tight.

"He's already spoken for," Ulric said, voice lethal. "And he has
no need for lesser stages when he already performs for a Lord."

The man lifted his hands in surrender, though the glint in his
eyes remained daring. "I didn't know this man belonged to
anyone."

"He doesn't," Ulric said, his mouth curving in a dangerous
smile. "He chooses to stay exactly where he is."

The man's gaze snapped to where Ulric's hand gripped
Auren's waist.

"And you are?" the man challenged.

Ulric's grip tightened just enough to make Auren's breath
catch.

"His Lord," Ulric said, sharp as a dagger's kiss. "And if you
value your tongue, you won't use it to make any more suggestions."

For a moment, silence pulsed between the three of them. Then
the man chuckled, stepping back with a graceful bow.

"My mistake."

Ulric didn't wait for more. He guided Auren away without
another word, his touch searing through the layers of cloth. As
they left, he leaned down and growled into Auren's ear, "I leave
you for one minute, and the sharks descend. Are you okay?"

"Yes, I'm fine. And lucky for you," Auren murmured with a

sly smile, "it would take a hell of a lot more than a shark to subdue me."

"How about a Kraken?" Ulric suggested.

"That is yet to be seen," Auren teased.

Ulric laughed and slipped his hand beneath the cape and pinched Auren's ass hard enough to make him jolt. Auren gave him a playful smack as the maître d' called them forward.

The ticket master held out his hand. "Passes?"

Ulric tossed him a heavy pouch of coin without blinking. "This will suffice."

But the man frowned, shifting awkwardly. "I'm sorry, my Lord, but this is a *private event*—ticket holders only."

Ulric's smile disappeared. Auren opened his mouth to suggest they leave, but Ulric held up a hand, cool and composed.

"Does my coin not satisfy?" he said, voice sharp. "Here, then."

He reached into his pack again and tossed another pouch— heavier this time. The metallic *clink* when it landed drew stares.

"You'll find no coppers there."

The man blanched, hands fumbling as he inspected the weight.

"I—I—" he stammered. "Be that as it may, my Lord, this event is for *couples only*. You and your companion would each need to return with a lady and—"

Ulric cut him off, lifting their joined hands into the light, Auren's fingers firmly clasped in his.

"This is my husband," Ulric said.

Auren's heart jumped. He turned his head quickly to hide the way his face flamed.

The man stared between them, visibly floundering. "I...I wasn't aware the law allowed for two—"

"Two *what*?" Ulric snapped, voice dropping dangerously low.

Before the man could finish that thought, another usher elbowed him sharply. He stumbled and cleared his throat.

"Just—just put them through!" he barked at the boy manning the velvet rope. "Balcony, west side. No one comes or goes."

"R-right this way," the mousy boy said, and blushed when Auren offered him a grateful smile as they passed.

"What was that about?" Auren asked as they were led down a carpet-lined hallway.

"Human nonsense. Prejudices over same-sex mating."

Auren cocked a brow. "They don't allow for couples like that? But..."

Piercing sky blue eyes returned to the forefront of his mind like the sting of a lionfish's quill. Elias had pursued him and...

"Of course they do. But privately. It's nothing for us to worry about. Don't let it bother you, Auren."

The sound of his name coming from Ulric's mouth snapped him back to the present, and he squeezed the Kraken's hand in gratitude.

The busboy led them up a sweeping staircase, while glittering chandeliers reflected the shimmering threads in their clothes.

The theater was breathtaking.

Scarlet drapes pooled from the ceiling like blood poured from a goblet, framing the wide stage in heavy, velvet folds. Every chair gleamed with lacquered wood and plush crimson cushions. Ornate crystal chandeliers threw pools of honeyed light across the audience below.

The boy who had escorted them led them not to the rows of seating, but up a winding staircase to a private balcony. Their view was perfect. High enough to see the whole stage, yet intimate, removed from the bustling crowd. Thick velvet curtains draped each side, hiding them from the adjacent balconies. Auren could hear other guests settling in—the muffled rustle of clothing, soft bursts of laughter—but he couldn't see them unless he leaned precariously over the edge. It was all very, very private.

Auren pressed closer to the railing in excitement, pointing eagerly at the stage as an orchestra settled in the pit below, tuning their instruments in a discordant hum.

"It's like the puppet show!" he whispered.

Ulric chuckled, sinking into one of the two ornate chairs at the front of their balcony. He stretched his long legs out, lounging like a king surveying his court.

"Oh, this will be much better than a puppet show," he said with a sly smile. "This is the Royal Theater. Though..." he glanced around at their lavish space, noting the nest of scattered throws and low, sumptuous couches, "I don't recall so many... pillows."

Auren looked around too, a little bewildered. Besides the two chairs near the railing, the floor of their balcony was littered with silken throws, thick cushions, and plush ottomans, creating a sort of luxurious nest.

"Maybe it's because tonight's a special event?" Auren suggested. "Maybe it'll go super late, and the guests are supposed to lie down for the later performances. Like an overnight party."

Ulric raised an eyebrow but didn't comment.

Auren's attention snagged on something else. Two tiny vials set into a shelf in the wall, their contents gleaming semi-translucent, yellow-tinted like olive oil.

"What do you think *those* are for?" Auren asked, pointing.

"I have no idea," Ulric admitted, frowning.

Before they could speculate further, there was a polite knock, and a silver tray was delivered, piled with olives, cheese, crackers, and slivers of cured meats.

Delighted, Auren set to sampling one of everything, firing a hundred questions at Ulric in rapid succession. About the instruments, the costumes, and the history of the theater. Ulric answered them all with infinite patience, smiling like a man content to simply *exist* beside him.

Then, with a low sweep of the conductor's hand, the lights dimmed, and the performance began.

It was glorious.

Vibrant music crashed from the pit as dancers exploded onto the stage. Acrobats gracefully flung themselves through the air, and shimmering costumes caught the light like falling stars. The tale that unfolded was simple but enthralling: a lover searching for his lost beloved across endless seas, mountains, and deserts. It was told not through words but through the sheer poetry of movement, each leap and turn a verse in the story.

Auren was utterly captivated. He leaned forward in his seat, breathless, forgetting where he was as he let himself fall into the story.

The music swelled into a frantic crescendo, the violins screeching a final, broken note. The two lovers were torn apart, their bodies straining for each other, their wailing notes raw as the velvet curtains swept across the scene like a closing grave. The last thing Auren saw was a hand reaching out, and then it was gone.

A tear slid down his cheek before he even realized it.

"It's not over, is it?" Auren asked in horror.

"No, this is just a break," Ulric said, then laughed at the obvious relief on Auren's face. "Don't worry, I've seen this one. It has a happy ending."

"Oh, thank gods," Auren said, slumping in his chair.

At intermission, Ulric slipped away and returned moments later with two bottles of wine tucked under one arm and a mischievous gleam in his eye. They sampled them freely, letting the warm buzz settle into their bones as they nibbled from the tray of delicacies. Auren, flushed from the drink and the thrill of the first act, whispered excitedly with Ulric about his favorite parts. The two of them were leaning in so close that their shoulders touched, laughing low like co-conspirators.

When the show resumed, Auren sank back into the plush chair, wine glass in hand, heart thudding with anticipation. Once again, he was utterly swept away.

He gasped out loud when the final scene exploded into a breathtaking display. Firebreathers spinning ribbons of flame through the air, dancers leaping around a coach pulled by living horses adorned in costume. The two lovers reunited in a triumphant, soaring song of forgiveness and devotion, their voices rising in perfect harmony as the orchestra thundered.

Auren's heart felt so full it might burst. He didn't even realize he was crying again until Ulric nudged a handkerchief into his fingers. He wiped his cheeks and gave a little laugh, more than a little embarrassed.

"You didn't tell me it would be so beautiful."

"Some things are better when discovered for yourself."

The lovers shared one final kiss centerstage, surrounded by the glow of swirling embers, and the curtain fell to a rapturous standing ovation. Auren clapped until his palms stung.

He didn't want it to end. He didn't want any of this to end. Not the night. Not this feeling. None of it.

And yet, even as the actors bowed and the orchestra struck its final chord, a voice boomed overhead:

"All general admission, please make your way to the exits. Our esteemed ticket holders are invited to remain seated."

Auren turned to Ulric, wide-eyed. "Is that us?"

Ulric frowned slightly but nodded. "I suppose so. We are in the private balconies—and I gave enough gold to buy the cast." He smirked. "I've never been to an exclusive show. Let's see how it plays out."

They waited.

As the primary audience filed out, Auren noticed something strange. Those who remained on the main floor all wore white owl-shaped masks, completely obscuring their faces. He could hear movement in the other balconies, too—the shifting of cushions and murmured voices—but the heavy curtains kept their neighbors hidden from view.

"Maybe it's a secret part of the story? A special ending about the lovers?" Auren asked excitedly.

"Maybe," Ulric said, but his brow remained furrowed.

When the last stragglers left, the theater dimmed, this time plunging the audience into near-total darkness. Only the faintest pools of light illuminated the stage.

The music began again.

Auren stiffened.

It wasn't like the previous music. No soaring strings or triumphant horns. This was slower. Sensual. A pounding beat of low drums that thrummed in Auren's chest.

He leaned forward eagerly, sure some thrilling stunt was about to happen—an acrobat leaping from the rafters, or a parade of exotic beasts.

"Auren..." Ulric's voice was cautious. Auren turned to see the Kraken holding one of the tiny vials from the shelf in his hand, turning it over with a frown. "I think maybe we should leave."

"What? Why?" Auren said, half laughing. "It's just starting—"

He didn't finish the sentence.

The curtains pulled back. And onto the stage poured half a dozen performers—completely nude.

Auren froze.

It was... carnage. Beautiful, *sensual* carnage.

Their bodies gleamed with oil, glowing under the torchlight, muscles sliding against one another like creatures from another world. Every dancer wore a mask. Elaborate things of masterful craftsmanship, each modeled after an animal. It obscured their identities but somehow made the performance all the more wild. Some wore slivers of lace so sheer it hid nothing, accenting the shape of their bodies—an invitation to revel in the sex that oozed openly through the air.

Naked and half-naked, the dancers tangled together in a writhing rhythm. Hands caressed slick skin. Mouths found the hollows of throats, the curves of hips.

One woman dropped gracefully to her knees, her mask tilting up as she looked at the man before her. The crowd held its breath, a hush falling over the theater as she leaned in and parted her lips around the thick length of him. Her hand moved in time with the low, pulsing drums, guiding him deeper into her mouth with a practiced, sensual grace.

Auren's jaw dropped. His cheeks burned with helpless, hot color, his heart pounding so hard he heard it above the music. He clutched the edge of his chair so hard his knuckles went white.

Ulric shifted uncomfortably beside him.

"I'm sorry, Auren," he said roughly. "I didn't know— We can leave if you want."

But Auren couldn't tear his eyes away.

Heat coiled low in his belly, spreading to his hips and filling his groin.

No... he didn't want to leave.

The scene on stage only grew more explicit. The performers, the sheer *enthusiasm*, and the pleasure painted openly across their faces was a tapestry of eroticism. The way they worshiped each other with touch, mouth, and tongue.

It was raw. Human. Hungry.

The air smelled of sweat and sex, and it was more dizzying than the wine.

And it awoke something in Auren that he hadn't known was sleeping.

He wanted it.

He wanted *him*.

Auren turned, unable to help himself. And there was Ulric, sitting rigid beside him, his strong throat working as he swallowed, hands clamped tightly on his knees. Ulric, who had touched him, held him, protected him—Ulric, who was trying so hard to hold back.

Auren was a man—and Ulric was a man—and there was nothing between them now but choice.

And Auren was ready.

He wanted to feel everything. *All* of Ulric.

He turned, meeting Ulric's wide, worried eyes across the darkness, and made a decision.

Tonight, he would dare.

Chapter Twenty Three

Ulric

ULRIC STOOD ABRUPTLY, HIS LEGS FILLED WITH beehives. This wasn't how he expected the night to go. He'd intentionally avoided this sort of thing. Maybe they could leave now, do some other activity to exhaust Auren before retiring.

But with one look at the prince, Ulric knew they were past the point of no return. The second Auren turned those fire-lit eyes on him, wide and blazing with intent, Ulric knew he was doomed.

The music thrummed through the theater like a second pulse. It filled the air between them, pulling them like a death grip of a riptide. There was no escaping it.

And then Auren, his wild, wonderful Auren, *pounced*.

Ulric's back hit the velvet wall of their balcony with a muted thud, and before he could even think to protest, Auren's hands were at his waist, yanking loose the clasps of his belt.

"Auren—" Ulric rasped, trying to catch his breath, "we don't... this isn't—"

Auren didn't stop. His fingers worked the buttons of Ulric's shirt, undoing them one by one as heat bloomed between them.

"Do you want to stop?" Auren demanded, sharp as the gleam in a Great White's eye before the attack. "Tell me now, Ulric. Say the words."

Ulric opened his mouth—but nothing came out. Nothing except the wild thudding of his heart—and the aching, desperate need flooding his veins.

Auren smiled. "That's what I thought," he murmured.

Then he dropped to his knees.

Ulric's breath hitched painfully as Auren pushed the cloak off his shoulders, baring him to the cool air. The sound of cloth sliding down his arms and pooling on the floor may as well have been the collapse of a mountainside, the avalanche loud in Ulric's ears. Somewhere nearby, he heard the faint sounds of other couples beginning to lose themselves to the music. The muted gasps and sighs filtering through the velvet drapes. Bodies shuffled on the main floor as the remaining guests joined the debauchery happening on stage.

Ulric didn't care.

He only cared about the man at his feet.

Auren worked methodically, loosening the ties of Ulric's trousers. Each tug of laces sent sharp jolts of arousal racing up his spine. By the time Auren finally freed him, Ulric was already hard. Aching so badly it bordered on painful.

Auren looked at him through amber lashes, hands braced on Ulric's thighs.

Ulric's jaw clenched as he braced against the wall.

"Auren—" he managed, rough and shredded. "Gods—"

And then Auren leaned in, wrapped his hot, wet mouth around Ulric's shaft, and the great Sorcerer of Atlantis fell apart. A broken, guttural sound tore from Ulric's throat. His head thudded back against the wall with a muffled *bang* as pleasure exploded through him.

"Wait Auren not so fas——Fuuuuuuck!"

The warning died on his lips when Auren leaned forward, taking in more of him, eyes bright and curious. Ulric's body jolted like lightning had struck his spine.

"Auren—Oh Poseidon, have mercy—"

He gritted his teeth, fighting to keep still, to not overwhelm the beauty between his legs. But Auren moaned, like the taste of Ulric was what he'd been craving all night. Any thought of taking it slow died on arrival.

"Fuck," Ulric hissed, grabbing the velvet curtain for balance as Auren worked him. The prince was warm. Eager. Mouth made of silk and heat. Inexperienced, yes—but that only made it better. There was something ruinous about how naturally Auren moved, how instinctively he adjusted to every twitch, every sharp breath. Like he was meant for this.

Like his body was made for me.

Ulric's knees buckled. He barely caught himself on the arm of one of the chairs.

"You're going to kill me, spriteling," he gasped.

Auren only hummed in a self-pleased sort of way, the sound vibrating up Ulric's length until he thought he might come undone right there. And Ulric knew he wasn't alone in that feeling.

He could hear it—the sounds of bodies moving, of laughter, of gasps and cries and shuddering pleasure. He could feel the thrum of the music vibrating through the floorboards and up his legs.

But all of it—the noise, the theater, the city itself—faded to nothing compared to the heat of Auren's mouth.

Ulric tangled a trembling hand in Auren's hair, pulling it free from his whale-bone clasp, until it spilled like molten copper across Auren's bare shoulders.

"Gods, you're perfect," he gasped.

He would remain in control. But damn it all, this Mer was testing the limits of Ulric's four hundred years of perfect restraint. And when Auren glanced up at him through those lashes, cheeks hollowing around the base, Ulric made a sound that belonged nowhere but the deep.

With a challenge in his eyes, Auren swallowed him down. *All* the way. Ulric throbbed as the tip of him touched the back of Auren's tight throat.

"Fuck—" Ulric groaned, one hand finding its way into Auren's hair, fighting not to thrust mercilessly into that mouth. "Auren, you don't have to—"

Auren pulled off with a filthy pop. "But I want to," he said. "I want to know what you taste like. I want all of you inside me." He went back down, as if he meant to ruin Ulric. Ulric was more beast than man now. Reduced to a tangle of nerve endings and need. Unraveling one breath at a time beneath the mouth of a man who was becoming his undoing. He gripped Auren's hair tight, using it to drag the prince's mouth back and forth, nearly pulling all the way out before shoving back into his throat.

All the while, Auren hummed, breathing hard through his nose as spittle dribbled down the sides of his mouth. Ulric wanted to stay in this moment. To burn it into memory. If this were all he ever got, he would die knowing that Olympus had once bowed to him, mouth open and eager.

And when those ocean-blue eyes met his, watery from the intensity of it all, Ulric fell apart.

He spilled into Auren's ready mouth, hips twitching, teeth gritted to avoid shoving in so hard he'd bruise the poor Mer's lips. Auren took it all, greedy, devoted, throat bobbing as he drank Ulric in.

Ulric gasped, feeling as though he'd shot out three times his usual load. When he pulled out, an echoing jolt of pleasure shot down his spine as he watched Auren lick his lips clean.

Ulric's knees gave, and he crumpled into the chair, panting like he'd just swum the entire breadth of the Pacific.

Auren crawled into his lap, straddling him, his flushed face split into a grin so wicked and triumphant Ulric wanted to kiss it right off him.

"Still think we should have left?" Auren teased.

Ulric groaned and yanked him into a bruising kiss.

He tasted himself on Auren's lips, tongues tangling in an explosion of sensation.

"You beautiful menace," he hissed. "Now it's my turn to have my way with you."

The Kraken's hands made quick work of stripping him bare. But that didn't mean he intended to rush the next part. Not now. Not after Auren shattered every wall between them. No, Ulric would savor him and draw out every second into an eternity. Slowly, he pushed Auren back, letting his greedy gaze drink him in.

Gods above.

Auren stood before him, bare and flushed, cock hard and leaking against his stomach, thighs trembling from need. The low light from the stage accented every line of him, honed and perfect. A body made for worship.

And Ulric planned to do just that.

He tugged Auren onto his lap, his back against Ulric's chest, their bare skin slick and electric where they touched. Ulric reached around, wrapping a hand around Auren's aching cock, stroking him slowly, idly, just enough to draw a ripple of pleasure down Auren's spine. Enough to keep him gasping, whimpering every now and again, those sounds punching straight through Ulric's chest like spears.

"Watch the show," Ulric commanded, steering Auren's gaze forward. "Don't look away while I touch you."

Below them, the show roared on.

Bodies writhed together on the main floor, the scent of sweat and lust thickening the air. Auren watched the stage as Ulric watched *him*—the way his mouth parted in breathless awe, the way his hips rocked into Ulric's loose grip without even realizing it.

The first man and woman took to a high podium, gleaming with sweat, bodies heaving.

Ulric saw it coming before Auren did—the inevitable crescendo. He heard Auren's sharp intake of breath as the man grabbed the woman's hips, lining himself up with her entrance. He thrust into her with a guttural roar, and the woman cried out in duet, wild and feral.

The wet sound of it echoed across the hall.

Auren stiffened in his lap, staring with wide, stunned eyes.

"What did he just—?" he choked.

Ulric leaned in, lips brushing Auren's bare shoulder, dragging his teeth lightly across the overstimulated skin.

"He penetrated her," Ulric murmured, dark as silk. "If he keeps that up, he'll spill inside her."

Auren's thighs clenched on top of him. More precum oozed out as though his cock were crying for release. Ulric groaned as the fresh dribble slicked his hand where he still idly stroked Auren's length.

"Is that how... how they...?" Auren could barely get the words out.

"Mmhmm," Ulric hummed, licking a slow, teasing stripe up the length of Auren's throat to his ear. "That's how it's done."

"Does she... does she also..."

"If he's any good, she'll find her own pleasure too."

To punctuate the words, Ulric bit down on the nape of Auren's neck, earning a startled, choked cry.

Someone on the neighboring balcony whooped with laughter and shouted, "That's right! Give it to him!"

Ulric chuckled darkly against Auren's back, but his focus was absolute. Every little sound Auren made—every twitch, every breath—wound him tighter and tighter. The underground pressure of a volcano on the cusp of spilling onto the earth.

The performance below turned feral, rhythmic slaps and cries echoing through the hall, but Ulric hardly noticed. He had a far better show in his arms.

When Ulric let his hand slide lower, thumbing Auren's dripping slit, Auren writhed helplessly in his lap, grinding his ass on Ulric's thighs.

He couldn't wait anymore. He needed that mouth again.

Ulric grabbed Auren by the waist, maneuvering him before retaking his seat, the men now chest to chest.

"Give me that wretched mouth of yours," Ulric growled, fisting the back of Auren's neck and dragging him down.

Auren gave it to him, tongue first. Their kiss was messy, all heat and teeth and sensation. There was nothing soft or romantic about it. Ulric groaned into him, biting Auren's lower lip hard enough to make him gasp, then chasing the sound with his tongue, stealing every broken breath he could.

Auren pressed in harder, grinding down with a helpless, shuddering noise. Ulric caught his ass with both hands, squeezing, spreading, baring him completely to the cool air.

"Ulric..." Auren gasped.

The Kraken rumbled deep in his chest. "What is it, spriteling? What can I do for you?"

Auren whimpered, struggling for words. "Please... with your fingers. Like before."

Ulric feigned ignorance, just to see him squirm. "Whatever do you mean, my prince?"

Auren opened his eyes to glare at him, cheeks flushed and lips swollen.

"You know exactly what I mean, you grouchy old Kraken," he hissed.

Ulric laughed. "Of course, my prince. Anything you desire."

He stood, gently easing Auren off his lap before walking to the little shelf in the wall, uncorking one of the glass vials. The slick, semi-transparent substance gleamed in the low light.

"What is that?" Auren asked.

"Lubricant. It'll make things… easier for you."

Auren's pupils dilated.

Ulric dipped his fingers into the oil and resumed his seat, beckoning Auren to straddle him. His prince obeyed without hesitation, legs bracketing Ulric's hips, their hard cocks sliding together.

Ulric smeared the oil across Auren's ass, working it in with long, tantalizing strokes, not caring about the mess. Auren's breath hitched when Ulric's fingers pressed harder, spreading him open.

"So beautiful," Ulric rasped. "So fucking perfect."

He ran his fingers up and down the crevice, relishing in the perfect shape of Auren's ass. In the dimple of muscle he felt there.

"Do you like this, my prince?"

Auren's face was buried in Ulric's neck, hands braced on his shoulders. He felt a slight nod.

"You like having your ass played with?"

Another nod, hands tightening with urgency.

"I need to hear it spriteling, or I might just end it here."

Ulric removed his fingers, as though to tease. But he should have known better. Should have known that it wasn't a fawn perched upon his lap, but a wolf.

Auren let out a desperate sound, a mix between a moan and a growl, before digging his fingernails into Ulric's skin and biting the side of his neck so hard that Ulric shouted in alarm.

"If you try to play games with me, old man, you'll find I am not very forgiving in this moment." Auren hissed, immediately licking the place where his teeth had been. And like an obedient lover, Ulric returned his fingers to that oil-slick crevice.

"Yes, my prince."

He explored further until he found the core of Auren's need.

He circled the tight muscle with one finger, teasing, testing Auren's limits.

"Please..." Auren cried, grinding down.

Ulric pushed the first finger inside.

Auren jolted in his lap, letting out a high, breathy moan that had Ulric's own cock throbbing painfully between them.

"Good boy," Ulric murmured, stroking him with his free hand to keep him calm. "Take it."

He worked the finger in and out slowly, letting Auren adjust before adding another. Stretching him wider, deeper. Auren whimpered. Rocked his hips greedily into the sensation.

"Gods above," Ulric grunted. "You're so fucking tight."

Auren only moaned in response, leaning his body back, eyes fluttering shut.

Ulric couldn't resist—he leaned forward, biting gently at Auren's exposed nipple as he worked a third finger inside. Auren's whole body jerked, hands clawing at Ulric's shoulders.

"U-Ulric—I—!"

"I've got you, spriteling," Ulric soothed, even as his fingers moved in deep, scissoring motions, dragging cries from Auren's lips.

Auren ground down hard against him once, twice—and with a helpless, gasping sound, he came, spilling hot and fast over their stomachs and chests, body convulsing around Ulric's knuckles.

Ulric held him through it, murmuring praises into his hair.

"That's it," he whispered. "That's it, my sweet sea-sprite."

He didn't pull away. Didn't rush. He held Auren, blissed-out and trembling in his arms, soothing him through the aftershocks.

They sagged against each other, both slick with sweat. Somewhere below, the stage descended into chaos—no longer the clean acts of performers, but pure, primal carnality. Men slid inside women, bodies gleaming with oil and desire. Moans and the wet slaps of skin against skin filled the air like distant applause. Ulric wasn't sure anyone was truly watching anymore. The performers weren't acting now. They were *indulging,* feasting on pleasure like ravenous creatures.

"Ulric…" Auren's breath was a ragged whisper against his throat, his sweat-soaked hair clinging to his flushed face. "The men… with the women," he gasped between breaths.

"Yes?" Ulric murmured, fingers still stroking lazy circles against Auren's sweat-slick back.

"Can such a thing be done… between two men?"

Ulric closed his eyes, battling the raw surge of need that threatened to strip him bare.

But Auren was sharp and caught the hesitation.

"Can it?" Auren pressed, urgently now.

Ulric swallowed, his cock throbbing with each stuttered heartbeat.

"It can," he admitted hoarsely.

Auren's brows drew together in that infuriating, beloved stubbornness.

"Then why haven't we?"

Ulric ran a hand down Auren's spine, feeling every tense muscle.

"I don't want to hurt you," he said. "For you, it could be… painful. It is not like with my hand."

Auren's mouth hardened into a grim line, and for a moment, Ulric thought he would fight him, but his gaze softened as he placed a tender kiss against Ulric's Adam's apple.

"I am a man, Ulric," he said with a firm resolution. "And you are a man."

He cupped Ulric's face in his hands, thumbs brushing along the sharp lines of his jaw.

"If you truly respect me," Auren continued, "then you'll let me decide where my limits lie. You'll trust me to know my body, to know what I can take."

Ulric opened his mouth to protest, but Auren shook his head, silencing him.

"Yes, this body is new, but strength isn't new to me. I know my balance. I know my power."

He softened then, a small, wry smile tugged at the corner of his mouth.

"I know my strengths, Ulric. But I also know my weaknesses."

Auren leaned in, stealing a tender, lingering kiss.

"And you," he whispered against Ulric's lips, "are my *greatest* weakness."

Ulric shuddered violently, barely holding on.

Auren pulled back to look him in the eyes. "Let me decide my limits, Kraken."

Ulric dragged a trembling breath into his lungs. "Are you sure?" His voice cracked.

Auren nodded. "Yes. I want it. I want *you*. All of you."

The floodgates shattered. And now Auren would know what it meant to tame a Kraken.

"Then do as I say, and bend over that balcony, spriteling."

Auren nearly stumbled over the silken pillows at their feet in his urgency to obey.

"Hands on the railing. You'll need something to hold onto."

His prince obeyed, hands braced on the polished wood, legs trembling in anticipation.

Ulric grabbed the vial of oil again, slicking his hand liberally. He worked one finger inside Auren, then two, stretching him until he could ease in a third. He took his time, massaging the tight muscle, coaxing Auren open. The prince whimpered, clenching the balcony in a death grip, a curtain of hair tipping over the edge.

Ulric swallowed a growl at the sight of him—red hair wild, muscles flexing, thighs shaking from need.

"If you want to feel me so badly," Ulric rasped. "Then you will feel every. Fucking. Breath."

Auren rocked back against his fingers, greedy and shameless. "Please," he gasped. "Please, Ulric. I need—"

Ulric pulled his fingers free and slicked himself.

He lined up behind Auren, gripping those slender hips, thumbing the slick cleft of his ass. He positioned himself at that rosy bud, letting Auren feel the heat of his length. To warn his body of the impending invasion.

"Relax, spriteling," Ulric murmured, voice thick. "Breathe for me. Let your body open."

He pressed in. Slowly, his tip strained past the resistant ring. The intrusion dragged a strangled gasp from Auren's throat. His shoulders bunched up, muscles rigid with resistance.

Ulric soothed him with kisses to the back of his neck, murmuring praise against his skin, even as he clenched his teeth at its tightness. "Good boy. That's it. Take me in."

Bit by bit, Auren's body surrendered, muscles yielding.

Ulric pressed in deeper, stopping only when Auren's knuckles whitened against the railing. He waited until the prince's body melted around him. They moved like that—inch by inch, breath by breath—until Ulric was fully sheathed.

"There," Ulric panted against his spine. "That's it. You've got it all, my prince."

Auren whimpered, legs trembling so violently that Ulric had to wrap an arm around his hips just to keep him upright.

"Stay strong," Ulric grunted. "I'm going to move now."

He pulled out slightly, watching the way Auren's stretched hole clung to him, the dark length of his cock shining with slick. Ulric pushed back in, then again, and again, as Auren's body adjusted, as resistance turned to welcome. Each slow thrust tugged at his cock as it glided through the tight, gripping ring of Auren's entrance.

Every movement tore a desperate moan from Auren's mouth.

"There you go," Ulric whispered hotly into his ear. "Now you're doing it. Taking me so well."

Below them, the stage roared with noise: cries and grunts and wet flesh colliding. Ulric forced Auren to look down, tilting his head toward the chaos.

"Watch them," he rasped. "Watch how they fuck. Know that I'm doing the same to you."

Auren let out a broken sound that wasn't quite a moan, wasn't quite a sob.

"That's it. My beautiful sea-sprite. My prince."

Auren was shaking so hard now Ulric was half-carrying him, holding his hips steady as he drove into him, the slap of skin against skin lost in the riotous noise of the theater.

"Is this what you wanted?" Ulric demanded. "To be filled? To be claimed?"

"Yes," Auren gasped. "Yes, gods—Ulric, don't stop—"

"You're mine," Ulric growled against his ear. "I'll fill you, spriteling. I'll spill myself deep inside you and *you'll keep it.*"

Auren cried out wordlessly, back arching, fingers clawing at the wooden railing.

Ulric felt the finish racing toward him, felt it building in his spine, coiling at the base of his cock. He reached around and grabbed Auren's dripping length, stroking him roughly in time with his thrusts.

"Come for me," Ulric demanded. "Now, Auren. *Now.*"

Auren came with a choked cry, spilling hot and thick across the floor, his whole body spasming in Ulric's arms.

The sudden, tight seizing of Auren's body was too much.

Through clenched teeth, Ulric drove in until his hips met Auren's ass and spilled inside him, wave after wave of thick, molten release. He ground in deep, locking them together, shaking from the force of it.

For a few stunned seconds, there was only the sound of their panting.

Then—

A hush. The sensuous music had stopped, as had the sound of slapping bodies. Ulric lifted his head blearily, just in time to see the stage performers *staring at them* from below.

A long moment.

Then they burst into raucous laughter and applause.

"Oh, Poseidon fuck me," Ulric groaned, yanking the velvet curtains closed.

Auren, already sliding to the floor in a heap of exhausted limbs and ruined bliss, laughed breathlessly.

"I think we may have distracted from the evening's entertainment," he teased, voice hoarse and delighted. "I suspect we caused a minor scandal."

Ulric brushed a damp curl from Auren's forehead.

"If they spent the evening staring at you, I can hardly blame them."

Auren curled into the cushions scattered across the floor, utterly wrecked, utterly beautiful, slick with sweat and leaking Ulric's release.

Ulric crawled after him, hauling him into his arms, pressing kisses into the damp fall of his hair. Ulric was in love with a prince of the sea. How had he ever lived without this? How was he supposed to let it go now, when it was all he had ever wanted?

As he cradled Auren against his chest, Ulric felt the clock ticking in his bones. The gods would come for him soon. But after holding his beloved like this, he would meet them smiling. And as Auren's breath grew even and Ulric held him, he whispered a silent prayer.

"Let me stay like this.
Let me have this moment.
But if I must vanish... let it be here. With you.
With love.
With the salt of your kiss still on my lips.
All I ask, my darling, is that you—
Drown me Gently."

Chapter Twenty Four

Auren

AUREN WOKE TO THE STUFFY HUSH OF MORNING.

Sunlight filtered through the heavy velvet drapes in thin, glowing bands, cutting across the haze of the theater. Dust motes floated in the still air, dancing lazily in the beams. Somewhere nearby, a curtain rustled. Bare feet padded against plush carpet. A few low groans echoed as other couples began to stir from their nest of scattered cushions, some laughing sleepily, others wincing with the weight of the previous night still aching in their bones. Nobody had come to kick them out last night. No announcement that the theater was closing, leaving the inhabitants to succumb to the debauchery of the night.

Auren blinked, his head fuzzy, his limbs heavy and sore.

He lay on a nest of fine silk pillows and padded mats, the luxurious kind. His whole body ached in places he hadn't known could ache. His thighs burned. His hips throbbed. His cock was sore in the best, most exhausted way imaginable. And his ass—well, there were bruises there that would sing for the rest of the day. He tried to roll over and winced.

Nope. That's not happening.

He chuckled to himself as the early light cut through the lingering scent of sweat and moth-eaten curtains.

So it was a slumber party, he thought hazily.

Only this one lasted late into the night, with bodies tangled in every shadowed corner and pleasure spreading like wildfire with every pluck of the violin.

He and Ulric lost themselves in each other twice more after the performance ended, wrapped in the heat of their private alcove, their limbs entwined as if they might never separate. The velvet curtains muffled the sound, but the rest of the theater had turned into a chorus of moans and murmurs, sighs and screams. Their hosts, Auren suspected, were under no illusions about what kind of guests they were housing. At some point, during a lull between kisses and whispered words, a gentle knock interrupted them. Auren cracked open the door and found a wash basin, fresh towels, and a folded cloth left respectfully outside.

Even now, he could hear the faint bustle of theater staff beyond the curtains—servants ferrying clean linens and trays of sweet breakfast rolls to other guests. The quiet sound of plates clinking. Murmured greetings. Warm, practiced hospitality.

This must cost a fortune, Auren mused, still lying there half-numb.

Not only for the accommodations, but also for the discretion. Auren didn't know much about human society, but he assumed that only the noblest of them could afford such a night, and they wouldn't want word of their proclivities widely known.

And Ulric is among them.

He remembered the way Ulric had been addressed, "Lord." The title meant something here. Auren wanted to know how Ulric had come by it. How much of himself he'd integrated into human society. He wanted to know it all, but mostly, he wanted Ulric to be the one teaching him.

Ulric lay behind him, one arm slung across his waist, their legs tangled beneath the covers. His face was tucked into the curve of Auren's shoulder, as if he'd been trying to breathe him in during the night. His hair was a wild tangle, and his breath stirred the skin at Auren's neck.

But something was off. As Auren blinked into clearer focus, he felt it—the irregularity of air. Ulric's breath wasn't right.

Too shallow.

Auren frowned. He shifted, easing out from under the weight of Ulric's arm.

The sorcerer didn't move, his arm flopping lifelessly to the blankets.

When Auren rose on one elbow, the light fell across Ulric's face —and dread pooled in his stomach like acid.

The Kraken's skin was pale. Not his usual shadowed warmth, but paper-thin and grey-blue at the edges. Almost translucent. His lips were parted and slightly purple.

"Ulric?" Auren whispered.

No response.

Auren grabbed his shoulder, shaking him roughly. "Hey, Ulric."

At last, Ulric stirred. He opened his eyes slowly, blinking like a man waking from a long, heavy dream. He tried to sit up and winced.

Auren caught him before his head lolled into the leg of an ottoman.

"Don't move too fast," Auren said, heart thudding.

"I'm fine," Ulric muttered hoarsely.

"You're full of shit," Auren replied, trying to keep his voice steady.

That earned a faint smirk. "Language, your highness."

"You're paler than sunbleached wood," Auren said, not bothering to keep the worry from his voice this time. "We're going back to the cabin. You need your tonics."

Auren cursed himself for not thinking of it sooner. Ulric was hanging onto this human shape by a thread, drinking the tonics almost every hour. Of course, since they hadn't known they would be staying the night, Ulric hadn't brought enough. He'd gone too long without a dose.

Ulric waved him off. "I just need to sit up. Maybe drink something."

He tried to stand, legs unsteady beneath him, but even the simple act of reaching for his trousers proved too much. Auren saw the last hint of color drain from Ulric's face—just a moment before he collapsed. Auren ducked under his arm, catching his weight and holding him upright until the dizziness passed.

"It's... fine," Ulric said, though he sounded half-conscious as he said it.

"Sit your ass down, I'll help you then we're getting the hell outta here," Auren said, not bothering to hide the worry and frustration from his voice.

He dressed Ulric, with little to no protest from the old Sorcerer, which scared Auren half to death. A fully well Ulric would never have let his prince kneel and lace up his boots.

He's falling apart.

"Let's go," he whispered as they exited the theater. "Lean on me."

And Ulric, who never leaned on anyone, didn't argue.

The streets were bustling with midmorning trade. Merchants shouted over one another from crowded stalls, and the scent of fresh bread filled the air. Children darted between carts. Baskets swung from arms. Wheels clattered over uneven stones.

Auren worried the press of bodies would jostle Ulric, that even the smallest bump might send him to his knees.

But somehow, they weren't touched.

It was as though Ulric's frailty cast a ward around them—people gave them a wide berth, glancing sidelong as they passed, whispering behind cupped hands. Whether it was the inky tattoos that now faded along Ulric's arms or the ghost-white pallor of his skin, Auren didn't know.

He tightened his hold and kept walking.

Ulric leaned into him, more than Auren expected. He felt the drag of the Kraken's weight in every step. His body felt... empty, somehow. He was heavy, yes, but not as heavy as he should have been. It was like his bones were hollow. He seemed to lack any substance at all—and the thought unnerved Auren. Just last night, Ulric felt solid as stone, unshakable as the seafloor. And now... he was a pale wisp, barely able to hold his own weight.

Auren tightened his hold.

It took twice as long as usual, but when they finally arrived at the cabin, Auren let out a sigh of relief. He helped Ulric to the edge of the bed and wrapped a blanket around his shoulders. The room was warm, almost uncomfortably so, with the noonday sun beating at the walls, but Ulric shivered like a man standing waist-deep in snow.

"Where are your tonics?" Auren asked, already opening cabinets.

"Green bottle," Ulric rasped. "Middle shelf. Smells like mint."

Auren found it, uncorked it, and held the vial to Ulric's lips. He drank with effort, grimacing at the taste, but some color returned to his face shortly after. His breathing evened. The tremble in his hands stopped. Not gone entirely—but enough.

"Better?" Auren asked, crouching before him.

Ulric nodded, running a hand down Auren's cheek. "You're wasted on me."

"Don't you dare," Auren snapped. "You don't get to say dramatic things while looking like death warmed over."

Ulric chuckled hoarsely. "You're not as soft as you look."

"And you're not as strong as you pretend."

They stared at each other for a long moment. No more jokes. Just breath and bone and truth in the space between them. Finally, Auren spoke the words eating away at him from the first moment he saw Ulric's strength falter.

"Ulric... please. You can't keep going like this. Let's return to Atlantis. Get your strength back. Get your magic back. We —I can talk to my mother. I can talk to the courts; they'll listen... about us." He placed a begging hand on Ulric's knee. "I don't want to go. You know I don't. But I can't stand by and watch you make yourself sick over this."

When Ulric didn't respond, Auren's confidence grew; maybe he was getting through to him.

"The courts will see that, we—that this won't affect our duties. You're still Court Sorcerer, and I am still the prince. Our responsibilities won't change. We can help each other." Auren added hopefully, but Ulric still wouldn't make eye contact with him. "Then, when things settle, we can come back here. We can make trips to the surface whenever we want. You can teach me more about this world and..." Auren gulped. "We can be together."

Ulric's large hand clasped over his, squeezing it. When he looked up, there was something unreadable in his eyes.

"Let me rest awhile. Then I would like to walk with you along the sand. Would you grant me that request, my prince?"

"Of course. Anything." Auren said right away, not liking how Ulric's voice had changed. There was sadness, and Auren was desperately looking for its source so he could banish it from this world.

They settled into the bed together, curtains drawn to block the sun, and held one another. Ulric fell into a fitful sleep right away, but Auren couldn't do it. Instead, he lay there, stroking lazy circles through the hair along Ulric's chest, worry knotting his insides.

The sand was cool beneath their feet. Ulric had slept most of the day, and even still, he looked exhausted. The tide receded, leaving behind glistening ribbons of seaweed. They walked slowly, side by side. Auren kept glancing sideways at Ulric.

"You alright?" Auren asked.

Ulric nodded. "I am fine, spriteling." He tried for a teasing tone, but it fell flat.

Auren rounded on him, planting his feet in the sand with a determined glare.

"Enough, Ulric. You have to tell me what's going on. Is it the drain on your magic? Is that what's happening? Then why am I not sick? What in Poseidon's sea is going on?"

He didn't mean for his voice to rise, but it had.

"I can't... keep watching you do this to yourself... for me."

Ulric let out an exhausted sigh.

"Holding this shape is... difficult for me right now." He admitted.

"And me?"

"I've been... helping you in that regard as well."

Auren's stomach sank. He knew it. So Ulric was using his precious strength to hold them both in this form.

"And you refuse to return to Atlantis because of what my mother would say? C'mon, Ulric, you can't expect me to believe that. I know you. You might be her Sorcerer, but you've always swum by your own currents. What's really going on?"

Even as he asked it, he didn't know if he was ready to hear the answer. Ready to pop this utopic bubble they'd lived in these past few weeks.

Ulric didn't respond with words, but with a pleading look. A look begging Auren not to ask him that exact question.

"Sit with me," Ulric said, and whether he wanted to talk or because he could no longer bring himself to stand, he settled himself in the sand. Auren sat beside him, leaning his head on Ulric's shoulder without putting too much of his weight there.

"I can convince the courts, Ulric… and even if I can't, then— I'd run away with you," Auren said in a whisper, but by the hitch in the Kraken's breath, he knew Ulric had heard him.

The Kraken exhaled, the sound low and rough, like something being dragged from the deep. He didn't look at Auren when he spoke.

"I thought I could carry it," he said, voice strained. "Bury it. Bear it alone without allowing it to burden your shoulders. But after everything…" He finally turned, meeting Auren's gaze. "I can't."

Auren searched those endless obsidian eyes.

Ulric leaned closer, his voice mixing with the song of crashing waves.

"I need you to know," he said. "Before anything else happens… that I'm in love with you."

Auren's throat tightened. His first instinct was joy. Then terror.

Because Ulric didn't say things like that.

Not unless he thought there wasn't time to say it again.

Auren swallowed hard. "I'm in love with you, too."

He reached out, cupped Ulric's cheek, and felt the faint

warmth of him beneath his palm. A stinging invaded his eyes, and he hated it for blackening this moment. But there was something here with them—something dark and lurking, ready to snatch this moment away, and Auren felt like he was fighting it blind.

"But why do you sound like you're saying goodbye?"

Ulric gave a soft, bitter smile. "Because I don't know what tomorrow holds."

"Don't," Auren said sharply. "Don't say that. I won't let them tear us apart, Ulric. No matter what Atlantis has to say, I'll be here. By your side."

"I know," Ulric said, leaning into his touch. "But I had to tell you... just in case."

He took Auren's hand and pressed a kiss to his knuckles. "I'll fight for every breath," he whispered. "But if anything happens... I need to know you heard me say it."

Auren's heart cracked down the center.

He pulled Ulric close, arms tight around his back, burying his face in the hollow of his neck. The ocean breathed for them. The wind curled their hair. They held one another in the hush between night and morning, hearts pressed tight, souls opened like wounds.

They returned to the cabin as dawn began to warm the sky.

Ulric fell into bed with a tired groan, and Auren crawled in after him, tucking himself into the crook of Ulric's body. The Kraken's arm wrapped around him automatically.

Auren stared at the wooden wall, eyes wide, body still trembling with unspoken fear.

This was love. It was comfort and heat and belonging. It was the one place he'd ever felt truly at home.

And it terrified him.

Because people didn't say things like Ulric had said unless they were preparing to disappear.

Please, Auren thought, gripping Ulric's hand tightly in the dark. *Please don't go.*

As his eyes drifted shut, he caught the faint shimmer of ink vanishing—another of Ulric's tattoos dissolving, leaving the skin bare.

Ulric was fading.

Auren closed his eyes.

And fell asleep in the arms of the man he loved, terrified it might be the last time.

Chapter Twenty Five

Ulric

Ulric awoke to the sound of gulls and the hot breeze of an open window. His limbs felt heavy, and each breath was harder than the last, like treading water for hours. He breathed deeply, expecting the salty smell of the sea, but there was none. No ocean breeze carried by the wind. No lingering scent of Auren's skin. Ulric took a deep breath through his nose, but detected nothing. It was as though that very sense was stripped from him.

What would go next? His hearing? His sight?

He tried not to think about it as he rolled over, feeling the faint rays of the sun on his bare back. It was warm already, the kind of heat that promised a good day for drying herbs or letting washed clothes stiffen on the line. A lazy sort of heat that wrapped the cabin like a cocoon.

How dare this world be as beautiful as this, even as his world was falling apart, right before his eyes?

And as he forced himself upright, the most beautiful thing in all of creation turned its head and smiled at him. Auren sat cross-legged on the floor, a peeled orange in his lap and a book in his hands. His red hair caught the morning light and glowed around his face.

"Good afternoon," Auren said, returning his focus to the citrus.

"Is it that late already?" Ulric groaned, letting the blanket fall from his chest. He didn't need to look to know it was almost devoid of all tattoos.

"It is. But I figured you needed the rest," Auren said without looking up.

"Mhm."

They sat for several silent heartbeats, with nothing but the sound of orange rinds falling to the floor and the faint snap of the curtains.

"You're staring," Auren said without looking up.

"I'm allowed," Ulric replied.

"You're being creepy."

"That's my right, too."

Auren snorted and threw a piece of orange at him. It hit Ulric's shoulder and rolled onto the blanket.

"There, eat. I peeled that with love."

"You peeled it with nails like a savage," Ulric said, inspecting the decimated orange slice.

Auren leaned over, stealing the piece from Ulric's fingers with his teeth. "Says the man who once told a room full of nobles I had mistaken a trident for a backscratcher."

Ulric didn't even flinch. "To be fair, you were scratching your back with it."

"I had an itch. And no one was supposed to be watching."

"You were in full ceremonial garb. On a balcony."

"And you let them believe I didn't know what a weapon was."

Ulric leaned back into the pillows with a smug smile. "I thought it added character."

"You're insufferable."

"I love you, too."

They bickered like that back and forth, eating fruits and talking of nothing. Every time Auren made a sharp remark, Ulric gave one back, even if it took effort. He laughed, even when it made him dizzy. He listened as Auren told stories of his childhood, about sneaking out of the palace to talk to Iska and carve rude words into the coral walls. Ulric taught him human games using cards and dice. By late afternoon, Auren was winning every round.

"You're losing your edge, old man."

"Yes, celebrate your shallow victory against a fatigued opponent."

"Do I detect the smell of—" he took an exaggerated sniff, "Yes, there it is. Smells like a sore loser."

Ulric grabbed Auren by the back of the neck, smashing their mouths together for the first time that day, though it felt like they hadn't touched in lifetimes. Auren made a startled little sound, and Ulric wished for the strength to pour his love onto this man using every inch of his body.

But he just couldn't....

"You're lucky I find you so appealing, spriteling."

Auren stuck out his tongue, and Ulric dove to snatch it into his mouth. They laughed into the kiss together. Lost in the simplicity of the moment.

They didn't speak of what might happen tomorrow. Or the next day. Or the next. They didn't mention Atlantis, or the court, or Poseidon's judgment waiting like storm clouds on the horizon.

Every time the words hovered on Auren's tongue, Ulric reached out and touched him—his hand, his cheek, the back of his neck—and the question would pass unspoken. It was kinder that way.

The truth would come. Ulric didn't need to summon it with words.

The sun was high, and the tide had gone out. Ulric was tired of being indoors all day, despite having no strength to do anything else. When he asked for a walk, Auren didn't hesitate. He tucked his shoulder beneath Ulric's, steadying him as they moved slowly along the shore. Ulric's chest tightened at the natural way in which Auren stepped in to care for him. To hold him in a time of weakness. It led Ulric down a rabbit hole of "what ifs" that left him sick to his stomach. What a pairing they would have made. Nothing in all the seas would have stopped them. Their power, their union, their love, unmatched by anything, even the might of Poseidon.

How different things might have been.

But that was for the next life, and Ulric was already mourning for how much he'd miss in this one.

Because even as he faded, the world was so painfully alive.

Seagulls shrieked overhead. The surf crashed in gentle rhythm. The sand clung warm to Ulric's feet. Auren pointed out every strange little shell, every floundering crab, and shimmer of fish between rocks. He talked just enough to keep the silence from turning heavy. Never too much. Always watching Ulric from the corner of his eye, offering a hand every time Ulric's breath hitched or his knees faltered.

"You know," Ulric said as they paused to rest on a flat, sun-warmed boulder, "if I had met you earlier in life, I would've done things differently."

Auren rested his chin on his knees. "I would've called you a grumpy bastard and avoided you for years."

"Fair."

"You would've rolled your eyes at all my human treasures and told me half of it was garbage."

"I would've moved things around just to piss you off."

"Don't you dare touch my collection."

Ulric gave him a sideways look. "You have a dozen rusted forks and a shattered lantern."

"If you didn't know what they were, you would have kept them too. And they have *charm*."

Auren laughed, but it didn't reach his eyes. He looked like he was fighting not to ask the question heavy on his mind. Ulric didn't stop him.

"Do you regret coming up here?" Auren asked. "I mean not the beginning of it." His demeanor shrank at even the mention of Elias. "But the stuff after. Staying with me up here instead of dragging me straight back home?"

Ulric reached over, took Auren's hand, and kissed the inside of his wrist. "I would have leapt out of the water to come to you a thousand times over. You are—"

He hesitated, the words clawing at the back of his throat. But Auren didn't rush him.

"You're stubborn," Ulric murmured. "Loud. Reckless. And somehow still... gentle. You have an inquisitive mind and are fierce in ways that make even the gods pay attention. You've taken everything this world gave you and turned it into something bright. And you look at me like I'm more than... just a pawn of the court." Ulric smiled faintly. "And no one's ever taken care of me like you do."

Auren looked startled. "I don't... do anything special."

"You do everything," Ulric said. "You listen. You learn. You see this world with the kind of courage nobody else dares to."

He let his fingers trace the inside of Auren's wrist, memorizing the shape.

Auren said nothing. But he squeezed his hand tightly. They

stayed like that for a while, hands clasped, foreheads almost touching, the tide hissing in retreat.

Slowly, Ulric got to his feet, brushing sand from his pants.

"Let's head back, I can teach you another game of cards—" Ulric's sentence died in his mouth.

He thought he had more time.

He thought he'd feel it coming. The moment when the gods reached out to take their due. That there would be warning—thunder, waves, some dramatic sign befitting the end of a Kraken's final chapter.

But when it came, it was in the middle of a sunny afternoon.

There was no storm.

No howling wind.

Just the cry of a gull, and the sudden, breathtaking pain lancing through his gut.

Ulric stumbled, grabbing at Auren's shoulder. He gasped once, then dropped to one knee.

"Ulric?!" Auren cried, catching him—but not fast enough. Ulric crumpled forward, eyes wide.

The sand was warm beneath his palms. Too warm. His vision swam.

"Auren..." he rasped.

Auren fell to the ground beside him, hands gripping his arms. "What is it? What's happening?!"

Ulric looked up, barely able to hold his head steady.

"Go... back," he whispered.

"Do you need a tonic? Which one? I can run and get—"

"No." Ulric rasped. "Go home. Go to Atlantis. I can't hold it anymore."

And as the sunlight spilled across the sea like ambrosia, he thought—

This should've happened at night.

The world shouldn't have looked so delighted by his demise.

But it did.
And now...
Now he had to say goodbye.

Chapter Twenty Six

Auren

"ULRIC!"

His name tore from Auren's throat as he fell to the sand, hands sliding beneath the Kraken's shoulders, trying to keep him upright. Ulric was trembling, skin ghost-pale, every breath coming ragged and wet.

"Stay with me—please, come on, talk to me!"

Ulric's tattoos were vanishing. One by one, those ancient symbols, marks that once pulsed with magic, dissolved like ink in water, leaving pale, bare skin in their wake. The lines on his chest faded beneath Auren's fingers. His arms. His throat. Gone.

Ulric's lips parted, his breath a ragged gasp as though each tattoo that faded was a vital part of him. On his forearm, a final tattoo flared white-hot, casting sharp light across the sand. Auren watched, stunned, as the ancient glyph pulsed, not fading like the others, but glowing brighter, glowing defiantly, as though the very ink of it had caught fire.

It wasn't burning out.

It was burning to speak.

One last message.

"What does it say?" Auren asked, his voice shaking. He knew it was important. That this one was different. "Ulric—what does it say?"

Ulric grit his teeth, voice rasping. "Oath... breaker."

Auren's eyebrows knit in confusion. What oath? What had Ulric done to— but his thoughts were erased as Ulric's body went slack in his arms. Like he wasn't trying to get up anymore.

"No, no—don't you dare," Auren choked. "I've got you. I'll get you back to the cabin. I'll give you your tonics—"

Ulric shook his head. "Auren, listen. You have to go. Go back to the sea. I can't—can't hold it any longer."

Auren reeled. "No. No, I'm not leaving you. All you need is a tonic, and it'll get better," Auren gently laid Ulric's head on the sand, standing, ready to take off at a run. "I'll be back with—"

Then pain.

Agony.

It lanced through his neck and into his throat, as though claws sank behind his ears and dragged down, tearing him open. He staggered, eyes wide, clutching his neck as his knees buckled. He gasped—no, *screamed*—as the fire spread into his legs, his calves cramping, bones grinding beneath skin that didn't feel like his own.

And then—just as fast as it had come—it vanished. A shaky, phantom ache lingering in its place.

Ulric looked up at him, eyes full of pain and—*guilt*.

"It's what I've been holding back," he rasped. "All this time… I've kept it off you."

Auren's heart broke open. This was what Ulric had been bearing. The weight. The agony he took upon himself to give Auren just a few more days in a borrowed body.

"Come with me," Auren begged. But Ulric didn't move— didn't even try. Panic flared sharp in Auren's chest. "Then I'll carry you, you stubborn ass!" he shouted, looping Ulric's arm over his shoulder. "I'll carry you—we'll make it to the water, just hold on—"

But he barely managed a few staggering steps before Ulric let out a cry that ripped the sky open. His body jerked, twisted, and then *erupted*.

A sickening sound split the air as his clothes shredded apart. Muscle rippled, and from his back erupted all nine tentacles— slick, black, massive. They curled on the sand like wounded things, recoiling from the heat of the sun as though it burned. The Kraken had returned in full. The sight stole Auren's breath—and what remained of his strength.

Another scream burst from his lips as he hit the ground, clutching his ribs as pain flared again. Gills tore open on his neck, his vision fractured with pressure. His Mer form clawing its way to the surface.

"No—no, I can't—"

He couldn't hear himself over the roar of the tide, as though the sea were calling him home.

"Go!" Ulric's voice wasn't human anymore. It echoed, reverberated—deeper than any voice should go. "It's taking all I have to keep it off you. Please, *go!*"

Auren couldn't breathe. He couldn't *think* through the panic.

"I *won't* leave you!"

"As soon as you hit the sea," Ulric growled, "you'll transform. I won't have to hold it anymore. I'll have enough strength to follow. But not unless you go. *You have to go first.*"

Auren's chest heaved. Gills tore wide, fluttering. The pain was unbearable—but Ulric was right. He could *feel* it. The second he submerged, the transformation would be complete. Ulric could release him. And they'd survive this.

"You'll be right behind me?"

Auren's voice was a raw, bleeding wound.

"Yes," Ulric gasped. "I swear."

"I'll be waiting."

Then, with legs barely steady enough to hold him, Auren turned toward the ocean-

-and ran.

Sea and sand blurred in his vision as the world tilted. Auren held onto consciousness by sheer will alone. Each step a war against his own body. But he didn't stop until his feet slammed into the first rush of incoming tide.

The moment salt water touched his skin, the pain hit him full force. Auren screamed as the ocean yanked him under. His body convulsed. His vision went white.

He felt it then—the release. A protective grip around his body, one he hadn't even known was there, let go. Ulric had been holding him the entire time. Without that shield, the full weight of Poseidon's blood ripped through him. Tore him open and reshaped his flesh.

There was no mercy of unconsciousness this time. Auren felt every twist of sinew and bone, every searing shift beneath his skin as his legs fused, his spine elongated, and his scales erupted. The gills at his neck flared wide, and fins split from his hips and wrists like living sails.

It was agony.

His scream dissolved into bubbles. Water flooded his ears. Still, even in the white-hot hell of transformation, Auren waited.

For a splash.

A pulse of magic.

The humming ripple of someone entering the sea behind him.

He waited, breathless in his gills, tail twitching where it had reformed—sleek and green and opalescent, as though it had never left.

The water swirled around him. Silent. Empty.

Nothing came.

No surge. No shadows in the deep.

Only the crash of white-capped waves above him and the shifting tide around his body.

Please. Please. Please.

But with every heartbeat, every passing moment—

The dreadful words in the back of his mind surged forward. Until they were no longer words. But screams.

He isn't coming.

Auren's tail curled weakly beneath him, twitching in disbelief. His chest heaved as if he still needed to breathe air. The truth hit him with the weight of a sinking ship.

Ulric was gone.

Not following. Not behind him.

Gone.

Ulric said he would follow. When Auren transformed, he'd have the strength to meet him in the water. He swore.

He lied.

Auren's heart lurched in his chest. He was helpless. Powerless. His magic was hidden somewhere inside him—dormant, unreachable—coiled deep in his blood like a sleeping beast. Useless. Stagnant. It couldn't do a damn thing to help him.

A scream clawed its way up Auren's throat, hands tearing at his hair in rage — And then, like a mountain falling, realization crushed him.

The tattoo.

The final mark.

"Oath Breaker."

Weeks ago, in the cave, Ulric's voice, quiet and distant:

"Those of the Kraken people chosen by Poseidon's will to wield his magic… do not take mates. We serve. That is our calling. That is our promise."

Auren's lips parted.

How had he not seen it?

How had he not put it together?

By falling in love with him…

By coming on land to save him…

By choosing Auren over Poseidon—

Ulric had broken his sacred oath.

And now…

Now he was paying the price.

Auren let out a sound that didn't belong in this world. A wail of grief, rage, despair. He curled beneath the waves, clutching his chest.

But something inside him hardened. He would not let this be the end. He surged upward, a trail of foam and fury in his wake.

No. I refuse. I won't!

With one violent thrust of his tail, Auren shot through the water, slicing toward the surface like an arrow loosed from a bow.

He broke through the shattering waves, flinging his body to shore.

He landed hard.

Auren's tail hit the sand with a sickening thud, the impact dazing him momentarily. Gravity laughed at him, the weight of his Mer body dragging along the beach like a dying thing. Heavy. Mired. A creature who had no business being on land.

The sand was scorching, searing into his skin. His human footprints, made only minutes before, vanished under his weight as he clawed forward. His elbows and palms scraped raw. He didn't care.

He didn't stop. Auren dragged himself forward—up the slope, through dune grass and sun-dried kelp, back toward the place where Ulric fell.

Auren would find him.

He would drag them both back to the sea if it killed him.

"Ulric!" he cried, wasting breath he didn't have. His voice cracked like a whip across the empty shore.

No answer.

The wind whispered. The waves crashed. But no one called back.

"Ulric!" he screamed again, throat raw, the salt from his tears stinging the open, gasping gills at his neck.

Still nothing.

Auren forced himself further inland, fingers digging trenches in the sand. His tail caught on a rock and tore open along the scales. Blood smeared the dunes in streaks as he dragged himself.

Auren didn't care.

He didn't care if every human on the island saw him. He didn't care if he suffocated. He didn't care if he died doing this.

He had to find him.

And then—

Not a body. Not a shape.

But a shadow.

A mark in the sand like a scorch or a stain. The outline of a collapsed man, but lower—lower the silhouette of nine long, coiled tentacles sprawled across the beach like ink spilled from a dying god.

Auren choked.

He reached forward, trembling, and touched it.

Sand.

Just sand.

Blackened grains, fine as powder, warm from the sun. But it had shape. *His* shape.

Auren's fingers clawed through it, trying to find something

beneath—bone, cloth, anything. But there was nothing. No weight. No resistance. Just dust. Ash. Absence.

"No."

His voice cracked. Broke.

He grabbed at the sand again, holding it in both hands, letting it sift between his fingers like spilled time.

And truth descended on him like a messenger of death. Ulric was gone.

"No, no, NO!"

Auren's howl split the sky.

"DAMN YOU!" he screamed. He was gasping now, all the breath gone from his body. Wasted in his wails. But the cursing didn't stop in the confines of his mind, even as his body began to reject the land it rested on.

"Damn you, Poseidon! Damn your oath, damn your laws, damn your fucking judgment!"

He slammed his fists into the earth. He clawed at the sand until his palms bled, until the black grains were embedded under his nails.

"You took him!" Auren sobbed. *"He broke the rules for me... and you punished him for it!"*

His tail thrashed behind him, kicking sand and rocks, drying fast in the heat. His gills fluttered, gasping. His whole body screamed for the water, but Auren stayed.

He crumpled over the mark in the sand, clutching the last remnants of the only man who had ever truly loved him.

"You bastard," Auren whispered with the last of his held breath. "You left me. You said you'd follow. You said you'd be right behind me..."

He curled around the mark as if he could shield it.

Hold it.

Hold him.

He buried his face in the sand, fingers tangled in the shape of Ulric's memory.

"Please come back..."
But no one came.
No great hand reached from the sea.
No dark figure appeared on the horizon.
Auren closed his eyes, and his final breath—shallow, dry, too thin for gills—shuddered through him.
And as the blackness crept in, his last thought was not of the pain, nor the rage.
It was of eyes like the deepest trench.
And a kiss soft enough to tame storms.

Chapter Twenty Seven

Auren

D*RIP*.

Drip.

Drip.

Auren winced as raindrops pattered on his eyelid.

Drip.

Drip.

Drip.

No. Not raindrops. These were too precise to be the scattering of rain. A steady stream of droplets fell deliberately over his left eye.

Drip

Drip

Drip

With each drop, awareness returned to him. Bit by bit, until he had the strength to flinch away from the intrusion and turn his head, sputtering. Auren coughed, spitting sand from his mouth. He inhaled—lungs, not gills.

He sat up, half expecting to find legs beneath him. He was disappointed to see a sand-covered green tail, the scales caked with blood, dry and cracked in the scorching sun.

"No, I did not transform you fully. I gave you breath, that is enough."

The voice came a little ways down the beach, carried by the early evening wind. The sky shifted into a pale peach and blue. The hushed light made the sand appear flushed pink. All except the tendrils of black curled around Auren. It was still there, a shadow left imprinted on the sand. All that remained of a mighty sorcerer who had dedicated centuries to an ungrateful god.

Tears sprang to Auren's eyes.

"The sea does not need your tears. It has enough salt," the voice said again, a woman's.

"And what makes you think I'm offering them to the sea?" Auren snapped, anger and grief mixing in a toxic pool in his stomach. "Poseidon has taken enough; he does not get my tears. They're for..."

But he couldn't bring himself to even say the name.

Auren looked at the human woman, his eyes aching as though he'd stared into the sun for too long. Her skin was dark, smooth, and her legs were bare beneath a delicate short burlap dress. The way she tucked her knees to her chest made her appear young, almost childlike with seashells woven into a mane of flowing black hair. But when she turned her silver eyes on him, Auren knew this was no girl. That this was no human.

"Mother."

"Hmmm." She hummed, with a pleased little tilt to her head that once again made her glow with youth. "I rather like that. At home, you only ever address me as the queen."

Auren didn't know what to say. His relationship with his mother had always been that of queen and prince. But seeing her here, in human form, something about her rigid, steely grip seemed to relax. Her muscles loosened, finally allowing for the kind of relationship mother and son ought to have.

"Why did you save me?" Auren asked, wincing as every inch of his lower body hurt.

"Does a mother need a reason to save her youngest son?"

"No. But I am sure you have one."

She sighed, long and hard. The wind caught a few strands of hair, which danced in the air. Instead of answering him, her eyes grew distant, maybe a little tired. It was the first time he'd ever seen his mother this way.

"I forgot how nice it is. The wind. The warm breeze. Sand between my toes," she said, wiggling her toes in solemn delight. "But I made my choice. A long, long time ago. Now, my precious son, it is time you make yours."

At Auren's wide-eyed look of shock, she threw her head back and laughed, a trilly sound like the call of birds. Not the Queen of the sea.

"Did you think you knew me so well?" She laughed, slender shoulders shaking. "No, I'm afraid you don't know me at all, and I do not know you. That is my fault."

She twirled a finger in the sand.

"As Queen of the sea, mother of Poseidon's heirs, I don't make it a habit to reveal my heritage. But I suppose, Auren, that as you stand on the cliffside of a choice, the same cliffside I once stood on - I can impart this wisdom."

Auren stared at his mother, and it felt like he was seeing her for the first time. Not as an untouchable entity, but as a person. As his mother.

"I was born on land, the daughter of a sea merchant. I came into this world with legs and no tail." She shuffled her long legs as though reveling in the feeling of them. "When my father's ship was lost at sea, my entire family succumbed to the ocean's wrath. And I would have been part of that number if I hadn't been offered a choice. A choice to live lifetimes, to bring about the next generation of half-gods into the world, to witness things a sheltered human girl could scarcely imagine. I had a choice, and as I stood on that cliffside, I chose to jump."

Auren listened without interruption. But her words struck a sort of sorrow he hadn't expected. Had she really been given a choice? Bear the burden of being one of Poseidon's chosen, or drown. In Auren's mind, that wasn't a choice at all. Yet now, he faced a very similar fate.

"I tell you this so you know the gravity, the permanence of your choice. I gave up my human life in exchange for another. I cannot take that back." She straightened, then, "Nor do I want to. I am satisfied with what the centuries have given me, most of all my wonderful children." She smiled at him then, and fresh tears prickled the corner of his eyes.

"Make a choice you won't regret, my son. I have given you temporary breath on the surface, but it is a small blessing. You must choose quickly."

With that, she stood, brushing sand from her legs. The motion was so natural, so human, that Auren was taken aback. She approached him, all youth and elegance, as the wind rippled the hem of her dress. Her gaze drifted to the scorch-mark silhouette in the sand.

"He made his choice," she said. "Now it's your turn."

Auren's chest cracked open. "He saved me."

Tritheya nodded. "He did."

"He broke his oath for me," Auren said.

"He did."

"He..." A fresh sob overtook him. "He loved me."

His mother's voice softened. "Of that, my son, I have no doubt."

Hearing it from her broke him open all over again. He folded over the sand, weeping. Tritheya laid a hand on his back.

"Choose, Auren," she said, her voice like a lullaby. "But do not forget... no matter the path, you are the descendant of a god." Then Queen Tritheya bent low, placing a soft kiss on his forehead. Auren closed his eyes, sinking into the moment, and when he opened them, she was gone.

He stayed crouched over the shape of Ulric, trembling, teeth gritted against the war waging inside him. Anger and grief battled for dominance like waves pounding on a cliffside, trying to tear it down inasmuch as the rocks held their ground.

Choice. As though he had one. What was his choice? To say farewell and return as prince of the sea? To die on the sand in the shadow of his lover?

That wasn't a choice, because no matter which way he went— Auren's life was over.

No.

No.

No!

His hand gripped the blackened sand. He snarled, slamming his palm into it.

Fuck this.

He didn't want peace. He didn't want closure.

He wanted Ulric.

Auren thought of Ulric's hands, large enough to protect him but gentle as a spring tide. He thought of the kisses. Of the whispered confessions. Of how alive Ulric made him feel. That love still existed. It wasn't gone. And that love had power.

Somewhere deep in Auren's blood, his magic slept. Coiled. Hidden. Waiting patiently for the sea god's call on his thirtieth birthday.

But Auren didn't care about Poseidon's will. He didn't care

about any god that stood in his way. Fuck them. This magic, this power, it was *his*. And it was time to come out.

"Get out," Auren yelled. "Come out. Now!"

He reached inside himself—not gently, not with coaxing, but like a man ripping open his own chest. He seized the slippery, ancient thing that pulsed inside him. It didn't want to be touched. But Auren didn't care.

"You cannot hide anymore," he said through gritted teeth. "You don't get to stay quiet while he's gone."

He clawed at his chest, imagining his own will reaching into his blood, digging out divine power from his veins. It splashed around, trying to escape him, like a fish in a barrel. But Auren seized around its belly, squeezing with brutal strength, demanding it submit to him.

He pulled the whale bone clasp from his tangled hair—Ulric's gift. The runes etched into its curve shimmered with echoes of magic.

Auren stabbed it into the center of the lifeless sandy shape.

"Bring him back!" Auren yelled, then shoved his unwilling magic into the bone clasp.

All of it. He wouldn't leave even a single drop.

It was like trying to force a large bony fish through a small hole. It squirmed and resisted, pushing at the edges, fighting him.

"I said GO!"

The black grains began to sizzle.

The magic began to mold. To bend and twist through his veins, syphoning into the whale bone in his grip. It turned from a bony fish into something softer. Something easily molded by Auren's will. Like an octopus, capable of forcing its bulk through even the smallest opening.

"That's it— you obey *me*."

Auren poured everything into it—every ounce of grief, fury, love. Every kiss. Every memory. Every whispered promise.

"I am the prince of the sea," Auren hissed. "And I will not bow to anyone. Not a god. Not magic. Not death."

The sand flared hot.

Then molten.

Like melting glass, it shifted, rippling under his will. It resisted. It fought.

But Auren didn't stop.

His hands shook from the force of channeling, gripping the whale bone like it was his only tether to his realm. His blood hummed, a current surging from his chest to his fingertips. The sand began to shape. Stretch. Elongate.

It was taking form.

A shape he knew in his bones.

Ulric's.

All nine tentacles curled outward like the petals of a great bloom, reaching for him. The body rose from the earth—man and monster in glass, hardening in the sunlight.

Auren didn't breathe as the molten sand twisted into Ulric's face. That jaw... those eyes.

The whalebone burned white hot in his hands, scorching his skin. The overload of magic spilled out in blasts of light and energy.

Just a little more, a little more.

Auren stood, thrusting the ball of white light towards the warping glass, demanding its obedience. He stood tall on his legs, chest heaving, hand engulfed in flames.

When had he shifted? His legs had returned. Human. Steady. He didn't even notice it happened. His whole being had been focused on this.

On his Kraken.

At last, the molten glass stilled, hardening in the dry air, creaking and cracking as it settled in its weight. With a final pulse of light, the whale bone shattered in Auren's hand. It was done.

Auren gasped, as though he'd been holding his breath. Maybe

he had. He wobbled, the drain of magic almost sending him back to the sand. But he kept his feet under him because nothing could have taken his eyes from the sculpture before him.

There he was. Ulric.

The likeness was made of black glass, shining in the setting sun, casting rainbows at his feet. It was perfect.

"My Ulric."

Unable to stop himself, Auren stumbled forward, falling into the glass embrace. It was ice cold.

"Come back to me."

He pressed his cheek into black glass. Eyes closed. Begging. Auren ducked his face into the familiar crook of Ulric's shoulder.

"Come back to me," Auren whispered. "Come back to me... my monster of the deep."

He shut his eyes. Held tighter.

Please.

A warmth.

A rush of heat beneath his palms.

Then a pulse.

A breath.

Glass cracked.

Cracked again.

And arms—flesh and bone and solid and warm—wrapped around him.

A voice rumbled in his ear, low, familiar, and choked with tears.

"Oh, my spriteling."

Auren sobbed.

And gripped his Kraken.

Epilogue

Auren

She was called Tritheya. With a mighty bow in the shape of the Queen, the ship was every bit as magnificent as her namesake. Auren thought it appropriate that he pay this homage to the Queen, his mother. For her gift of giving him a chance. A choice. And Auren had made his choice, even if it meant never seeing his mother again.

Because Auren was, irrevocably, unapologetically... human.

He'd given all of himself to bring back the man he loved. He poured all of his divinity into that whale bone to shape the sands.

Auren had cried then. They both had.

At the relief, the terror, and the humbling truth of their situation. Ulric harbored residual guilt regarding their permanent humanity. Auren knew he did; he saw it in the stoop of his shoulders, or when Ulric caught Auren staring at the shore for too long.

But Auren would have made that choice a hundred times over. If it were a choice between the sea and Ulric, Auren would have stood by as the sun god dried the sea into a desert. Because nothing called to him as strongly as the embrace of the Kraken.

"The waters look quiet, my Lord; it should be a good voyage."

"Should be," Auren replied, hair tied back, vest strapped tight with a long, emerald jewel dangling from one ear. "Get your men ready, we set off at high tide."

"Yes, my Lord," said the crewmaster who began barking orders at the men, as they pulled ropes, checked rigging, and fastened masts.

A hand slid to the small of Auren's back, and he didn't need to look to know who it was. It was in his smell—cold water and black oceans. It was in his silent footsteps and the teasing pressure of his fingertips.

"There is something rather attractive about the way you command the crew," Ulric whispered, leaning in to kiss the shell of Auren's ear.

"Would you like me to command you as well?" Auren teased, leaning back, resting his head into the familiar slope of Ulric's shoulder.

"You already do, spriteling. Mind, body, and soul." His hands crept to the front of Auren's corset vest, teasing the hem, slipping a single finger beneath the tight cloth.

"Easy, Kraken. The crew might be tolerant, but I don't think that extends to full-on exhibitionism."

Ulric growled at the notion.

"I cannot wait to get you over that balcony again."

Auren's heart fluttered, heat pooling instantly below his navel. Tickets had just gone on sale for the private theater's exclusive "show of pleasures," reserved for only the highest-ranking Nobles and Lords. Auren couldn't wait. Couldn't wait to be thrown back into those silks, bent over the mahogany railing and...

"Easy there."

Auren lurched forward. He hadn't noticed he'd begun rubbing his ass against Ulric's tenting front. He cleared his throat.

"Well, Captain, I say we shove off and get out to sea."

"Of course, Captain," Ulric said with a slight incline of his head and a glint in those abyssal eyes.

At sea, they were both captains. And on land, they were Lords. Ulric's vast stores of sunken treasure (far more than Auren had first imagined) had granted them entry into the higher echelon of human society. As Ulric's mate, that title of Lord was extended to him as well. Of course, they presented themselves as "business partners" to most, and as "comrades" to those they knew more personally. Humans had no concept of mates or the ties that bound one being to another. But Auren didn't mind dancing around the terminology. That's all it was at the end of the day. A label. Nothing that would affect the bond that tied Ulric to him on a cellular level.

And with the title of Lord came opportunities.

Auren was given space in the royal court: a vast studio carved from stone and glass, where light filtered through perfectly every sunrise. And he was also given freedom. The freedom to create. Ulric quickly learned that Auren could not pass a discarded thing without seeing what it *might become*. Driftwood warped by the sea, fragments of broken statuary, rusted metal hauled from old wrecks, coral snapped and cast aside—what others dismissed as refuse found new life in his hands.

Auren sculpted obsessively, tirelessly. His pieces grew stranger and more breathtaking with each passing month: figures caught mid-motion, forms that seemed to breathe, beauty coaxed from ruin. Before long, commissions followed. His work was installed throughout the palace, then beyond it—sent to distant courts, displayed in galleries and museums, some granted permanent homes where his name would outlast him.

Still, his habits never changed.

Auren could not stop collecting, just as he had under the sea. His chambers were filled with half-finished works and careful piles of odds and ends he refused to abandon. His collection was never complete. It could never be.

But when the noise of court grew too loud—when marble echoed with boots and expectation pressed too tightly around his ribs—Auren escaped to Tritheya, where the water opened wide and creation came easier. Her magnificent helm felt like a second home, and though sometimes melancholic, Auren would never be able to eradicate the salt from his blood. The sea was a part of him, however distant.

They departed from the harbor and onto the open, endless horizon. Once they were well and out to sea, they were joined by Iska, chattering and bobbing in and out of the waves at the ship's wake. The men hollered, whooping as she jumped for show. They saw her love for their Captains as a good omen and basically considered her a part of the crew. Auren waited patiently, knowing he'd swim with her soon.

"Sky looks awfully clear," Ulric said as Auren manned the helm, salt air blowing red strands into his eyes. But unlike the men, Ulric sounded disappointed by the prospect of clear weather. "You sure about this? I don't know how much longer I can wait to get you beneath me." Ulric said, once again, standing far closer than "co-captains" might.

"Do I hear doubt in your voice?" Auren asked in mock offense.

"Not doubt. But my paper-thin patience is about to break and drag you to the captain's quarters, storm be damned." Ulric leaned close, his voice rumbling like thunder.

Auren settled his back into the Kraken, sucking in his warmth before stomping on his boot and shoving him away with a hip.

"You're going to have to restrain yourself."

Ulric pinched his ass before whispering, "You'll pay for that, spriteling."

Auren was counting on it.

And Auren's instincts, as ever, were right.

The storm broke fast across the clear sky, thunder cracking like a war drum as gray clouds boiled above. The men groaned, tossing hats to the deck, curses flying as the ship began to pitch and roll. Wind shrieked through the rigging like a banshee.

But Auren—Auren could hardly hide the grin twisting his mouth. He'd steered them straight into the heart of it.

"Get below! Captain's orders!" he bellowed, crimson hair whipping around his face.

"But sir, the masts—we need more men to manage—!"

"I said that's an order! Trust in your captains!"

With a roguish grin and a playful threat of the plank, he waved the men below deck, shouting exaggerated curses at any sailor brave enough to hesitate. They obeyed, as they always did. Because this was tradition now.

The storm was for the captains.

Only the captains.

As the last hatch slammed shut, Auren turned to find Ulric already watching him—his grin as wild as the waves churning below.

"Now," Auren said, voice crackling like the wind between them, "it's our turn."

Ulric grabbed him without a word, hands fisting into Auren's damp shirt, dragging him in until their mouths collided with a fury that rivaled the sky. Rain lashed against their skin, but neither pulled away. The storm roared around them, but they only kissed harder.

This—this—was when they came alive. When the sky bled

into the sea, and the horizon disappeared. When memory blurred, and for a breathless instant, they weren't men at all, but gods—Kraken and Prince—echoes of myth.

Ulric's fingers worked quickly, tugging Auren's vest open, slipping beneath the fabric to feel hot skin against chilled rain. Auren's hands tangled in Ulric's hair, nails biting his scalp, their bodies pressed so tight together it was hard to tell where one ended, and the other began.

"Clothes off," Ulric purred against his mouth. "Now."

"Demanding," Auren panted, but he obeyed, yanking the drenched cloth over his head and off his legs, just as Ulric's teeth grazed his collarbone.

They were frenzied, half-mad as rain pelted their skin, heightening the sensation. They were clawing for each other beneath a wrathful sky when a sharp, indignant whistle cut through the chaos.

They both froze, blinking like boys caught sneaking kisses behind a chapel.

A second whistle, more insistent, echoed across the waves, followed by a trilling, unmistakable squeak.

Iska.

She surfaced beside the ship, bobbing with clear disapproval, spitting bursts of water onto the deck like a sulking child.

"She's rather impatient," Auren sighed, dragging rain-slicked fingers through his hair and trying not to laugh.

"She always was the jealous type."

He leaned in one more time, licking into Auren's mouth like a promise, the taste of rain and lust thick on their tongues. "Go to her," he whispered. "I'll manage up here. But have no doubt, my prince—I will have you when you return."

Auren stepped back, lips swollen, skin flushed with the heat only Ulric could summon.

"Well," he said, sass curling around every word, "with how desperate you look, I should keep you waiting more often."

Ulric tilted his head. "Desperate?"

"Mhm," Auren teased, backing toward the railing. "You're one thunderclap away from dragging me below deck by the hair."

Ulric lunged, grabbing him by the waist.

"Ulric—don't you da—!"

And without ceremony, Ulric hurled his naked body overboard.

Auren's shriek split the wind as he flailed dramatically into the waves, vanishing beneath the surface with a splash. Moments later, he burst up laughing, wiping water from his eyes.

"You ass! I was going to jump anyway!"

Ulric leaned casually over the railing, his single fang earring dangling on one side as he crossed his arms. "Then I saved you the effort, spriteling."

Auren flipped him off, still grinning, as the ocean shifted beneath him.

With a sharp chirp, Iska surged from below, lifting him easily onto her sleek, scarred back. She chattered, circling the ship with joyful leaps that sprayed salt into the air.

Auren clung to her, beaming and breathless. "My loyal girl," he murmured, stroking her side.

Above them, Ulric watched with that storm-swept smile of his —equal parts hunger and awe.

And in the rain, with the sea rolling beneath him and laughter in his chest, Auren never felt more alive.

And it was here, as Iska spun beneath him and salt kissed his lips, that Auren felt the last echoes of his past self. A self with a different body, belonging to a different world. A world of coral thrones and bioluminescent tides. A man of the sea, not the sun.

They had first discovered the final dregs of that ancient magic the last time they'd accidentally sailed into a storm. Where before his magic had been as numerous as the sands on the beach, now only granules remained. Auren felt those small grains now, humming beneath his skin.

It was, perhaps, a mercy from Poseidon. A final gift. A whisper of what had been lost.

He closed his eyes and let go.

The transformation was gentle this time. Skin shimmered, then shifted, softening into scales of emerald green. His legs fused, and the aching stretch of muscle gave way to fluid grace. The sea accepted him like an old friend. When he opened his eyes again, the world was brighter, sharper—alive.

He was Mer once more.

But not entirely.

Gills no longer opened at his throat. His chest rose and fell with the sharp rhythm of air, not water. Though his tail gleamed just as it had when he was a prince beneath the waves, it only came during the storms. When sky and sea were at war, and the veil between worlds thinned.

He could not breathe below the surface. That world was still barred to him. Lost.

So Auren surfaced often, like Iska with her blowhole, drawing great gulps of air before diving back down. The rhythm became second nature. Up, down. Breathe, glide. A shared cadence between a merman who had once belonged and a creature who had remained beside him anyway.

Together, they raced.

Through the waves, into the storm's heart, leaping high before crashing back down in twin arcs of green and black. Auren laughed as they spun, Iska clicking and chirping her joy, their movements seamless with the sea.

For a little while, they were just wild things. Free. Full of salt and speed and the memory of a world that still lived in their bones.

And even if he could never fully return, Auren had this.

Only after Auren was breathless—lungs burning and vision bright around the edges—did their play finally come to an end.

"I can see you eyeing that school of sardines," Auren panted, brushing water from his face. "Go hunt. I need to catch my breath before you drown me."

He pressed a kiss to Iska's wide, glistening nose, and she chirped in response, before wheeling around and charging into the school of silver fish.

With a final gasp of sea air, Auren turned and glided toward the ship, curling his hands around the rope ladder that swung against the hull. He paused there, floating for a heartbeat, eyes closed, calling to the sea, coaxing the magic that lived under his skin.

Muscle shifted. Fins dissolved. Skin changed.

When his toes met the bottom rung, he began to climb.

Water streamed from him, puddling beneath each step as he hauled himself aboard. The sea calmed somewhat, though the wind still tugged at the sails and the sky above churned, like it might crack open again if provoked.

He scanned the deck for Ulric, frowning when he didn't see him, until he tilted his head up.

And there he was.

Ulric's Kraken form clung to the rigging like something summoned from a sailor's nightmare. All nine of his great tentacles moved in seamless coordination, curling through ropes, securing knots, hauling lines that would take six men to move. Stormlight glinted off his bare chest, catching on every curve and hollow, while damp curls clung to his jaw. No ink marked the Kraken's skin. No tattoos, no sacred vows. Nothing to tie him to the god of the sea.

Auren watched in awe, mesmerized by the eerie elegance of it —how the long, boneless limbs didn't always wait for direction, how they moved without command, as though each thought for itself.

Ulric must've sensed the heat of his gaze, because he glanced down. "It's about time," he rumbled, and descended in a controlled sprawl, settling his bulk on the slick deck like some great beast preparing to pounce.

"Iska's off hunting," Auren started, voice light. "I think she—"

He never finished.

One of Ulric's thick tentacles shot out, fast as lightning, and wrapped around his mouth.

"Enough talking out of you," Ulric growled, stalking toward him. "You're mine."

Auren's pupils blew wide. His breath hitched. Every muscle went taut with high alert.

There was no mistaking the power difference—Ulric, ancient and godlike, his form rippling with restrained violence. Auren, bare-chested, flushed, with sea water clinging to every inch of skin. Human in every way but the defiant tilt of his chin.

Ulric could've snapped him like driftwood. Could've ruined him with a whisper. But all Auren felt was fire.

"I've been waiting far too long for this," Ulric murmured, and then Auren was flat on his back, the wet deck hard beneath him and Ulric's weight bearing down.

Tentacles slithered across the wood, forming a cage. One wrapped around his ankle, another cradled the small of his back. Ulric's hands gripped his hips hard enough to bruise. Hot breath ghosted over his throat.

"You're so small like this... so breakable. And yet you keep begging for more." Ulric whispered, eyes molten. "Do you know what that does to me?"

Auren groaned, voice muffled.

"Got something to say, my prince?"

A single sucker-lined appendage crawled up Auren's leg, teasing the sensitive skin of his inner thigh.

Auren made another sound, shivers climbing his spine, hips bucking with the need for more. More touch. More wet. More of him.

"Oh, how I love it when you sing for me. Sing, my siren."

Ulric released his mouth, and Auren drew in a sharp breath as another curling tendril slid up the crack of his ass.

"Do you intend to tease me all day? Or are you going to actually do something?" Auren goaded, but he did a poor job of hiding the desperate lilt in his voice.

Ulric's laughter rumbled against his ribs.

"Careful," he warned. "I am a beast from the deepest part of the sea. And right now, you're a very breakable human."

Auren smiled. "And yet you obey so nicely when I order you around."

Ulric lifted a dark brow. "Is that what you think you're doing?"

"Isn't it?"

He chuckled. "Spriteling, you've never had a shred of self-preservation."

"And you've never stopped lecturing me about it."

"No."

"Then why are you smiling?"

Ulric's hand tightened slightly.

"Because for all your reckless decisions, you made one exceptionally good choice."

Auren raised an eyebrow. "Oh?"

Ulric leaned closer. "You chose me."

Auren felt a thrill race through him and his heart beat faster.

"Someone had to."

A tentacle lazily coiled around his ankle, the smooth limb spreading his legs farther. Auren couldn't hold back the little whimper of longing mixed with the slightest tinge of fear.

Their time aboard the ship during storms had been rare and often brief. This was the first opportunity they'd had to explore each other this way—Ulric in his kraken form and Auren with both human legs.

Auren kicked out with one of those legs now, challenging.

A warning flickered across Ulric's face. "You're awfully brave for a human at a monster's mercy."

Auren lifted his chin defiantly.

"Y-you don't frighten me— Kraken." He put a harsh emphasis on the final word.

Ulric's mouth curved. "Bold words from a very small human."

Auren grinned. "I should warn you. I intend to put up a fight."

The look Ulric gave him was dangerously amused.

"Do you?"

"Mm-hm."

Ulric smiled, flashing sharp shark's teeth. "Good."

Auren sensed the excitement in Ulric's tone. The thrill of playing out this fantasy. But Auren wouldn't make it so easy. He kicked out, twisting and struggling. More tentacles wrapped around his joints, pinning all four limbs.

"Mmm. I like it when you fight. You're making it very difficult to restrain myself." Ulric growled, his black hair curling in wet strands around his face.

"Don't," Auren dared. "Wreck me."

The next moment, Auren felt himself go weightless as Ulric lifted him off the deck as easily as if he were a rag. Every part of him was supported, so that despite now hovering six feet in the air, he didn't feel the strain of gravity. Both his ankles were wrapped in a vicelike grip and pulled apart, exposing him in the most indecent pose, his erection in line with Ulric's face.

"It's a good thing the thunder is loud. Because I'm going to make you scream until you lose your voice, pretty siren."

Then he moved Auren's entire body to him, opening his mouth, and taking the entirety of Auren's length.

Auren cried out, mouth agape, rainwater sliding down his throat as he groaned. He reached to tangle his fingers in Ulric's hair, but two more of those powerful, rubbery limbs caught him, gripping his wrists and pinning his arms behind his back.

Ulric wasn't moving his head; rather, the tentacles were moving Auren's hips back and forth, gliding his erection along Ulric's tongue and down the channel of his throat.

"Fucking hell Ulric. You're a... a monster."

Auren tried to admonish him for the indecency of it. For the lewdness that had even Auren's cheeks flushing with embarrassment. The unceremonious position of his body, how exposed he was. It had Auren's toes curling just as much as the heat moving in languid strokes up and down his cock.

If any of the men saw...

"I barred the doors," Ulric said as though reading his mind. "Even if they try to come on deck, they can't."

Auren let out a high-pitched cry as the most subtle graze of teeth pinched his tip.

"Or," Ulric said, licking Auren's cock as though it were the most delicious treat, "would you rather they know? Would you want someone to witness you being ravaged by a monster?"

"You... you know we can't... I—ahh!"

Auren shouted in alarm as his body was rotated, and Ulric took one of his balls into his mouth, sucking at the sack.

"I can reach every part of you without having to tilt my head," Ulric said languidly, rotating Auren again like he was inspecting a valuable piece of pottery.

"Ulric, you son of a bitch put me down!" Auren yelled as he was held upside down, his hair reaching towards the deck.

"Mmm, is that an order, Captain?"

"Y-yes," Auren said, blood rushing to his head.

"As you wish. But not until I get a taste."

Before Auren could bark another command, two tentacles slid for the globes of his ass, their suckers gripping the skin and pulling them apart.

Exposed, open. Ripe for the taking.

And when Ulric's tongue licked at his puckered hole, Auren knew he was only moments from losing consciousness. Blood was rushing to opposite ends of him. Filling his cock and ringing in his ears as Ulric ate his ass while holding Auren upside down. When the Kraken's tongue pushed inside and swirled in a wide circle, Auren saw stars.

"Ulric I'm... I'm gonna..."

Auren didn't know if he was going to cum or pass out, but either way, he couldn't take much more of it. His cock swelled, and just as release came knocking at his door, the sweet warmth of Ulric's mouth disappeared. Auren whimpered at the loss.

"None of that, my prince. We aren't done here. I've imagined this far too many times to end it so quickly."

The sky spun as Ulric righted him, his head dizzy and limbs weak. When his back was once again resting on the deck of the ship, Auren blinked away the raindrops from his eyes.

"You're... cruel," he said breathily.

"You know nothing of cruelty. Yet."

Ulric descended on him, and when their lips crashed together, it was as though they were deep below the waves, and Ulric was searching Auren's mouth for his final breath.

They consumed one another, all mouths and teeth and tongue. At some point, Ulric grabbed Auren by the chin, turning his head aggressively, bearing his neck. He sucked then, hard enough for Auren to wince in pain as the tender skin below his ear was tortured. Ulric did this again and again, leaving his mark along Auren's neck and chest.

And Ulric's mouth wasn't the only part of him determined to leave its mark. Auren felt the suction-cup grip of the Kraken's tentacles curl tightly around his limbs, holding on and pulling at the skin, leaving behind a perfectly symmetrical row of red dots.

"Ulric you're... you're...mmm~"

"Yes?" Ulric hummed, but didn't remove his mouth from Auren's skin for long before diving back in for another taste. Auren felt like a starfish, spread in all four directions, unable to move.

"Please... let me touch you."

At his words, the appendages pinning his wrists let go, and Auren wove his fingers into the Kraken's hair, delighting in the handfuls of wet, silky strands. But the tentacles that released him moved to his chest. Auren looked down in time to see them line up with his nipples and...

"Ulric—Ahhhh!"

The tentacles slapped onto his chest, a sucker lining up perfectly with each nipple. Once attached, they pulled up with so much force that Auren's skin stretched a bit, and his back arched into the pulling sensation.

"Yes, yes, yes~!" Auren cried.

"That's it. Sing for me. Sing until you lose your voice crying my name."

"It's... It's too much." Auren said as the tentacles twisted and rotated over his sensitive nipples.

"On the contrary, I think it's not enough," Ulric groaned with longing. "There are still parts of you that this version of me has not seen. I will stimulate every inch of this body until you break."

Anticipation burned hot in Auren's stomach. Every muscle in his body begged for more, while simultaneously threatening to give out. Auren wanted to find where the line was—that razor's edge between insurmountable pleasure and unconsciousness.

The gentle glide of a single tentacle climbed up his leg, passed his inner thigh until the tip found his perineum, flicking at it like a tongue.

"Uuuuulric~." Auren twisted, trying to adjust the touch to where he so desperately needed it.

"Yes?" Ulric said, but even his teasing tone lost some of its edge. The Kraken above him was growing as impatient as Auren was. "Tell me what you need. I want to hear it from your pretty mouth."

"If I don't have you soon, I'm going to lose my mind."

Ulric made a sound like the growl of the ocean itself. At the same time, the tentacle at his perineum traveled lower, until it swirled around his hole, coating the puckered skin with its natural slick. The muscles of Auren's ass tightened on instinct.

"Every time I see you like this, I can't get enough. I want you like this forever. Spread for me. Begging me to wreck this perfect body."

"Please... ruin me."

With a groan, Ulric bent low, capturing Auren's mouth just as the tip of the tentacle pushed past his entrance and into his body. Auren moaned into Ulric's mouth.

"You have no idea what those sounds do to me," Ulric said between rushed kisses, all the while the tentacle slowly crept in deeper, filling Auren and stretching him.

It felt odd as it slid inside. The tentacle wasn't as hard as a cock. It gave when Auren's rim pulsed around it, soft and velvety. He didn't expect to feel it *move* so much as it twisted and rotated its way deeper.

Without meaning to, Auren's body tightened, clamping down on the intruder inside him.

"Relax for me, my love. I won't hurt you. Relax and let me show you things you've never felt before."

Auren took a deep breath, eyes closed, forcing his body to obey, to loosen and welcome Ulric in.

"That's it. There you go, now I can reach--this."

On the final word, Auren's entire body jerked, pearls of precum flying from his cock as the tip of the tentacle found his prostate.

"Oh gods~ oh gods~ " Auren panted. He was going to fall apart, he was going to...

The tentacle moved, sliding deeper, stretching his hole and pushing further into his body until... one of the suckers lined up with his prostate and—

"Look at me. I want to watch those eyes when you fall apart."

Auren forced his eyes open, tears mingling with the rain. The Kraken's volcanic gaze softened. "So beautiful."

And the tentacle pressed hard on his prostate, its sucker grabbing the bundle of nerves and pulling.

The world collapsed inward—his vision blurred, muscles locking tight as pleasure detonated inside him with white-hot force. His mouth fell open in a strangled gasp, soundless at first, then breaking into a cry that ripped through his throat like surf against jagged stone. His entire body convulsed. The sucker at his core pulled again, and stars burst behind his eyes. His hands scrambled against slick tentacles, helpless, lost, as his orgasm tore through him. Wave after wave wracked him—sweat, rain, tears indistinguishable as his body gave in, gave everything.

He sobbed Ulric's name like a prayer. Not out of pain. Out of awe. Out of *need*. Out of the unbearable, brutal beauty of being *seen* like this and *taken* like this and *loved* like this.

And when it was over, he trembled in the Kraken's grasp, wrecked and shaking, chest heaving like he'd barely survived the storm. Maybe he hadn't. Maybe this version of him was new. He felt different. Felt even more *one* with the creature above him.

Auren was only half aware of Ulric's tongue running from his abs to his chest, gathering his milky release before licking into his mouth, both of them sharing in the taste.

"Ulric... Ulric..." Auren all but sobbed, wrapping his arms around the Kraken's neck as the tentacle gently moved inside him, easing him down from oblivion.

"I've got you, my prince."

Auren trembled, suspended on the edge of ecstasy and disbelief. Rain slid down his flushed skin in rivulets, mingling with sweat, salt, and slick. He blinked up at Ulric through wet lashes, face slack with wonder and dazed satisfaction.

"Are you alright?" Ulric asked after a moment.

"Y-Yes~" Auren sang, "But I am not finished."

Ulric's gaze lingered on him for a long moment, his eyes

widening slightly in surprise, as though he couldn't quite believe Auren still had any stamina left after that ravaging.

"Spriteling." There was a warning in his voice.

"What?" Auren asked, entirely unrepentant.

Slowly, a slick tentacle wound its way up his body and wrapped around his throat, squeezing with enough pressure that Auren felt his pulse grow heavier.

Ulric's eyes were ablaze, revealing a flash of the ancient creature lurking beneath the man. Of the instinct he kept carefully restrained.

Ulric had once told him that Kraken mating was a violent, brutal event. It was more of a show of strength and dominance, with females fighting males, often nearly to the death, to prove their worth. Kraken females were significantly larger than the males, and they showed no mercy. The fights were brutal. Driven by instinct and desire.

Auren saw that instinct flaring in those eyes now, trained on him.

The tentacle around his neck tightened ever so slightly as Ulric spoke. "You should learn when to be afraid."

Auren didn't waver, didn't back down from his mate's challenge. "I've never been particularly good at that."

"No," Ulric agreed. "You haven't."

A fresh surge of lust coursed through Auren's veins.

"Show me," he demanded.

Ulric stilled. "Show you what?"

Auren swallowed, his nerves telling him they'd gone far enough. That he couldn't take anymore. But since when did Auren quit before his curiosity was satisfied?

"You. I want to see you. Like this, in this body. I've— I've never seen it before."

Ulric tensed, and another flash of that wild instinct sparked in his abyssal eyes.

"Are you sure, Auren?" He growled, his voice dropping several pitches. "I'm not the same in this form. Nothing like what you're used to with me. I don't want you taking on more than you can handle."

Auren flared at that last sentence, his pride demanding he rise to meet Ulric. But instead of arguing, he decided to play this game a little differently.

He rolled his hips, relishing in the way Ulric's eyes locked on his rippling muscles.

"Do you not want to see yourself inside this body?" Auren asked breathily. "Or are you afraid of how much you'll like it?"

There was a moment of silence, save for the patter of rain on the deck. Ulric locked him in a primal gaze, and in that moment, Auren knew—his plan had worked.

Slowly, Ulric's tentacles shifted, parting around the space where his human body met his monstrous form. A slit, subtle and hidden in the smooth flesh just above his groin, began to part—peeling back with a slow flex of muscle. Inside, his skin was a lighter shade of lavender, and pushing free of the pouch was...

Auren's breath hitched. "Oh... gods."

Ulric's cock slid free—thick, ribbed, and sheened in glistening lubricant that wasn't rain. The shaft was a deep purplish-gray, textured with ridges like those carved by ocean currents, and the head was a menacing black-violet, slick and swollen with arousal. It twitched, and a long streak of translucent cum leaked from the tip.

"That's... it's..." Auren's voice faltered. "Oh Poseidon, help me."

"I told you," Ulric said, breathless, the tension in his tentacles betraying just how tightly wound he was. But despite the clear desire detonating beneath his skin, Ulric offered him an escape. "I do not expect this from you, Auren. The females of my kind are quite large. My biology is made to compensate for that difference."

Auren heard the message in his words.

Ulric's monstrous body was built to reach and impregnate

females nearly twice his size. And Auren... Auren was less than half that.

Instead of answering, Auren approached the terrifying cock like a man nearing a monster's bared teeth. Equal parts excitement and dread. He reached out and touched the massive length, marveling at how it glided beneath his fingertips, already coated in a warm, clear slick.

"Is this..." Auren tilted his head. "What is this?"

"My kind produces it," Ulric said, leaning back against the railing, eyes heavy-lidded and wild. "To aid in... reproduction. Our females are enormous and can handle the size but lack the ability to secrete slick as female mammals do—" he groaned as Auren's hand tentatively stroked him—"Th-This helps."

"So you make your own lube," Auren deadpanned.

"Don't say it like that," Ulric groaned, almost scandalized.

Auren laughed through his nerves, but couldn't think of anything less funny. The game they were playing, the line they were riding— it was dangerous.

But since when had that ever stopped him?

He leaned in and dragged his tongue along the length of Ulric's cock in one long, reverent stripe. His tongue moved up and down over the ribbed ridges that rose an inch high.

The flavor hit his tongue immediately—briny, musky, rich with a mineral tang that was unmistakably oceanic. It was like licking the belly of the sea itself.

"Spriteling," Ulric gasped, and the tentacles now stroking up and down Auren's back *shook*. He'd never known those powerful tendrils to shake this way. Ulric was truly coming undone before his eyes.

Encouraged, he tried to take the head into his mouth, but it was far too wide. His lips stretched, straining, and even then, he could only suckle the very tip. But that was enough to make Ulric moan—head falling back, tentacles writhing with the effort of restraint. Precum dribbled onto Auren's tongue, and the taste made him groan in return.

"You like that?" Ulric rasped, one hand fisting in his hair. "Do you enjoy tasting what you do to me?"

Auren didn't answer with words, only redoubled his efforts, working Ulric with both hands while his mouth lavished the tip. He needed two hands to wrap around the enormous shaft, his fingers barely touching each other around the impossible girth.

All the while, Ulric's tentacles resumed their work, one stroking his cheek, another teasing his entrance. Auren sucked in a sharp breath when two tips pressed inside him at once.

"If... if you insist on trying this, then I need to prepare you."

Auren nodded while still suckling Ulric's flushed tip, rolling his tongue around in long, slow circles.

He didn't know what he was doing, but there was no stopping it now. He was more than a little scared. But—he trusted Ulric. Always had. Always would.

The two velvety-soft tentacles pushed deeper inside him, and already Auren's cock was hard and begging. The tentacles twisted and rolled over one another, even spreading apart, pushing his hole to its limit. Auren mewled as he sucked and swallowed mouthfuls of Ulric's precum.

"I could come just from watching your mouth suck on me like this," Ulric rasped. "We can end it this way. You don't have to—"

Auren popped off, wiping his mouth with the back of his arm, lips swollen from the stretch.

"No. I want you. All of you," he said determinedly.

Ulric nodded and laid Auren on the deck, the rain cooling his flushed skin as tentacles braced around them, shielding them like petals of a monstrous bloom. Ulric loomed above him, gaze burning.

All the while, the two tentacles remained inside Auren, keeping his hole open and ready.

"I've never wanted anything the way I want this," Ulric said, voice breaking with emotion. "Let me have you. All of you."

Auren's heart thundered. "I'm already yours."

With both hands, Ulric carefully spread Auren's legs, revealing the tentacles pulsing in and out of him. The way Ulric moved now —it wasn't rushed. Not the savage need that had him flipping Auren upside down only minutes ago.

This was careful. Like Auren was made of glass, and Ulric was terrified of cracking him.

Auren would never admit it, but he was grateful for his mate's tender caution, because when the bulk of his body pressed closer, and Ulric's hard, ridged cock stood straight and proud between them, Auren couldn't help the needle of fear biting into his skin.

Oh gods. Oh gods. There's no way. No way.

But he kept those thoughts to himself, afraid of pushing Ulric away. Afraid he might stop.

The tentacles inside him slowly pulled out, leaving Auren feeling uncomfortably empty and gaping. Ulric lined himself up, pressing the head of his cock against Auren's hole. It was hot despite the cool rain. And even with his hole opened wide and prepped by the tentacles, the pressure at his rim was immediate. And when Ulric pushed against him the tiniest amount, the sting that followed sent shockwaves through his body.

Auren's body was screaming at him, telling him to stop. That this was too much. Too far.

Still, he refused to back down.

"Breathe, spriteling." Ulric bent low, his breath a soothing balm against Auren's nerves. "Breathe through it."

Auren nodded stiffly, the muscles along his neck bulging with tension. He could hardly breathe through the tremors in his chest.

Ulric noticed.

"Auren, if you want me to stop, say the word, and I swear to you I will."

Auren shook his head, speaking through clenched teeth. "No. Let me... let me keep trying," he hissed through the pain.

Ulric nodded patiently as he pushed again, and Auren sucked in a heavy breath, eyes watering. Ulric kissed his cheek, tasting his tears as Auren wrapped his arms around his mate's neck, holding on for dear life.

And just when the pain was surely going to rip Auren in half, he felt a quick *pop*, and Ulric's enormous tip was passed his ring and inside him. The pressure eased some, but the burning remained.

"I'm inside you, Auren. You're doing so well. Look at you. So strong to withstand me like this."

Auren clung to the praise, chest heaving. Ulric didn't rush him, didn't push. And if he was annoyed by how long this was taking, Auren didn't notice as his mate patiently waited for him to adjust. To ask for more.

The longer Ulric was inside, the less tender his hole grew. Then the most pleasant soothing sensation began to outweigh the terrible burn. Auren realized that Ulric's natural slick also served as a numbing agent.

Ulric locked eyes with him, and without a word, Auren gave a nod, ready for more. His mate went slowly. Pushing deeper until the first ridge met Auren's hole. Once again, Auren grit his teeth as he was stretched impossibly wider, and then the ring slipped inside, and Auren was able to catch his breath.

Until the next one met his ass. Over and over, Auren's toes curled through the burn as each ring made its way inside.

Each time Auren thought he was full, Ulric gave him more. Another inch. Another breathless sound. Another dizzying wave of sensation.

The slick helped, and by the time the final one passed, Auren was sweating, eyes rolled back, arms too weak to hold onto Ulric anymore as they lay useless on the wooden deck.

When Ulric's hips finally met his ass, Auren was gasping, eyes clouded with tears, and his body shaking.

"It's in spriteling. You've taken it all." Ulric whispered against his throat. Auren blinked away the tears.

"It-it is?" he wheezed. It was hard to speak; he felt as though he couldn't expand his lungs all the way.

"It is my precious mate. You've taken all of me." Ulric reached down and ran a soothing hand up and down Auren's stomach. It felt a little off. "You're so perfect. It steals my breath to know you're all *mine*. That you're doing this for me."

Auren found the strength to look down and...

He whimpered.

The sight of them joined was obscene. Impossible. His poor ass was stretched to its limit, the rim pink as it struggled to take Ulric in. But what had Auren's eyes go wide was the significant bulge in his stomach. Ulric's mass was nestled inside him, so large it pushed at his skin to make room.

"Fuck..." Auren whimpered, "Oh fuck Ulric. Is that really me?"

"It is, my mate. Look how your body stretches to take all of me." Then he took Auren's chin, forcing his gaze away from the swell. "Are you okay? Tell me now."

Auren nodded. This was... so much more than he'd imagined.

Until this point, Auren's poor cock had flagged as he endured the burn of Ulric's intrusion. But now, seeing the way they fit together, his cock straightened to attention, seeking more of this impossible connection. It dribbled onto his stomach. He wiggled his hips, testing the pressure, and groaned as the delicious sensation curled his toes. As the swell in his belly moved separate from him.

"Are you sure, my prince?"

"Yes," Auren begged. "Please. Move."

Ulric obeyed.

He started slow, a gentle withdrawal, just until the first ring before sliding back in with sinful precision. Again. And again. Auren's cries rose with every thrust, his body singing with over-stimulation and hunger. Each push hit deeper, each pull made his body clench harder.

He was fully numbed now, or maybe he was beyond feeling. Maybe he relished the burn. Pain mixed with pleasure in an intoxicating concoction that would either kill him or send him into euphoria.

"Ulric~ fuck me," he moaned. "Wreck me. Brand me from the inside."

He was babbling now. A simpering mess of nerves and pleasure. Nothing made sense, and yet it all suddenly became vibrantly clear. He loved this beast. He loved him, and nothing else mattered.

Ulric's low, deadly hum vibrated through Auren's chest.

"You'll feel me for days, spriteling," Ulric rasped, out of breath. "You'll dream of this stretch, this fullness. No one else will ever touch you here again."

He flipped Auren over without pulling out, guiding him onto hands and knees. Tentacles coiled around his thighs, his wrists, his waist. One looped around his throat, not choking, but a reminder of who held him. Who owned him.

Auren cried out as Ulric pulled out further this time, allowing for that ridge to exit his body before plunging back in. His forehead pressed to the soaked deck as his body was driven forward with each thrust. The tentacles held him firm, kept him spread, kept him grounded.

Each time Ulric pulled out a little further, allowing Auren to experience every ridge of his cock, sending waves of pleasure each time one made its way back inside.

Weakly, he became aware of that funny feeling in his stomach as Ulric pounded him. With what strength he had left, he lifted his head, looking down — and gasped.

His belly bulged with every punishing bottom-out. Skin

stretched as his body took in Ulric's cock. The visual broke Auren's remaining sanity.

"Oh fuck—Ulric—fuck me~"

He sang. Cried. Whimpered until his tongue was hanging out, gasping through the pleasure.

"This body of yours," Ulric snarled, never breaking pace, "was made to take me. To withstand me. To beg for me."

Auren reached between his legs, touching that bulge in his stomach, moaning at the electric spark it sent through his core.

"I'm gonna—Ulric—gods—"

"I'm close," Ulric grunted, voice shattering. "I need—fuck—I need to come inside you."

"Do it," Auren sobbed. "Flood me. Fill me. I want all of you—every last drop—"

Ulric roared and slammed home one final time.

Heat exploded inside Auren as Ulric came—wave after wave of molten release pouring into him. It was too much. He felt it spill into his guts. Felt his belly swell, the sheer volume of it stretching his insides to their limits. His own cock jerked, and Auren came again, untouched, shuddering violently as his ass clenched around the twitching mass still sheathed inside him.

When Ulric finally pulled out with a slick, wet sound, Auren collapsed flat to the deck, trembling in a puddle of rain and release. Milky white cum dribbled from his spent hole in a slow, lazy stream. He lay there, gasping, body twitching with aftershocks.

The sudden emptiness... hurt. He whimpered, tears springing to his eyes for an entirely different reason. Quickly, Ulric gathered him into his arms, and one plump tentacle slid its way back inside Auren's gaping hole, soothing him from the inside as he came down.

"My mate. My spriteling," Ulric crooned, nuzzling into Auren's hair. "You were perfect. So good. So strong." He held Auren close, letting the rain wash over them, fingers brushing through his wet hair. After some time, Ulric's worried voice interrupted the patter.

"Talk to me," Ulric said softly. "Spriteling... you haven't said a word. Was I too much?"

Auren shook his head with a lazy smile. "No. I was just thinking..."

"Mm?"

"...I can't wait for the next storm."

Ulric barked a laugh, wrapping him tighter.

They cleaned up—sharing sweet kisses, trading gentle touches. Iska returned long enough for a nuzzle and a knowing chirp before diving again.

Once the deck had been thoroughly washed by rain and Ulric shifted back into his human form, they dressed and opened the hatches.

The crew returned to their stations, none the wiser—at least, not visibly.

As they set sail back toward the mainland, wind in their hair and sea at their backs, Ulric smirked.

"Think the thunder was loud enough to cover your moaning, little siren?"

Auren turned red. "Gods. Maybe next time we come out here alone. You think we can manage the ship by ourselves?"

Ulric leaned in and kissed his cheek. "Together, my prince... we can do anything."

And the ship, gleaming with salt and promise, carried them home.

~Fin~

acknowledgments

To Aly Hollis and Harlowe Savage—thank you for being unhinged enough to cheer me on through every twist of tentacle and tear-stained kiss. Your friendship and writing have made me a better storyteller (and monsterfucker).

To Laney, Dakota, Emma and Kristina—thank you for loving this story as deeply as I do. Your time, your feedback, and your unwavering support kept me going when the waves got rough. This book wouldn't be the same without you.

To my husband—thank you for your patience, your dedication, and your ability to live with someone who says things like "How many tentacles do you think could fit in your mouth?" at the dinner table. I love you more than I love morally gray sea witches—and that's saying something.

And finally, to the staff at my local Denny's:

You didn't ask questions.

You just kept the coffee coming at 3 a.m.

You're the real MVPs.

This book is for everyone who's ever fallen for a monster—and got horny. You know who you are.

about the author

Tereza Kane lives in the rattlesnake deserts of Arizona with her husband and six dogs. She teaches piano lessons by day and writes queer love stories by night. If she isn't cuddling with one of her fur babies or watching nature documentaries, she is likely in the container store buying an unreasonable amount of Tupperware, and someone should probably stop her.

also by tereza kane

Storm and Sea - Gay Mer Boys, Luca Vibes

Drown Me Gently - MM Little Mermaid Retelling

Curse Me Silent - MM Swan Princess Retelling

flipped fairytales

Drown Me Gently (MM - Little Mermaid) Tereza Kane

Curse Me Silent (MM - Swan Princess) Tereza Kane

Wish Me Freely (MF - Aladdin) Aly Hollis

Rob Me Blindly (FF - Robin Hood) Harlowe Savage

Dream Me Lovely (MM - Cinderella) Harlowe Savage

Carry Me Sweetly (MM - Thumbelina) Laney Arden

Deal Me Darkly (MF - Mulan x Puss in Boots) Jade Nioma

Freeze Me Slowly (FF - Jack Frost) Abigail Schmitz

Tame Me Fiercely (MF - Tarzan) Zia Tyree

Poison Me Fairly (MF - Snow White) Sarizona

Bury Me Endlessly (MFF - Atlantis) Kay Lalock

Claim Me Fearlessly (MF - Beauty and the Beast) Alexis Alamanzar

Free Me Truly (FF Lady and the Tramp) Cara Blaine

Kiss Me Cursed (MF Sleeping Beauty) Sierra Scandella

With many more to come!

Scan for an updated list